A GIRL CALLED
FLOTSAM

A GIRL CALLED
FLOTSAM

JOHN TAGHOLM

First published by Muswell Press in 2016

Typeset by e-Digital Design Ltd.

Copyright © John Tagholm 2016

John Tagholm has asserted his right to be identified
as the author of this work in accordance with the
Copyright, Designs and Patents Act 1988
Printed and bound by Clays Ltd, St Ives plc.

A CIP catalogue record for this book is available from the
British Library

ISBN 978-0-9954822-0-3

Muswell Press
London
N6 5HQ

www.muswell-press.co.uk

to
Hunter

'Who has fully realised that history is not contained in thick books but lives in our very blood?'
Carl Jung

CHAPTER ONE

Beatrice Palmenter felt she was losing her balance. Somewhere beneath her the water had shifted and begun to tug at her legs, a soft but insistent weight against her boots and she raised her arms to steady herself. To those watching on the foreshore she was a grey crucifix reflected on the water. A cormorant skimmed low over the glassy surface just as the ripples began to appear behind the cables holding the metal barge in the middle of the river. The tide had turned. In a few hours she would be standing in double her height of water and for a moment she wondered if she should wait to be submerged. She turned and looked back at the others, spread out along the muddy shore, dark shapes stooped at different angles, staring at the ground and dragging behind them black plastic bags.

Shortly after arriving she had wandered off from the group, walking into the river as far as her waders would allow, to stand with the smell of the dirty water almost tangible in her nostrils. The warm drizzle blowing gently from the east blurred the line between sky and water. The buildings on either bank receded and the view might not have changed much in a thousand years. The river moved more strongly against her legs, an invisible hand trying to attract her attention, to remind her that in the scheme of things she barely existed. She remained in the water, thigh deep in her hip waders, not wanting to rejoin the others. When she spoke it was to the open expanse of water in front of her.

'I can't believe it.'

'What was that Triss?' The peculiar acoustics of sound and water had carried her words, although spoken quietly and to herself, fifty or so metres behind her.

Beatrice lowered her arms to her sides and reluctantly began to make her way back to the foreshore. The water had disguised her height and when, having negotiated the broken bricks and discarded scaffolding, she stood next to her male companion, it was clear that she was considerably taller.

'I said I can't believe it.'

'That's exactly what you said earlier this morning, when you first woke up.'

She frowned and had to reroute her thoughts and assimilate the information that she was now being given. Even though Beatrice had been living with Joshua for three months and known him for double that time, she now looked at him as a stranger, hearing his statement as a foreign language, unable at first to deduce its meaning.

'Those were your words when you opened your eyes and looked at me,' he insisted, nodding at her, appearing to want an explanation.

And then she remembered and in so doing glanced away, towards a wall of damp bricks and green moss, where an old chain hung uselessly. She had woken to find him staring at her, dark-eyed and expectant and she knew then what she had been denying for months, almost from the moment they had met, that she should not be with him, that she was wasting her time. But it had happened and she had pushed her head back into the pillow and uttered the words he now prompted her to remember.

On the opposite shore a young child was running along the dirty beach, a beacon of life amongst the drab greys and she heard the exclamations of delight with metallic clarity across the water. She could not tell whether it was a boy or a girl, but she registered the freedom and the unfettered cries of joy.

Joshua was still waiting for an answer. She stared at him and knew that to offer an explanation would have been a waste of time, for he had already drawn his own conclusions. As it happened, the words that she had repeated standing in the water referred not to Joshua but to an incident that had taken place a few days earlier. As the water had pushed against her knees she had been berating herself for almost having believed the praise that she had been given, knowing that in truth it meant nothing and disguised everything.

In the muddy waters, her arms outstretched, she had closed her eyes in weary acknowledgement of scenes she could not erase. She was walking between tables set for a banquet, men in dinner jackets and women in long dresses, everyone looking in her direction, clapping her progress towards the stage and she saw it again in slow motion, the ill-defined hands, the indistinct faces and the music from her film now so familiar that she never wanted to hear it again. It wasn't her, Beatrice Palmenter, who was about to win a Bafta award for best documentary series, but a carefully constructed replica, perfect in every respect save for the fact that it didn't have a heart and many of its senses had been cauterised. She saw herself receive the golden mask, or at least feel its cold shape in her hands, her fingers in the eye sockets and then look out over the expectant faces of the audience.

'I can't believe it,' she had said and again her words were misinterpreted by those in front of her and the audience spontaneously applauded her modesty. Her short speech thanked those people who needed to be thanked and refrained from mentioning those she wished to hell and damnation, the list of which was considerably longer. It was, she mused to herself in the ladies' loo not long afterwards, an out of body experience during which she was able to watch her fabricated self go through the motions of success, gratitude and appropriate humility. What a sham.

Today, on the foreshore of the Thames, she was trying to put that person behind her. The golden mask was now propping open the kitchen door of her apartment and the debris that now lay about her, the accumulation of junk and treasure revealed by the departed river, was more real. At the prompting of a friend, she had volunteered to help a charity charged with cleaning up London's waterways and on this grey Saturday morning removing old tyres, rusting corrugated sheets, indestructible plastic and panty liners seemed a more honourable task than receiving awards in Piccadilly.

She shrugged her shoulders. 'I don't really know what I meant,' she said to Joshua. She was lying and she could see that he knew it. If she felt guilt it was the guilt of repetition for she had been here before, too often.

She walked away from Joshua to begin a struggle to release a supermarket trolley whose metal grilled sides had acted as a filter in the strong currents and were now clogged with the detritus of the river. Another pair of hands, not Joshua's, helped her pull it clear of the mud and they dragged it to one of the skips positioned about five metres in from what would be the high-water mark. At first it seemed a futile task, the old river too full of rubbish, ancient and modern but the work was repetitive and strangely satisfying and the hours went by as the water rose. She didn't speak, except to acknowledge help from other members of the group, glad of the silence and the innocent camaraderie. Occasionally she looked up, but Joshua was nowhere to be seen and for this she was grateful.

Then the sounds around her changed and she was conscious of a suppressed excitement close by and she saw three or four people gathered at the edge of the water. She made her way towards them noting that one of the group was holding a dark object carefully between his fingers, turning it slowly to show the others.

'It's a skull,' she heard him say. He pointed to the broken arch of one of the eyes and along the roughened gap where the nose had been and peering closer she could see his fingers tracing the fine, tightly meandering lines that joined the different sections of the dome. There was no lower jaw, but several teeth hung in the top part of the mouth and this, unmistakably, had been a human.

'What happens now?' someone asked.

'I'll have to call the police,' the man said, pulling off his gloves before tapping his pocket to locate his mobile. Without thinking, Beatrice offered to hold the piece of skull as he made the call. Like the other volunteers, she was wearing thick protective gloves and she placed the dirty curve of bone in the palm of her hand. This tiny reminder of a human had a strange impact on the group, which had now been enlarged by other volunteers and they stood, heads bowed in the fine drizzle, silent with their own thoughts. How many times had it washed backwards and forwards in the tides before emerging in this reduced form? Beatrice looked across the water and the child was standing opposite, quite still and she wanted to wave but the object in her hand caused her to pause. Moments later the figure was gone, scampering across the mud and gravel.

Later the police arrived, two men in uniform who slipped on latex gloves to solemnly examine the fragment before declaring that it would need to go to forensics. They took names and made a note of where the object had been found and then they were gone, the skull in a transparent plastic bag, their radios crackling as they walked back to the embankment steps. By now the river had risen to within a few feet of the metal containers and the group began to disperse, hosing the mud off their boots and pulling off their thick socks. Before long a tug would come and tow the rubbish away to a land-fill site down river to create a different archaeology for another generation to discover. Beatrice cleaned her waterproof gloves, placed them together but just before she laid them with the others in a large container she looked at the palm of the right glove, the one that had supported the piece of skull. She remembered the shape of the eye sockets and it was only then that she realised how small the whole skull must have been and that it might have been that of a child. She sat down again overtaken by an immense sadness quite out of proportion to the event and at one and the same time she understood why but chose, as she nearly always did, to ignore it.

Her phone chirruped and real life intruded. It was a message from her boss, the man who'd greeted her with such false pleasure at the award ceremony and who was now inviting her to a meeting the following day.

'We were all thrilled at your Bafta, Triss.' She remembered his open arms as she walked back to her table, swinging the statuette in her right hand. 'Yours was the stand out success of the night, in a category of its own. I'm – we're – thrilled for you.' She marvelled at these words, spoken by the chief executive, for he had been notably reluctant to let her make the films in the first place and, apart from the fact that he had once tried to get into her knickers, she was fairly certain he had never liked her. Certainly she had little time for him.

And was she delighted? Was it worth the effort of pushing the stone up the slope? How many of those who slapped her back that night had been willing to stab it only moments before?

'Of course,' she remembered saying, avoiding his eyes and shortly afterwards excusing herself to go to the lavatory.

She looked back at the text on the screen and the phone vibrated again. It informed her that the meeting would take place over lunch at a well known restaurant where being seen was more important than the food being served. She was now a trophy herself, a Bafta award winner and he wanted to display her whilst she still glittered.

The foreshore had now been swallowed up and the appearance of the river had changed yet again, fuller and more threatening, the currents pushing against the old wooden jetty and swirling angrily behind. Where the skull had been found was now under a metre of water and any other treasures would remain hidden until the river breathed in again and shrank back to offer another tantalising glimpse of the past.

Beatrice Palmenter sat on a bench along the embankment wall and despite the grey skies and the continuing drizzle, closed her eyes. Her breathing slowed and in that no man's land between sleeping and waking, a smile appeared on her face for only now did she make the connection between the eyeless mask of the Bafta statuette and the fragment of skull and in her mind the two images were merged, one mixing into the other and slowly coming towards her so that she entered one eye and through it to the other. She saw a child running, apparently weightless, her strides unnaturally long, her arms outstretched so that at any moment she might have taken off, so real that Beatrice involuntarily raised her arm in salute.

CHAPTER TWO

She runs because her life depends on it. She runs because her father's life depends on it. She runs because her mother had fear in her voice. So she speeds from her home on to a track which many years later will become Lombard Street and where one day the tip of the morning shadow of the NatWest building will fall, over the track where the lion and bison have lain hidden for ten thousand years and will remain undisturbed for a millennium more, on down the slow incline where her legs promise to go faster than she is able to follow, over the patch of mud where a year ago the Viking had dropped the arrowhead that would survive the Great Fire and the Blitz, the slope getting steeper now so that she can see the line of water at the end of the path that at some future date will be cobbled to withstand the tread of a million feet belonging to those who, like her, will travel oblivious over a bowl of Roman coins hidden for safety and forgotten until the tunnels for the Underground are excavated, the noise of the men out on the river being carried towards her on the cold, east wind which, even at her young age, she knows will speed their enemies' arrival, to come at last to the marshy shore hardly able to speak, to look breathless along the line of the bridge in search of her father, somewhere at its broken centre, replacing timbers that in years to come will be puzzled over by those who will wonder if they had truly belonged to the first London Bridge. The river is high and she can see it moving beneath her, carrying secrets in its belly, the whorls and eddies racing below through the cracks in the timbers, making her feel unsteady so that she holds out her arms to regain her balance.

She feels the wind catch her cropped hair and she is staring so intently at the men on the bridge that she fails to see her father only feet away. And then he snatches her up and tells her not to worry but to return home and look after her mother, all will be well. She looks into his eyes and embraces him. She knows about his fear for he has already lost a son and a daughter, her brother and sister. She smells his smell and is happy for that moment to rest in his arms.

She returns up the slope from the river, where St Clement's Church will one day stand, but just before the gentle incline claims her, turns and looks back at the scene.

Wooden pins and rope hold the final section of the bridge in place and she can see the men dispersing, some southwards over the ground where the market is held and where the market can still be found, others northwards into what will become the City, to return armed and protected and ready to give their lives for their families. The smoke from several encampments rises into the grey sky where, exactly a thousand years later, the fireworks will explode at the arrival of the third millennium.

CHAPTER THREE

In the end, it was Joshua who had ditched her, in his precise, designer's way.

'There's something missing in you, a part, a piece of machinery. Emotional, I mean.'

She watched him fold a napkin into a neat square and move the salt and pepper pots symmetrically to the centre of the kitchen table before continuing. He had not been at her apartment when she had returned home from the Thames but had reappeared early that morning, having prepared his ultimatum.

'I don't think this relationship is doing me any good.'

What Joshua was saying to her came as no surprise. She'd heard it before and not only from him and her impatience to have this chapter over and done with, zipped shut, was typical although what she was sensing now was not the chance of freedom once again, but a narrowing of options and a faint whiff of panic and claustrophobia. All she could do was shrug, whether in sympathy for him or for herself, she couldn't be certain.

'I know,' he said. 'You've got nothing to say. You can make films exploring people's feelings but you can't use the same approach to yourself.'

As admonishments went, it was fairly accurate and the reason she offered no defence was due to the fact that she didn't have one and so she gave another shrug, further confirming Joshua's indignation. He was a neat, tidy man and the process of moving his possessions from her flat was equally precise and orderly and so by late morning Joshua Myers might just as well not have existed in her life. She should have known this that first night she spent in his apartment in Camden, shortly after they met, when she tiptoed to the bathroom in the early morning and saw, next to the lavatory, the magazine which proclaimed on its cover "The Thirty Fonts You Can't Live Without".

The Tube jolted her awake and a distorted voice informed her that they were being held to regulate the service and that they would be moving again shortly. She would be slightly late, which irritated her because that is what he would have expected and no part of her wanted to be second-guessed by the man with whom she was about to have lunch. Ahead of her Graham Roth would be waiting, no doubt receiving visits from other tables, joking with the maitre-d', holding court in his inimitable way. She had worked for him for three years and it surprised her that never once had she been remotely seduced by this exterior charm, the blatant manipulation of those around him for his own ends. At a post production party at the conclusion of her first series, he had followed her towards the cloakroom and clumsily tried to kiss her and her resistance had taken them both by surprise. Life was complicated enough without sleeping with the boss, although she accepted that her denial of Graham Roth, Chief Executive of The Digital Corporation, was an exception rather than a rule. What made him any different from Joshua Myers?

She fought her way off the train, pushing between a group

of Japanese tourists for whom this overcrowded platform was more or less what they were used to but who wanted to take pictures of each other in front of the Tube sign. She skirted around them, part of a faster stream of people who knew where they were going, emerging into the light of Oxford Street and turning towards Mayfair. She noticed that a small line of Thames' mud was lodged under one corner of the nail of her little finger on her right hand and whilst puzzling at how it had remained there, felt oddly comforted that she was carrying a reminder of yesterday's adventure. She was familiar with the restaurant where he was waiting and knowing that Graham Roth did nothing by accident, wondered why he had chosen it as a place to meet, apart from it being a useful venue for showing off his prize winner. Would this be the second man she would cross swords with today?

The *Brasserie des Ouvriers* was neither a *brasserie* nor was it for workers, at least not in the sense the French used both words. This was *brasserie* Michelin-style, a film-set background for expensive food and whilst at lunchtime its diners certainly worked, they came from the world of finance, fashion and the media and had little connection to factory workers and lorry drivers. Graham Roth sat under a large mirror promoting *Ancre Pils* from Strasbourg. He didn't stand up when she arrived but merely offered her the seat with its back to the restaurant with an nonchalant wave of his hand. Even in this brief moment of greeting he took his eyes off her to see if anyone had registered her arrival. She didn't like the man and yet she was amused at how little time it had taken to once again reaffirm this fact. He gave the briefest nod to a waiter who handed her a glass of champagne and before she had said a word, he raised his glass to hers and the lunch began.

I am thirty-six years old, Beatrice Palmenter told herself and I am being lunched by one of the most powerful men in television and I am frankly indifferent and barely curious about what might follow. The component parts of why she felt like this were all contained within her, she knew, but they had not presented themselves in a pattern she could fully comprehend.

'Did you celebrate at the weekend, Triss?'

She was not fond of this reduction of her name and certainly not happy that he used it with such an assumption of intimacy. Thinking of Joshua, it crossed her mind that it was only men she didn't like that shortened it in this way. The mirror above her was hung slightly forward so that she could see the restaurant reflected and could watch the other diners playing their own games of question and answer.

'I removed panty liners from the shores of the Thames,' she said.

'Are you researching something for a new film?' he replied without missing a beat.

'Not as such. I was invited by a friend.' She straightened her knife. 'Do you know the Isle of Dogs?'

'Not intimately, no.'

'You should go. It's quite restorative.'

The verbal skirmishing continued over the hors d'oeuvres but the main course, both in terms of the food and the purpose of the meal, arrived at the same time.

'What do you have in mind for your next project?'

The way he asked the question made Beatrice aware that she didn't need to answer and so, not for the first time that day, she shrugged and gave the impression that it might be this and it might be that.

Graham Roth played with his sea bream, splitting the fillet in half and dividing it yet again before taking a neat mouthful.

'Do you remember what this restaurant used to be, in a previous incarnation?'

Of course she did, but she was going to wait for him to make the running, to declare himself as he surely would. In the distance she had glimpsed a possible motive for the lunch, beyond the celebratory.

'You once touched on it in a proposal.'

'I did, indeed.' She was about to add "and it was rubbished from a great height" but that would have given him too much advantage.

'Did you ever eat here when it was Chez Joseph?'

'I would have been a child,' she said, 'but I knew those who did.' The names were all on the list I gave you in my pitch, but you never read, she said in her head adding, also unspoken, why are you taking an interest again all of a sudden?

'I've dug out the proposal you outlined a couple of years ago. I wonder if we shouldn't revisit it.'

She waited, again unwilling to play the game until he'd declared his hand.

Once upon a time, in what now seemed another life, she had gone out with a chef who was beginning to make a name for himself and through him had met Joseph Troumeg, the celebrated food writer and restaurateur. He was in his early seventies then, but still carried about him the aura and glitter of the glory days when his name was on everyone's lips. He had recently sold his group of restaurants and was, much to his displeasure, slipping from the public eye to be replaced, well, by people like her old boyfriend.

'Hello, my name is Joseph Troumeg. The 'g' is silent,' he had said in a routine she knew he had repeated many times, 'unlike me.' And, unlike Graham Roth, he had stood to meet her and had given a small bow as he introduced himself before ushering her into the best seat in the restaurant. During the next two and half hours Joseph Troumeg gave a bravura performance, sketching out his life in elaborate and amusing detail, stopping now and then to hear about her job and praising her boyfriend for his fabulous cooking. The following morning she had Googled him and was fascinated to read many of the quotes which were word for word what he had said to her over dinner. She took her researches further, phoning several of his ex-colleagues and one or two journalists, but she only heard more or less the same potted history.

A few days later he called and invited her down to Deal, where he had a small house. How could she resist? The 'small house' turned out to be a double-fronted stuccoed villa just off the front decorated in what he described as 'magpie camp'. There was reason for this invitation to the coast, of course. He continued his smooth encapsulation of his life, before handing her a folder which had a studied photograph of him on the cover and the grand title 'JOSEPH TROUMEG: A LIFE IN FOOD'. It outlined a series of programmes in which he revisited some of his favourite haunts, told a potted history of his life and cooked appropriate dishes to camera. From the look of the folder it had been through a few hands, although the practised restaurateur made her feel that she was its first recipient. She saw him a couple of times in London, where he had a flat in Chelsea and came to like the man who happily described himself as the outsider who transformed British cooking and eating. Her fascination was not so much to do with his celebrity – he counted queens, princesses and film stars as his disciples – but with the smoothly polished and repeated history of his life and times.

She had no intention of doing a cookery show so she put together a proposal for a documentary which might easily have had the same title even though it had a rather different purpose, an exploration of why Joseph Troumeg, born in France, should have become so successful in a country not noted for its love of food or indeed the French. She wanted to explore the strange fascination with the restaurateur and investigate his background and influences. She showed the idea to Troumeg who was distinctly lukewarm. 'They don't want to know about all that,' he'd said. 'They want the glamour and the cooking and the fancy locations.' Nevertheless she had pressed ahead and shown the proposal to Graham Roth and this lunchtime she remembered his words as though they had been spoken to her yesterday.

'A bit old hat, isn't he? Hasn't he been somewhat overtaken?'

16

'I think there's a bit more than meets the eye,' she had replied. She couldn't have substantiated that remark for it was instinctual and not based on much fact, but her nose for these things was usually accurate. 'He's a fascinating man who would make a very good story, one way or the other. And he really did make a difference to the way we look at food.'

Graham Roth had shaken his head and that was the end of it. Until today. But she wasn't going to ask him why the change of heart. He took two mouthfuls of strawberry panna cotta before continuing.

'We've had an approach from an agent in association with a publisher. They think Joseph Troumeg is due for a revival. Isn't this what you think?'

'Not really. I thought he was an interesting man. I think he would have to be dead before we could revive him. Why do you think it might work now but dismissed it so quickly two years ago?' Her tone was just as cold as she meant it to be.

'Then, Beatrice, I judged the time not to be right. But things move on, do they not?' Graham Roth usually got what he wanted and although his response did not quite have the same edge as hers, it nevertheless contained the ultimatum, take it or leave it.

'It would be a different sort of cookery show,' he said finally.

She thought at first that she wouldn't respond to this, but her irritation got the better of her. 'But it wouldn't be a cookery show. It would be a documentary.'

'I'm sure you'd find a way of combining both formats,' he concluded. 'One way or the other, you won't be able to avoid food. Anyway, think about it and let me know.' With that he changed the subject and the meal quickly ran its course.

The Tube back was less crowded and she sat slumped in the seat, her left ankle propped on her right knee and wondered precisely where she was, other than on the District Line rattling along the side of the Thames to Aldgate. Graham Roth was offering her a chance to make the film that she had more or less proposed and not so long ago was keen to make. And now she was resisting the idea and she tried to establish why. One of the answers was easy: it wasn't the film Joseph Troumeg wanted and she would have to persuade him to participate. She realised, though, that she was in the grip of a larger malaise only part of which was caused by the whimsical and offhand way Graham Roth had offered her the project. She hunched lower in the seat and felt her body move as the train swayed its subterranean passage eastwards.

CHAPTER FOUR

She does not look back again, her bare feet carrying her up the hill away from the river and she thinks that what she can't see might never happen. There is a quietness about the house, her mother stooped at the workbench, her back to the door working on a tiny axe head outlined in gold which she had seen her beginning the night before. Her mother hugs her, kissing the top of her head before tracing its shape with the palms of her hands and she looks up and tells her, as she herself had been told by her father, not to be frightened. But as she does, she remembers only too clearly their recent flight from their settlement in the west, burned and pillaged by the invaders, her mother's workshop destroyed and her precious stones, glass, amber, garnets scattered in the earth to sink for generations. The girl runs the tips of her fingers around the gold rim of the axe and admires her mother for transforming a weapon of war into an object of beauty. Her mother continues to work on the small pendant but she herself is thinking of the men on the bridge which is, at one and the same time, the place she wants to be and where she does not. She slips out of the house and heads back to the point above the river where she often sits to watch the merchant ships arrive from places whose names she has never heard. From here she would watch her mother trade with the sailors, swapping a finished necklace or ring for a bundle of coloured stones, orange, ruby and emerald. But now the ships and sailors below have a different purpose and she wants to cover her face with her hands but can't help but watch what happens next. In some ways she knows already and is merely witnessing a confirmation.

By the time the Norsemen's longboats appear on the eastward approach of the river, the men had gathered on the bridge and the quays to the north, just beneath her. Somewhere her father is with them. She can see they are wiser now and better armed with their long spears and shields lined up in defiance of an enemy they are beginning to know and understand. In amongst the closely formed ranks, she imagines her father is thinking of the beauty that his wife creates, the amulets dripping with pendants, the fabulous geometric brooches, the bracelets in gold and silver, all the colours that sparkled in his life.

This time the defenders are determined to keep the bridge intact and a protective wall of shields flanks the down river side. The longboats come relentlessly closer, no fearful pause in their progress. On the brow of the hill, unseen to her father, she watches from what will later be the top of Pudding Lane. From this distance the viciousness of the battle is muted, although the sounds of clashing metal and the cries of the men carry distorted up the slope. She has lived twelve years, each one punctuated by conflict like this and the spectacle unfolding in front of her is just a normal part of her childhood. She can see the boats manoeuvre alongside the bridge in a vain attempt to attach ropes, each one repelled in a shower of spears. A longboat breaks away to land at one of the quays on the near shore and the roar of the Norsemen is frightening. In the various melees and with shields raised in front of their faces, it is not possible for her to make out her father but each man that falls sends a blow to her heart. A second wall of shields holds the attackers by the quay and gradually they are pushed back to the water, not turning to run but stepping backwards as they fight towards the protection of their boat.

Out in the centre of the bridge she senses the last moments of the life of her father are about to happen. Does she imagine how it ends? Does she see the axe that is thrown from the deck of a longship? She hopes that her father neither sees its flight nor feels its blow. He tumbles from the bridge and is dead before he hits the water, his body to float down river to slowly decompose, to wash in and out with the tides, the parts of this loving father, carpenter and farmer, deposited here and there on river bed and foreshore, his skull finally coming to rest in the mud at the mouth of the Walbrook, close by where the Cannon Street railway bridge will stand and where, precisely nine hundred and three years later, it will be wrongly identified as that of a Roman soldier slain and beheaded by a Celtic attacker and offered to the river in sacrifice.

Somehow she knows what has happened even if she hasn't seen it. When the longboats have departed and the defenders regroup to repair their wounds and assess the damage wrought by the attack, he is not one of their number. A search up river fails to produce his body and they know what she knows, that he has been taken by the waters and lost forever. On the hill she accepts that she will never see her father again, grateful for their final moments on the bridge. When eventually she comes home to have the news confirmed, she embraces her mother and senses in that moment that she is different, that she has been handed, unspoken, a new responsibility, the gift of continuity.

CHAPTER FIVE

Beatrice Palmenter could not have told you what she had been thinking as the train arrived at Monument, but in the few seconds it took to orientate herself she became conscious of a feeling of dread, a weight pressing on her chest, a physical reaction to an unspecified event. She found that she was gripping the red shiny armrest for support whilst trying desperately to remember what she had been thinking, or dreaming, in the moments before. However unpleasant her lunch with Graham Roth she couldn't imagine that it would produce such a response and she folded her arms across her chest for protection and comfort. As the Tube continued on its way, the unease began to subside and she became more alert to the feeling and its possible cause. The images in her mind were unformed and just out of reach but they seemed just as real as the carriage in which she was travelling. She was returning to an apartment which would contain the smell and reverberations, real or imaginary, of another failed relationship, having spent two hours with a man whose judgements and manner she thoroughly disliked. Although he had offered her a project that she herself had proposed not long ago, he had done it without affection, the production simply a way of holding on to her so that he, himself, could benefit from her status. It was easy to see how both events might have depressed or angered her, but then she had actually wanted the end of the relationship with Joshua and rather liked the idea of making a film about Troumeg. But contained in her feelings was fear and she knew that neither man had the ability to produce this in her. The Tube passed onwards, under the City to Aldgate and she emerged blinking into the bright afternoon sun, none the wiser nor, as she was ready to accept, willing to question any deeper.

Joshua might just as well have never existed. He had removed all trace of himself from the flat and his absence had the finality of death. She wandered from room to room and concluded that even a forensic expert would have been hard pushed to find evidence of his domicile.

She had a message on her landline from the friend who had introduced her to 4Shore, the charity she had helped at the weekend.

'Hi, it's Amanda. Thought you'd like to know about our dramatic find by the Thames. The police have just let us know that it isn't recent and therefore they don't want to know about it any more. But they think it might be very old, so they've sent it to a, let's have a look, an osteoarchaeologist – bit of a mouthful – to have it dated. They confirm it's probably a child, which makes you think doesn't it? Give us a call when you can.'

There was a chirpiness about Amanda Lodge which clashed with Beatrice's mood and, she thought, with the information she was conveying since her friend was the proud mother of a one year old boy. Amanda was an extremely able producer with whom Beatrice had worked on two drama-documentaries and her effortless good humour and attention to detail had made them natural companions. Beatrice sat on the edge of her bed and thought about the information she had just received, about that other distant life and she lay back on the pillows and stared at the ceiling. The room was hers again now and she could lie here without fear of offending or irritating anyone. She didn't have to accommodate the whims and foibles of a partner, or listen to music she didn't like or face the prospect of an evening with his friends. She could do what she wanted and whereas once upon a time this would have pleased her, it now brought a continued sense of foreboding. Restless, she got up and paced the room and registered the distant bells of St Leonard's sending out their message of hope, or warning, she wasn't sure which. She reached up to a top shelf for a box file and took out its contents and spread them on the bed. Here were the details she had amassed of the childhood and career of Joseph Troumeg which she now re-read, along with the notes from the conversations with some of his friends and colleagues. She preferred his title to hers – Joseph Troumeg: Set Menu – but it didn't quite convey the feeling that Joseph Troumeg's life had been neatly portioned and presented to the public by the man himself, a series of pre-prepared finished dishes. It was the very neatness of this history that alerted her for this was a resumé prepared by an expert in the art of presentation and, she thought, obfuscation. But how, she asked herself, was he any different from other celebrities who, over a period of time, came to believe the half-truths and lies they peddled about themselves?

Joseph Troumeg, according to his own embroidered account, was the result of anti-Semitism, the union of a French woman and an American journalist. How often had she read his words on his own genesis: "My mother was a beauty by all accounts, probably Spanish in origin, hence her unusual height, but unmistakeably – and unashamedly, let me tell you, Jewish. Cultured though the French undoubtedly are, they are not keen on Jews and in the mid-30s she suffered the sort of prejudice that we might find intolerable now, although, believe me, it still goes on. My father had been covering the approach of the Civil

War in Spain and was now trying to alert the world to what was happening in France but America then was not concerned about France or Jews. Nor, I suppose, was England. It seems they met in a street at the foot of Montmartre, when she was being abused by a gang out looking for Jews. He stepped in and – *voilà* – before long, *moi*."

This account had about it an undoubted ring of romance, touched with drama and intrigue and it had been often repeated, not least by the man himself when they met in Deal three years earlier. He had come to Britain in the late fifties although all the stories of these years begin with the same throw-away quote "...why one should have come to Britain to learn about food in those days, I can't think." She found, in a cutting about his *stage* at the Dorchester in his twenties, comments which had followed him through life, polished to perfection along the way. "She was a fine and distinguished lady, but she'd been doing the same old dishes for longer than she could remember. Sure, I learned the disciplines of the kitchen but when I suggested changes I was regarded as an upstart and sent back to my station with a flea in my ear. Although I was young I had already discovered in France tastes and techniques that were way beyond what was on offer here. For this I am grateful for my parent's housekeeper, Monique, a true gem of a woman, who first set free my culinary imagination."

And so the story of Joseph Troumeg's conquest continued, the establishment of Troumeg Fine Dining, one of the earliest bespoke caterers, where Joseph Troumeg would visit the homes of the great and the good and cook personally for their dinner parties. Then the early books and, in the sixties, the first of what would be many Joseph restaurants, franchised here and in America. She read it all again, the growing success, the accumulated wealth, the houses in Chelsea, Knightsbridge, New York and France, the TV series, the gradual creation of an iconic figure. It was a life unencumbered by a partner or the demands of children, blemish free except where Troumeg himself injected drama for the sake of effect. Beatrice had, nevertheless, fallen under his spell, for he was charming and attentive and the narrative of his success was compelling and immediate, packaged like an oven-ready screenplay to be simply heated up and served to an expectant audience. Why couldn't she just dish this up again? It was what Graham Roth would have been all too happy with, a mix of celebrity interviews, foreign locations, beautifully shot food with a dash of Joseph Troumeg's wit.

Unable to give perspective to what she had been re-reading, she broke away from the potted history laid out on the bed to return Amanda's call.

'Joshua has gone and Roth has offered me the Troumeg project,' she declared without preamble.

'Is there a connection?'

'Well, I'm free of one and free to do the other.'

'So what's the problem?'

'I don't really know.'

'So, let me get this straight, as far as I can see you didn't really want to be with Joshua anyway and you used to be keen on the Troumeg film. Am I missing something?'

'No, I think it's me that's missing something. Anyway, tell me about our find in the Thames.'

'You don't want to talk about it, then?'

'Well, yes and no.'

'I've heard that before. So, the skull then. Probably a child and since I left the message they've sent me more details. This osteoarchaeologist at the museum is – hang on a mo' – Doctor Harold Wesley and he's doing some tests at the moment. Says we can call him for progress.'

Beatrice copied down the contact number and then abruptly switched back to the earlier conversation.

'You know I can't bear Roth and maybe that's stopping me making up my mind. I don't know what's wrong with me.'

Amanda Lodge, at the other end of the line, noted her

friend's hesitation and regarded it as a positive development for the instinctive, confident Beatrice Palmenter often committed herself too quickly and then had to suffer the consequences of her actions for a long time afterwards.

'Wouldn't you have to do a fair bit of research,' she volunteered, 'a lot of it in France? Maybe this would give you an opportunity to have a break from what's been going on here.'

'Or maybe it would just be a continuation of what I've been doing before. Joshua thinks, thought, that I was good at exploring other people's feelings, but not my own.'

'And you think he might be right?'

Some part of Beatrice hoped that Amanda might have dismissed such a notion and she was rather disappointed by her querying response and so, even though she was on the phone, she shrugged her shoulders and said nothing.

'I gather from your silence that there's an element of truth here.'

'For God's sake, Amanda, I thought you were a friend. Of course I think there's an element of truth,' here imitating her friend's voice... 'it's just a bit hard to admit to.'

'Yes, well, can't you tell Roth that you need a couple of weeks to give some shape to the project before you give him a definitive answer and spend a bit of time in France for some r and r? What else are you going to do? And if you decide to do it as a drama, you know who to ask to produce it...'

'To tell you the truth, I don't know what drama there is in the story in the first place. It's only a hunch I have that maybe there's something contained in his history that might add a little zest to the over neat version of his life.'

'But you're good at that, Beatrice. Follow it. But don't give up on thinking what dear departed Joshua had to say.'

'And I thought you were a friend.'

'Oh, but I am, Beatrice Palmenter, I am.'

Although she was not prepared to admit it, Amanda's intimation that she should perhaps take time to look at herself had taken Beatrice aback and for the moment, as she had been doing for as long as she could remember, she wanted to shrug it off. She looked down on the Commercial Road and the lines of traffic inching forwards opposite each other under the imposing stare of Christ Church and did what might have been expected of her and changed the subject by phoning the number of the expert at the museum. It took a little time to be put through to Dr Harold Wesley who she imagined might be a crusty septuagenarian rarely allowed to see the light of day. In this, as in other recent assumptions, she was proved wrong.

'Hello, Harry here,' a pleasant voice told her.

Beatrice explained that she had been part of the group that had found the skull and it was clear from his response that he was only too glad to talk about the discovery.

'It's very old,' he said and she could hear the excitement in his voice, 'probably Anglo-Saxon, although we're still waiting final analysis on that. From the few teeth we've got, he or she was in good shape and had a pretty good life, although we're still not sure what happened in the end. Clearly a child, although we can't be sure of the sex.'

'I'm astonished you can tell so much already.'

'Oh, believe me, there's a lot more to come,' he replied, clearly pleased.

It was a surprise when he asked her if she wanted to come to the museum to learn more and she readily agreed, but it was an even greater surprise when, after she'd said yes and rung off, she burst into tears.

CHAPTER SIX

She searches the banks of the river up from the bridge, following its sinuous turns as far as the remains of the settlement where she was born, where the drunks and the homeless now shout their abuse in the gardens by the watergate, but there is no sign of her father's body. At this point the current of the river stops and rests before flowing outwards again, taking her with it, all the time looking at objects floating in the water. She knows about death and she is proud that her father had died in battle but she wants him to be buried with the other dead, along with the possessions he loved. It would be dark in an hour and she knows that her mother will be worried and she begins to run again, her bare feet in the soft mud left by the departing water, a lone spirit in the marshy ground.

When finally she returns, they are burning the bodies and the flames lick into the evening sky, the sparks drifting away with the wind. She sees her mother revealed in the light of the large bonfire, framed in the doorway of their home, her face calm and accepting of her fate, comfortable that her husband's sacrifice had not been in vain, but for them all. Her mother worked with flame and fire, softening the gold and silver, creating the alloys that her clever hands turned into beautiful objects. The smoke rises and she sees that her mother is once again holding the small axe pendant in her hand, turning it over between her fingers, occasionally rubbing the golden outline. It is not quite a relic but a token of the man whose body is no more. Later, when she thinks her mother is alseep, she cries for her father, her body curled tight to contain her sobbing. Her mother comes over and gently strokes her hair and kisses the tears from her cheeks, holding her hand until her breathing changes and she lets go her sadness.

In the morning the ashes are raked cool and then placed delicately and solemnly in twelve pottery urns, one for each of the men who were killed. She watches her mother walk forward towards the nearest pot and place the tiny axe head on top of the ashes it contains. Later the urns are carried and then buried in graves just outside the walls that will later become the Barbican.

The community gathers around in support and some ask if she might spend time with them, bringing offerings of food with their consolation. She knows her mother is an important figure, for there is deference as well as sympathy in the manner of those that visit. Her mother has always made her aware of their position, independent, owners of land and, above all, possessed of a skill prized and demanded by others, near and far. Her first husband, she had told her, had made jewellery and when he died at the old settlement, in the first month of their marriage, her mother had taken over, proving to be a greater craftsman. As a widow she had power, but no protection and soon she married again and, hardened once, she was able, the girl knew, to absorb this second blow and take it in her stride.

On this bleak day, when the house no longer contained the physical presence of her father, but where she could still imagine him walking in through the door, her mother reaffirms their status and tells her that life will go on, that she is treasured and that the gods would look after her father and their future. She looks upwards and can see the pride in her mother's face and while she takes solace in this, feels again that something is changing inside her that was sacred to just her, a separateness that had begun the moment, unseen, her father had tumbled lifeless into the river. She feels it even more when she begins to explore the down river shoreline that afternoon, up beyond where Wapping police station would later be built. She looks eastwards and knows that not far beyond the horizon the men who had killed her father would have returned to their settlements. She cannot find her father's body and decides that he is gone forever, that he will only exist in some corner of her mind to be visited every now and again, for comfort or remorse.

She sees a ship being brought in on the tide, an unusual shape and size and the men on its prow, delighted that their destination is at last clear, steering for the jetties to the right of the bridge. What had only a few days earlier been a scene of battle is now returned as an arena of commerce.

She breaks into a run, banishing her thoughts, eager to see what the traders are bringing and to hear their stories of other lands.

CHAPTER SEVEN

It had taken the best part of a week for her mother to phone her congratulations, not that these were given directly.

'Your father would have been very proud of you.'

Eileen Palmenter was not given to praising her daughter and Beatrice was hard put to think of any time her mother had shown unalloyed pleasure at her achievements. This was a fact of life that had to be tolerated, even though at times, when she was younger, it was difficult.

'I'm told these Barta Awards are quite prestigious, although I can't say I've heard of them.'

'Bafta, mother.'

'That's what I said, Bafta.'

Eileen Palmenter spoke with an accent that was related to no part of this country, or any other for that matter, but pockets of its type were alive and well and could be found clustering in the Home Counties.

'I'm coming to town and I thought it might be a good idea if you bought me lunch. Don't you think that's a good idea? Shall we meet in John Lewis at the usual place?'

There had never been anything motherly about Eileen Palmenter and her daughter, an early arrival in her life, had largely been raised by nannies and au pairs. As much as Beatrice tried to distance herself from her mother, there was a blind persistence about Eileen Palmenter which she found hard to deflect and no matter how much she resisted her gravitational pull by creating her own world, her mother remained an immovable and consistent obstacle.

'I'm pretty busy at the moment, mother.'

'Oh, come on Beatrice, I'm sure you can't have started your next project just yet. It would be nice to have some company.'

Why does she always do this to me, thought Beatrice, unable to come up with a quick and effective lie to put off her mother? So she capitulates and finds herself agreeing to meet later for lunch in one of the several restaurants in John Lewis so favoured by women who, once a week, dress up and take the train to town to shop. When they kiss, they barely touch, her mother offering her body in a stiff, forward movement, her arms by her side, so that physical contact was kept to the minimum.

'Are you sure you're ok, dear? You look a little pale,' is the opening salvo and before Beatrice could answer, 'I've bought a darling little dress for the summer. You know Joan and I are going on that cruise around the Mediterranean and this will be perfect,' revealing through the packaging the corner of a pale blue outfit heavily patterned with pink and white flowers.

'It's very nice, mother.'

'I didn't think you'd like it.'

Joan was another replacement companion for Beatrice's father, who died when his daughter was twelve, one of a succession of women Eileen uses to escort her on trips and holidays.

'I might be going to France,' Beatrice said, picking up the theme.

'Oh, we must meet. I'm sure the boat will dock at one of those lovely French ports, Toulouse, you know where I mean.'

Beatrice nodded.

'And will you be alone?' her mother added. 'Anthony?' she asked, with a little tilt of her head.

Anthony was the only boyfriend her mother remembered, an expert on classic cars, rather conventional and liked by her mother because he always wore a tie and was overwhelmingly polite to her. There had been a least half a dozen so called boyfriends since, but when the subject of partners was raised, which it was at every meeting, Anthony was her default setting.

'Alone, mother.'

'What is it about you and men, Beatrice? Anthony was such a nice boy. Don't you want to settle down?'

Beatrice knew only too well that it was not possible to have a rational conversation with her mother about this and she deliberately chose not to engage.

'It's partly work,' she said.

'Such a shame.'

To what this referred, Beatrice wasn't sure. Perhaps it was merely a generic comment about her daughter, a blanket expression of disappointment. Eileen Palmenter's grasp on her daughter's life, only marginal at the best of times, became increasingly slim in the years after the death of her husband.

'Don't you want to know what I might be doing in France?'

'Where, darling?'

If the remoteness of her mother and the absence of her father had done anything, Beatrice told herself, it was to give her a resolve to create a different sort of life for herself, regardless of the wishes of her mother.

'Television. Well, I suppose it's fine until you marry,' had been a typical response. 'Although what your father would have said, heaven only knows.'

Beatrice's father had been an actuary, a profession she never understood until one evening, after she'd been teased at school for not knowing, she had asked. Jim Palmenter sat his daughter down and in measured tones told her that it was a job which looked into the future by assessing facts about the past. He was involved with pensions, money people saved for their retirement and he showed her complicated graphs about how long people lived in order, he said, that he could estimate what future liabilities might be like for his company. She didn't understand everything but she recalled the conversation at his funeral not long afterwards when it seemed unbearably sad that a man whose life was expected to last a lot longer should unexpectedly be cut so short.

'I found a skull by the Thames over the weekend.'

'Darling, really, I'm eating.'

Am I my mother's daughter, she wondered and not for the first time? On the way home, though, she realised that the lunch, however tortuous, had served one purpose, for it had, by chance, flushed out a decision on France. On her return to the flat she looked up Troumeg's number in Deal and called, but the line appeared to be disconnected. She tried his Chelsea apartment where a rather sharp female voice told her that he no longer lived there and that she was so tired of receiving calls for him that she was going to change the number. Finally Beatrice called his agent, a long-suffering woman with a smoker's voice.

'Goodness only knows where he is,' she said. 'One minute he was here, then he was gone. It's typical. He's done it before. Have you tried his Paris number?'

Beatrice had read that he had a home in France, but no further details so she copied down the number and address.

'I have to tell you, though, these details must be at least twenty years old.'

Beatrice sat and looked at the number. The lunch with her mother rested uneasily on her stomach and the life of Joseph Troumeg lay scattered on her bed. When the telephone rang it made her jump in surprise.

'Is that Beatrice? It's Harry, Harry Wesley from the museum. I was wondering, well, curious to know if you could remember exactly where the skull was found?'

'Good afternoon, Harry. Yes, it was marked in a couple of places, a tagged steel rod where it was picked up and with a cross reference on the embankment itself. There was a GPS recorded of the location as well, which 4Shore will have.'

'I was hoping you might show me yourself. But would you like to come to the museum first and I could explain what we've done so far?'

There was an assumption on the part of Dr Harold Wesley that she would be free and rather than challenge it, as she might usually have done, Beatrice agreed, glad to shelve the life of the all-too-perfect restaurateur in favour of one far from complete life still in the process of being pieced together.

The new building had been constructed around the remains of the Roman wall which once upon a time guarded the northern approaches to old London, now the Barbican. Beatrice looked at the wall and thought it was like a stone quilt, patched, repaired, extended over the years to produce a solid record of time passing, useless now except as an ornament of curiosity but still powerful.

'Ah, you must be Beatrice. I'm Harold, Harry Wesley. Pleased to meet you.'

He was wearing a dark blue T-shirt over faded chinos and dirty white trainers edged in grey, not quite what she expected but why should doctors of archaeology come in tweeds and brogues which is what she had imagined. He set off and gestured her onwards with a backward wave of his hand, through two security doors swiped open with a card on a short chain on his belt. At least he had the air of a distracted professor, she thought, arriving in a room of smart grey benches lit by a series of angled lamps giving very specific white light.

'This is a sort of bone mortuary,' he said, launching straight in, 'where we do our post mortems. Slightly late, of course, but better late than never. And, at least in what we do, with no criminal to prosecute at the end. Mind you, we're always on the look out for villains.'

She continued to follow him to the furthest bench where, lit from below with an opaque white light, and again from above, rested the yellow brown skull. Beatrice was stopped in her tracks the moment she saw it and raised one hand to her mouth, a gesture noted by the doctor.

'Perhaps you don't like this sort of thing? Some people don't.' It wasn't spoken sympathetically, more as a matter of fact.

'No, it's not that.' But what it was, she couldn't quite say except, to herself, that she couldn't just regard it as a remnant of bone, a relic of history but as the basis of a person.

She was surprised when he picked up on this unspoken thought. 'We become attached to one or two fragments that come in here, especially those we can, well, put some flesh on as it were.' He slid onto a high stool in front of the skull and brought to life the computer on a telescopic arm to his right. It revealed a computer image of the skull which he now animated so it turned through three hundred and sixty degrees.

'And what about this one?'

'Well, we haven't formed a relationship just yet. These things take time. This one is still playing hard to get.'

Nothing about the skull could indicate to Beatrice that this had once been the head of a boy or girl but the more she stared at the place where the eyes had been she imagined the face of a young girl that would have existed around them.

'Why, when you seem to know so much already, can't you tell the sex?'

Dr Harold Wesley lowered a microscope above the skull and in another backward gestured, offered the seat to Beatrice so that she could look down on a detail of the skull revealed on the computer screen.

Adjusting the microscope, the image showed the line of bone just above one of the eye sockets. 'The whole shape of the skull, the eye sockets and the development of the teeth, even the few that we have, show that it was probably pre-pubescent, or at least on the edge of puberty.'

For Beatrice Palmenter, her eyes moving between the computer image and the inert skull, there was no doubt it was a young girl and she wanted to reach out and touch the remains as an act of affinity.

He then shifted the microscope and increased its magnification. 'Here you see a close-up of the upper jaw. Shame we haven't got the lower but for our purposes this is fine to be going on with.' With a small wooden stick, he pointed at the screen where one of the remaining teeth looked like a stranded iceberg. 'There's no evidence of a third molar here, which would indicate that whatever the gender it was younger than about seventeen.'

The forensic explanations continued under the cold white light, the stick now tracing the edge of the tooth. 'There are no Harris Lines here, which, if there had been, would tell us that for periods of the life of this individual there was severe malnutrition. And the examination of the dental enamel confirms this.' His tone was all matter of fact.

Again Beatrice looked at the screen and then the skull, amazed at one and the same time at how much the examination had revealed and just how little of the life of this young person was available to them.

'There is just the slimmest of chances that we may find other pieces of the skeleton when we return to the Thames. If we're lucky, DNA testing will confirm a connection and, if we're luckier still, they will be parts more likely to tell us the sex. It's a long shot, as it always is when a thousand years has come and gone, but that's what's exciting, don't you think?'

For the first time Dr Harold Wesley looked directly at her and she could see the animation in his eyes.

'Do you have a name for her?' she asked.

He shook his head. 'You've decided it's a girl?'

She looked at the skull and thought of it washing backwards and forwards in the dirty water of the Thames until coming to rest in sight of the tip of the Isle of Dogs under the gaze of the grandiose buildings of Greenwich.

'We'll call her Flotsam,' she said.

Dr Harold Wesley glanced at her and nodded his agreement.

'Flotsam it is. It's a word without gender, anyway. But let's go back to the Thames to be sure, shall we?'

CHAPTER EIGHT

Life goes on, just as the river rises and falls. She takes comfort and strength from its certainty, just as she does from her mother who has returned to her work bench. She sees how she has coped with the death of her husband, tackling what is in front of her, seeing possibilities in the future and not yearning for the past. She watches her mother work at the brooch she has been making for several months, squinting at a detail in the design in the low light. She shares her mother's excitement as she seals the pattern with gold so that the magnificent stone at its centre has the setting it deserves. Her mother tells her about the brooch and the red stone which she had bought on the quays a year earlier. It is deeper, she says, than any of the garnets she has used in the past, richer and more lustrous. Her mother explains that as soon as she had seen the stone she knew she would use it as the centrepiece of a brooch she would make and give to her daughter the day she became a woman. Her mother puts her hand on to her head and tells her that she thanks the gods for the gift of a child who seems so wise. Her mother moves her fingers over the smooth stone mounted in a gold shield and she takes her mother's other hand, not for comfort, nor in fear, but to register the start of a journey that she knows is just beginning.

She tells her mother about the arrival of the merchant ship and how she had gone down to the quay to watch it dock, the crew stepping on to land for the first time in perhaps months. She tells of her wonder at the treasures that lay on the deck and how she drifted amongst the new faces to observe the unloading. She hears the Danes have retreated to their camps in Essex ready to attack again. These fierce men appeared to live to fight, intent on the gold and silver in the town's mint and the position on the river with its bridge and docks. She admires her mother who must live with the threat of death, a black crow on her shoulder. Later she goes down to the docks with her mother and watches her seek out the merchants. She admires these sailors who travel great distances to other lands, browned by the sun and winds, bringing with them their strange smells and exotic goods. One or two boats she has seen before and they have travelled, her mother tells her, hundreds of miles, bringing woven cloth and pottery and taking away finished goods, including her mother's jewellery. She knows she has inherited from her mother the fascination of this intermingling of people, the excitement of barter and exchange. She can see the foreigners admiring her mother, noting that she is a woman of substance and position, with her neck rings and pendants and the beads on the sweep of her dress distinguishing her so that men would bow before entering a trade. She absorbs this, aware that her mother is beginning a new journey as well. Today she is shown rough pink stones which sparkle with tiny silver points, but they are too rough and she watches how her mother declines them before moving along the quay. Later some of the men get drunk and she hears their strange songs coming from the taverns and boarding houses just up from the river.

And then her mother is stopped by a man who lowers his head before speaking. He asks if she is the woman who makes the jewellery sought by all who came to this port. The question, she knows, demands no answer and he produces a cloth tied with a bow which he opens carefully to spread its contents before her mother. She knows this is no accidental meeting and she sees her mother pick up the bands of gold wire, polished stones in yellow, pale green, glass and garnet with pieces of silver. There is something between the man and her mother that she can't quite understand but she knows that the man has deliberately sought out her mother, that he knew her from the start. She suspects that he has heard of the death of her father and she watches her mother pull her cloak around her, avoiding his eyes, to examine the precious materials in front of her. He speaks and offers her mother a deal, proposing that she takes them all in return for creating a necklace so beautiful that it would be remarked on whenever it was worn. He is sure that she can achieve this during the month that he will remain in the port. He brings the four corners of the cloth together, reties the bow and hands the bundle to her mother who turns to her, stoops down and kisses the top of her head. The wind catches in the sails of the boats.

CHAPTER NINE

She heard the strange monotone of the foreign telephone and imagined it ringing in the heart of Paris, all other sounds suppressed, the camera moving over the rooftops, the ring getting louder all the time, the location becoming more specific, eventually dropping through open French doors where a light wind is blowing the lace curtains, to the noisy telephone where, in close up, it is stopped by a hand powdered with flour. 'How dare you interrupt my cooking.' The words are spoken out of vision, clearly the voice of Joseph Troumeg. The title of the film now appears, JOSEPH TROUMEG: A LIFE IN FOOD, the letters rearranging themselves like Scrabble pieces until order is achieved.

But there was no answer. She saw from the address the agent had given her that Troumeg's apartment was in the 19th and not one of the smarter *arrondissements* down closer to the Seine. She Googled a map of Paris and saw that its location was to the north-east of the Gare du Nord, not far from the Bassin de la Villette. When she had begun seeing him, three years ago, he had told her how he despised mobile phones so she knew that to catch him she would have to try at regular intervals during the day in the hope of finding him at home. She felt an interest stirring in her again and she was grateful, for now at least, that she was not encumbered with a partner with whom she would have to negotiate her movements.

Beatrice had arranged to meet Harold Wesley by the Cutty Sark in Greenwich at midday but the pursuit of the elusive restaurateur had delayed her and unless she hurried she would be late. She need not have worried, for the osteoarchaeologist – she enjoyed saying the word – lived up to her stereotype of an absent-minded professor by arriving half an hour after her, complaining how hard it was to get to this part of the world. She estimated that he was probably five years older than her and he appeared to be wearing the same clothes as the day before. He was fiddling with a GPS receiver as she led him to the foreshore. The tide was just about to reach its lowest point and the river looked forlorn and diminished in the weak midday sun. Even from the embankment steps she could see the short steel rod marking the spot where the skull had been found and the GPS device confirmed this as they arrived. Only now did she realise that he'd had the exact position of the discovery even before he had phoned her. Dr Harold Wesley was engrossed to the point of exclusion and he began a close examination of the area around the marker, placing coloured needles in the ground to show his progress.

'You're the film maker, aren't you?' he asked with his face still to the stony, muddy ground.

'I am, but that's not why I'm here. Did you look me up or did Amanda tell you?'

'Both.' He crouched lower, pulling on a pair of thin rubber gloves, before picking up a small object and turning it over in his hands. 'Might be human,' he said, more to himself than her. 'So why are you here?'

'I could say because it's not television, but that wouldn't be entirely true. I wanted to know more about...' she nearly said "the skull" but stopped herself... 'the girl, Flotsam.' Using the name for the first time felt good, almost a mark of respect.

He appeared not to have heard. 'Ah, this is interesting,' he said, holding up what looked like a small glass marble. 'Might be old, but nothing to do with Flotsam. Why are you glad it's not television?' Still not looking at her.

'It makes a change to be curious about something without compressing it into the form television would like.'

'I think I understand you.' He carried on quartering the foreshore, the area around the marker rod now a series of grid lines. 'But you're quite good, aren't you?'

She presumed he had read about the Bafta. 'I've won an award, if that's what you mean. Aren't the chances of finding anything relating to Flotsam pretty remote?'

'It would be a chance in a million to find more of the skeleton, but it would be a dereliction of duty not to try. That's my job, if you like. I'm compressed by its demands, just as you are in yours.'

Beatrice was quite surprised at this declaration which, again, was made with his back to her.

'There was a skeleton discovered not far from here,' he continued as if he hadn't made the last remark, 'revealed only at the lowest tide. We had less than two hours to lift it before it would have disappeared for maybe another year. It was about three hundred years old and we managed to find quite a lot of the skeleton nearby. He'd probably been murdered, struck on the head with a sharp object anyway.'

'What do you think happened to Flotsam?'

'That's the fascination, isn't it? It's my job to give these bones the life they once had. Not easy when there's a thousand years between us.'

Beatrice smiled, for wearing a different cap, she would have pounced on this man's statement as the beginning of a film about the dead of the Thames, or some such title, but now she could just listen and put that part of her to one side. She watched him pick something else from amongst the debris and place it in a plastic bag. Perhaps he was aware that she was looking at him because he turned towards her and then stood.

'Getting to know Flotsam won't be easy, but we'll try.' Out of the diffused white light of his laboratory, Dr Harold Wesley had more colour in his face.

'I hope I can help.'

'Well, I've found one or two more bone fragments, but so many animals have been dumped in the river over the years it's hard to tell what you've got until you get them back to the lab.'

'What are you working on now?' He had returned to not looking at her.

She pondered her reply. 'Have you heard of Joseph Troumeg?'

'Sure, the food fellow. What's he done?'

'I thought I would make a programme about him.'

'You don't sound too convinced.'

Was she surprised that she'd conveyed her doubts so clearly? 'You're right,' she said. 'I'm still at the research stage, but I have a hunch he might be interesting.'

'We're in the same line of business, then. Examining other people's lives.'

At this point she almost admitted that some of those people might say she should look at her own life, but she gauged this might be too familiar.

'I've been told that I'm more interested in the dead than I am with living,' he said and she heard him chuckle. 'Could be right.'

'I know what you mean,' she said, and then corrected herself. 'I don't mean about you, but I sometimes wonder if it isn't easier to delve into other people's lives than it is into your own.'

She had come to the conclusion by now that although Harold Wesley appeared not to listening, he usually was and that, sooner or later, he would respond. In this case, it was later.

'Look at this,' he said and she leaned forward to see what he was holding. 'It's a flint spear, or at least it was attached to the end of spear and bound in place. It's survived better than the iron and bronze versions.' He handed the knapped flint to her and she felt the edges, still sharp after all these years. 'And do you think they're right, these people who tell us we should examine ourselves a bit more?'

'Not always.' She waited. 'But sometimes.'

He took out a camera and photographed the grid that he'd created and then in a notebook quickly sketched the squares, marking those in which he had found the different objects.

'It's the routines that are so comforting, don't you find? But I suppose that's the same with all jobs.'

She wasn't sure exactly what he meant, but she attempted to reply in kind. 'When I'm directing, on location, or in the gallery, I'm wearing blinkers so it's easy not to think about anything else.'

'My point exactly.'

They were the only people on the foreshore, at the blunt end of a great meander which brought the river almost back on itself. At the top of the loop the huge docks had been built to join both sides of the Thames. She thought again of Flotsam, the life of a girl on these very banks, whose story they were now in the process of piecing together.

'I wonder if Flotsam saw life in the same way that we do?'

'Why not. If she's as old as we think she is, then she may have been lucky and been born a high ranking female. You'd be surprised how advanced the Anglo-Saxons were. Women's liberation wasn't just the product of the late twentieth century, you know.'

She didn't know and rather like her preconceptions of what an osteoarchaeologist might look and act like, her imagined view of Flotsam was somewhat wilder than a description which would include the words "high ranking".

'What I meant was, did she have the same idea of self that we do? Did Flotsam ever examine herself like we're being told to do all the time?'

'I doubt it. Probably too busy staying alive. But then I'm only an expert on ancient bones.'

He wanted to take more photographs from the bank and while he did so Beatrice tried Troumeg's number again but without luck.

'Who were you phoning?'

'I was trying the apartment of the elusive Joseph Troumeg in Paris. I need to go and see him.'

'My parents once went to his place in Mayfair. I don't think he's got it anymore. What's he doing now?'

'He wants me to make a series about his life in food.'

'But you don't?'

'Not really. I don't have the patience for that sort of film making.'

'Which is what?'

'Troumeg showing people how to make fancy dishes is a different prospect to a documentary about his life.'

'Do you look down on food programmes?'

'No. They're hard to make, but it's not what interests me.'

'Well, it seems you have to catch your main ingredient first.' And he chuckled again and Beatrice found herself joining in.

'From what I've read of him he would be a *dorade royale*.'

'What's that?'

'It's a type of sea bream with a rather distinguished nose.'

'And does he have a distinguished nose?'

'Not exactly, but he is rather pleased with himself and he cooked me sea bream once and told me about the different varieties.'

'I thought there was only one.'

'Me, too, which is probably why I'm not going to make a food series.'

'Will you have to go to Paris?'

'I'll certainly have to go to France. He was brought up there and I want to find out whether what he says about his childhood is true.'

Harold Wesley looked at her now. 'Do you have reason to doubt his version?'

'I suppose I do a bit.'

'How come?'

'It's all too neat.'

'Isn't that what happens to everyone's backgrounds the older they get, especially if they're well known?'

'I know, I know. It's just a hunch I have.'

'Useful, hunches. I rely on them.'

'Really?'

'With so little information available to us we have to make some deductive leaps, the sort of thing that the most sophisticated equipment can't do.'

Beatrice realised that in the months that she had known Joshua she had never had a conversation like this. 'Well, let's hope we're both lucky with our deductive leaps.'

'By the way, most people call me Harry. Are you always Beatrice?'

'Some people call me Beatrice. My mother always does, in the way that mother's have. I hate Triss, which I'm afraid I get a bit. What do you think?'

'What about Beattie?'

'I don't mind that.'

'Well, Beattie it is then. You look like one.'

'I shall take that as a compliment, shall I?'

But Dr Harold Wesley was already pulling out his steel needles and packing his kit, his back to her again and the river had turned and would soon wash over the ground he had so painstakingly searched. And so it goes, she thought, the washing in and the washing out, the sifting of evidence, the revealing and the burying, history moving further away with every tide, every new encounter.

'Thank you,' she said as they walked away from the river. 'I enjoyed that very much.'

'Me, too, Beattie, me too.'

CHAPTER TEN

She begins to bleed under what is now Cannon Street railway bridge, close to where platform two will one day end, at a point where she thinks her father might have come to rest. Perhaps she had willed it to happen here so that her father could share this important moment. Almost from the first morning after his death she had felt different, a series of new sensations in her body and this sign seems to be the result. She is bleeding for her father, just as he had bled for her. Her mother had told her it would happen, had taken her into her arms to explain that it was nothing to fear but to celebrate. It meant that she had moved from being a child to a woman and if and when she wanted, she could have children. Her mother had described how this happened, gently taking her to the next stage in her life. The blood on her legs confirms this and she wipes it away with tufts of grass. In the centre of the river a blackened log with two broken and bare branches floats slowly by and she narrows her eyes and imagines it is her father acknowledging this rite of passage. She raises her hand and waves in return and thinks it might be the last childish gesture she will ever make.

Her stomach aches and she hugs her knees close to her body for warmth and watches the log until it disappears from view.

On her return she doesn't enter the house, but hesitates and watches her mother at work from the entrance. Leaning over her bench, deeply absorbed in what she is doing, she at first fails to register her standing there. When she does look up, she knows that her mother recognises what has happened. She sits her down and goes to fetch a cloth which she tells her to wear until the bleeding stops and then, kissing her forehead, tells her to wait for she has something special for her. Once more she returns with a cloth, but this one is gold, folded and tied with crimson thread. The glow from the material seems to light up the mother's face and she senses this glow is transferred to her when she is handed the bundle. For these seconds reality is suspended as she slowly opens the cloth thinking this alone was the most beautiful of presents. When she comes to the brooch she hardly dares touch what she has revealed. Slowly her hand moves forward until the tip of her forefinger rests on the deep ruby stone. She feels its smoothness and marvels at the depth of its colour. Cautiously she picks up the brooch and holds it carefully to her chest and looks up to her mother, who nods her approval. It affirms all that her mother has told her, that she is important, that she is the equal of any man and that she would inherit all that belongs to the family. When she pins the brooch to the rough cloth of her tunic, its power and beauty seem to flow into her and although she wishes her father was by her side, she can feel their final embrace on the bridge. Tears form in the corners of her mother's eyes and now it is her turn to become the comforter.

That night she dreams she is running down the hill towards the river, so light that each of her strides takes her a great distance and brings her to the water in no time at all. The bridge is empty and she stands alone at the centre, at the point where she had last seen her father. She runs her fingers over the stone before unclipping it and holding it in the palm of her hand. She then kisses it before tipping it down into the water.

She wakes sweating and feels under her bed for the gold cloth. Her head sinks back in relief when she sees the brooch is still there, the polished red at the centre reflecting the outline of her face.

CHAPTER ELEVEN

Beatrice awoke from a deep sleep to find herself in the armchair by the telephone. The light told her it was late afternoon and her watch confirmed that it was shortly after five. She had returned home from her meeting by the Thames with the intention of phoning Troumeg's apartment yet again, but she could neither remember sitting in the chair nor whether she had made the call. She tried the number once more, but without success and sank back in frustration, the setting sun reflecting in a window on the other side of the road. She stared at the rectangle of orange light, deepening in intensity until it slipped away and was absorbed into the London brick of the market building, the shadows darkening all the time.

She then made a series of calls to the list of friends and acquaintances of Joseph Troumeg that she had accumulated two years ago asking if any could help track him down. Some of them knew of the Paris apartment and nearly all confirmed that this was not the first time the man had evaporated before their very eyes. Why not just go to Paris and hope for the best, she asked herself? If he couldn't be found, then she could enjoy a long weekend. Because, she answered, he might also be in New York, or San Francisco, or simply not answering the phone in Deal.

She picked up her mobile and scrolled through her contacts until she came to Ben Tynan, a predecessor to Joshua and a relationship which had suffered the same fate. She had once worked with him at The Digital Corporation where he was a producer specialising in investigative programmes, many of them to do with cyber security and internet fraud. He had left to form Scope, a firm offering advice to companies and individuals who feared hacking and the electronic theft of valuable data. He was the company's owner, executive director and only member of staff.

'And what brings you back into my jungle?' Ben's response to hearing her voice was flat and cautious to the point of hostility. 'What do you want?'

At this point, not ten seconds into the call, Beatrice realised it had probably been a mistake.

'C'mon Beatrice, you didn't call to see how I am,' he said, breaking the silence. 'Which is fine, by the way, since you ask.'

She had no option but to respond. 'Yes, I wanted some advice, but I see now that I shouldn't have called.'

'Same old, same old. Better get it off your chest, then.'

'Do you know an easy way of finding out if someone has recently left the country and not yet returned?'

'You're aware of my day rates, I think?'

She waited. They had seen each other for several intense months but it had been clear to Beatrice early on that this was a relationship doomed to failure, entered into in all good faith but floundering for the usual reasons in a familiar routine. He was good looking, clever and, for a man, reasonably astute but it had been unwise for her to exploit him by getting back in touch.

'Well, I'm glad to hear just a little embarrassment in your silence. What's the name?'

'Troumeg. Joseph. I think he's in France but lives most of

the time in London and Deal.'

'And you're making a programme about him.'

'I might.'

'Poor him. When might he have left?'

'Probably not long ago, this year say. I can't be certain.'

'Unlike you, Beatrice. I'll get back to you. This number?'

Did she feel any shame at exploiting this man whom she had hurt when she abruptly ended their relationship? Beatrice Palmenter had to admit that she didn't but her decision to call him, clearly motivated by self interest, did puzzle her. Was she really that blatant? It was part of a pattern, though, which contrasted sharply with the conduct of her professional life which was increasingly successful and more controlled, as if one was in direct proportion to the other. She had cleared the decks again, banishing Joshua to the same graveyard as Ben and she was free to pursue her next project about which her thinking was clear and methodical. Within a few minutes of having spoken to Ben she had banished the memory of his tone of voice to continue the pursuit of her subject.

According to the family history as recounted by Joseph Troumeg, his mother met his father in Paris a few years before the war and Beatrice assumed they were both living in the capital at the time. If she could confirm this then it would further justify a journey to Paris. She scoured the information she had in her possession and went on-line in an attempt to find evidence of where exactly his parents might have been living when they met. She gathered from the official state web site that records of birth, death and marriage remain confidential for a hundred years unless a birth certificate can be produced showing a direct line of descent. She was sure that Ben could find a way around this but knew she couldn't phone him and set this task as well as the other. Well, for the moment at least.

She found in an early interview in the *Daily Telegraph* that Troumeg's mother's name was Odile Leval and his description of her was typical. "Odile," he said in the piece, "was ideal.

The perfect mother, at least to me. I remember her watering my red wine at dinner at a very early age. She always treated me as a grown up." Beatrice could only assume that Odile had married – here she checked the article again – at some point either before or after she had become pregnant with Joseph.

Ben Tynan phoned back ten minutes later. 'According to passport records, Joseph Troumeg left London two months ago on Eurostar. It appears he has not returned. And no, I can't tell you if he was going to Paris, or Lille or, indeed, any other part of France or Europe.'

And he was gone, his anger confirmed by the abrupt arrival of the dialling tone. This was no more than she deserved and yet she felt irritated for it meant that it would be more difficult to ask him for further help. The mild discomfort she experienced at her contradictory behaviour she pushed to one side.

She returned to the map of Paris and assumed that Joseph Troumeg, a man prone to disappearing at a moment's notice without telling his friends, was somewhere to be found in this random gathering of streets. She phoned the apartment one more time without success before booking a Eurostar ticket for the following morning. She found a hotel not far from the canal, a reasonably short walk from the Gard du Nord. She located the Mairie for the 19th *arrondissement*, where she imagined a futile attempt to discover more of the family background of Joseph Troumeg against the united ranks of French bureaucracy, before printing out a map of the district in order to orientate herself. She returned to the scraps of information scattered about her room and saved on her computer, the abundant, well worn threads of Joseph Troumeg's life. She realised she was beginning to stake out her ground in the same way that Dr Harold Wesley divided the foreshore of the Thames, placing a contrived pattern over random pieces of information in order to bring about a semblance of order. She thought of the expert alone with his bones in his meticulously clean laboratory under the white lights attempting to confirm some facts about a life a thousand years older than that of Joseph Troumeg and infinitely more difficult to access. There was a momentary regret that she would be away from his investigations while she conducted her own and she pondered phoning him for a progress report. That she didn't might have had something to do with the result of her call to Ben, the thought of spoiling a relationship, although she didn't consciously register this until later when she was packing a small bag for her journey.

For now, the facts at her disposal about Joseph Troumeg reminded her that the man so hard to pin down was once a ubiquitous presence, hard to avoid. "He has transcended the world of food to become an international celebrity," gushed *The Times*, adding he was "as well known as Coca-Cola." If she had read that quotation once, she had read it twenty times, often repeated by Joseph Troumeg, usually referring to himself in the third person as an admiring onlooker of his own success. Beatrice wanted to shake this cosy recycling of facts, but she was finding it hard to find a way through the shiny smooth shellac finish of the story as presented.

The land line rang to interrupt her frustrations.

'Harry here,' he announced and she checked her watch to see that it was almost seven.

'Are you still working?'

'Sort of. Thought you'd like to know the radiocarbon dating analysis has come through.'

'Sure.' She knew, though, this wasn't the main reason for his calling.

'To within a hundred years one way or the other, she lived around about the turn of the first millennium. So, late Anglo-Saxon like we thought.'

'Incredible.'

'If you like I could tell you more over a drink?'

Beatrice experienced a faint wave of apprehension at the request, one she received at regular intervals and was usually adept at dealing with and didn't know how to respond.

'It's ok,' he said in the face of silence, 'it was only on the off-chance.'

'Thanks,' she said after a while, 'but would you mind if I said no. I'm going to Paris tomorrow and I've got to get myself organised.'

'Another time, then?'

'Yes. Sure. I don't know how long I'll be away but I'll give you a call as soon as I'm back. And thanks for the information about Flotsam.'

Beatrice Palmenter went into the kitchen and began preparing supper, her tall figure stooped over the stove, slowly slicing mushrooms and garlic and feeding pasta into a pan of boiling water. It was only as she sautéed the softened spaghetti, adding the other ingredients and stirring in the butter, that she saw that she had cooked enough for two, an understandable mistake since she had been used to cooking for Joshua. When she sat down she had the urge to phone Harry Wesley and take him up on his offer, but the moment was gone and she ate alone with the white spire of Christ Church bright in the window behind her. Somewhere a bell chimed the time.

CHAPTER TWELVE

The bell tolled a warning.

Where the eight streets meet, as they do today, the draped body is carried on the back of a cart, to be buried with the other victims outside the walls beyond Aldgate. The girl watches its progress from a rise in the ground where the Royal Exchange now stands, and she holds her tunic to her face, as the others walking alongside are doing. This is the fourth body she has seen this week, for the pox is spreading quickly, as it had the time before, taking hundreds in its path before disappearing as it arrives, silently and unseen. She runs back to her mother but the news that the line of death is getting closer has already reached her. Her mother had warned her to stay away, but she had chosen to ignore it for there is another dimension to her these days, a singularity of purpose that she could not ignore. When she arrives home her mother is working on the sailor's necklace, arranging the stones in a semi-circle first one way then the other, trying to decide which colours worked best together. She stands and watches the variations, her mother's fingers slowly changing the patterns, each time looking across to seek her reaction. The workbench, spread with pieces of bronze, silver and gold and coloured stones in pottery bowls, is the heart of calmness. Outside the plague is taking its toll on neighbours and the Norsemen are likely to attack again but in here time is being held at bay and they are suspended in a different reality.

The sailor comes later that afternoon. The way her mother is with him alerts her to a change she cannot fully explain. He inspects the progress of the necklace, praising her mother's skills and saying that her reputation was deserved. The man not only speaks strangely but brings with him different smells, hard to identify, but which draw her to the faraway places that exist in her imagination. She can see that her mother is happy and she asks if the sailor has a wife. Her mother holds her face in her hands and smiles when she shakes her head.

The following morning, down at the quays near the bridge, she wanders among the crowd looking for the man. There are half a dozen ships moored in line and the tide is high. Barrels of water are being rolled on to the ship furthest away and she sees that it is being made ready to leave. The ropes fore and aft are loosened and the craft is pushed away with long wooden poles until it catches the current and begins to drift down river. Through the bustle of activity on the dock she sees the sailor, who returns her stare with a slight nod of his head before turning away. She doesn't move but continues to watch him as he instructs others to load the boat he stands alongside, moving between groups, clearly in charge and occasionally glancing back in her direction. There is a familiarity about him that is almost conspiratorial and she knows then that he will play an important part in her life, but she cannot decide how.

In the centre of their home the necklace takes shape, the stones mounted in gold and hanging close together on oblong spirals, also of gold, threaded on copper wire. She sees her mother work day and night, aware that the necklace has to be finished before the sailor departs. When finally it is complete the work surface is cleared so that it can be laid out in all its glory on the black velvet bag, the focus of the room. It appears to have a light of its own and when the sailor comes he stands before it without speaking. She sees him look at her mother before stepping forward to pick up the necklace and place it around her neck. The man nods his approval and something passes between him and her mother and the girl slips away and walks down to the river and watches for her father, neither sure of what was in front of her or what she has left behind.

CHAPTER THIRTEEN

Even though she knew Paris, Beatrice felt that she was entering the unknown. It wasn't a feeling she could give any shape to, a generic sensation without apparent logic.

The Gare du Nord is a station of tourists and pickpockets. Not long ago she had filmed in Paris and several of her crew had lost wallets here and in the Metro. Beatrice was careful, then, to take her bag off her shoulder and tuck it under her arm for the walk towards Stalingrad, over the lines leading into the Gare de l'Est and her hotel. It began to rain and the reflections of the Quai de la Seine were lost on the peppered surface of the canal. The programme she had made here was called 'The Revolution is 40', about the students who had taken part in the riots of 1968, many of them now leading comfortable, middle-aged lives in smart apartments, their radical days long behind them. How quickly events become history she thought, making some facts clearer with perspective, but clouding many more.

She dumped her stuff at the hotel, a non-descript affair with a view on to the Bassin de la Villette but only via a narrow gap in the buildings opposite. Still, she wasn't here for the sightseeing although she was eager to see where Joseph Troumeg lived. It was no more than two streets away and as far as she could make out, his flat was on the top floor of an ornate block entered through a gated doorway to an inner courtyard. His name wasn't against the bell for 4b on the outside and nor did he respond when she pressed its brass surface. Some part of her had expected to run into him and she hung around hoping this might happen. Several factors had made Beatrice Palmenter a good producer and the greatest of these was persistence. If Troumeg had owned the flat for some time, which her phone calls to his friends the day before had confirmed, then he would be known in the local food shops. She tried the *boulangerie* without luck, then the butcher but it wasn't until the *charcuterie* that she found a response.

'*Monsieur* Troumeg? Sure. When he's here he always buys our special *assiettes*,' a florid faced man told her, his hand pointing towards a plate layered with cold meats and dotted with olives and herbs. 'He had one yesterday. A good customer.'

'Do you know how long he was staying for?'

'He didn't say. He comes and goes. I shall tell him a pretty young woman was looking for him, shall I?'

Beatrice gave him her card and he spoke her Christian name, relatively common in France, in the French way, but stumbled over Palmenter, trying to pronounce the 'l'. She thanked him, excited to know that she wasn't far behind her prey, but puzzled that Troumeg hadn't been to the *boulangerie* to pick up bread for breakfast. She deduced that he might have had breakfast in one of the local cafés so she chose the nearest, drew a blank but picked up the trail in the third. Pretty women can get answers to questions that many men can't.

'*Bien sûr*,' a young waiter said to her. 'He was here this morning. Always sits over there watching the canal, or reading his paper.'

'Did he look as though he might be going away today?'

'How would I know? Didn't seem to be in a hurry. Same as usual, really.' All this said with a smile on his face as he wiped the tables. She hesitated before giving him her card and she registered the look on his face as she did.

'It's a business matter,' she said.

'I'm sure it is, *mademoiselle*.'

She took a coffee and sat at a table on the covered terrace, watching the entrance to the flats, the sound of the rain pattering the canvas above her. After an hour she gave up but decided to ring the bell one more time. She had just crossed the road when she was astonished to see Joseph Troumeg appear around the corner. He was reading a newspaper and as he came nearer almost collided with her. She was too surprised to warn him but looking up at the last minute he recognised her.

'Ah, there you are,' he said, taking his keys from his pocket. 'C'mon.'

She followed him into the courtyard.

'You won't like the stairs,' he said, as though their age difference was the other way round. At the top he opened the door to his apartment and gestured for her to enter. The living room was small, but very light with a double aspect, a pair of long windows on one side and, directly ahead, French doors which seemed to lead to some sort of terrace.

'Shame it's raining, but do go ahead and look at the garden. It's the reason I came to live here.'

Beatrice couldn't believe her eyes. A small lawn stretched out in front of her, with a magnolia tree on one side and what looked like an apple on the other. There were two beds of flowers, bounded by a low box hedge and along one side ran a stone terrace with a balustrade looking across to curved leaded roofs opposite.

'Remarkable, isn't it? It's one of the best roof gardens in Paris. Or anywhere for that matter. I don't see enough of it.'

'But where do the roots go?'

'Sideways. There's about two and half feet of soil to play with. Not a lot, but enough. I have dinner up here in the summer.'

When she looked at him he was holding two glasses of champagne.

'Welcome.'

'You act as if you knew I was coming.'

'Some people call me a witch.'

'Or some person called you to say that I'd been asking questions about where you'd gone...'

Although she'd barely touched her drink, he topped up her glass and led her back into the small living room. 'I bought this place with old francs,' he said, ignoring her statement, 'and although there were lots of noughts on the end, it was surprisingly cheap. The garden was leaking, you see and nobody wanted the liability.'

'So how long have you had it?'

'I bought it with the newspaper serialisation of my first book.'

She remembered the quote, having read it several times and completed it: 'A place where I can go and retreat, like a trap-door spider.'

'You know me so well.' And then, with a change of gear, 'let me take you out tonight to a little place around the corner. Perhaps the best food in Paris at the moment.'

This was Joseph Troumeg, master of ceremonies, maitre'd, restaurateur supreme, setting the agenda, smoothing the path, making his guest feel important and giving the impression that all this was meant to happen.

'Oh, and well done about the Bafta, by the way. I saw your series and it was exceedingly good. How did you get those women to talk like that?'

Because in some ways I almost felt like one of them, she almost replied, which was a surprise since she had never articulated the thought before. 'It took me some time,' she said instead. 'Being a woman helped and, of course, I had an all women crew.' She had spent a month getting to know the women in the refuge before ever introducing a camera.

'Battered women seem to ask for it, don't they.' Joseph Troumeg wasn't posing a question but making a statement and from another man it might have produced a different response.

'That's the point. At some stage in their lives they've had the self-respect knocked out of them, so they don't think they're worth anything. As you say, they expect abuse.'

'And you think they are worth something?'

'Indeed they are.'

'Why were you interested in the first place?'

This conversation seemed to be the wrong way round but Beatrice found his directness difficult to escape. She was used to asking the questions, of using question and answer to her own ends.

'I met a woman who was being abused...'

'And it rang a bell with you?'

She didn't know why he'd jumped in and asked such a challenging question and she was thrown off guard.

'Not that I was aware of. But I was supportive.'

'Of course not,' he continued. 'I'm sorry I asked.'

Nevertheless, Beatrice was left strangely wounded by the question for she had always believed she had conveyed the very opposite picture, a young woman in charge of herself and her destiny.

'What I meant, I suppose,' he said, unabashed, 'is that personal experience always lends a certain weight to any project and I just wondered if these women felt that you were a fellow traveller, as it were.'

'They were certainly happy to have a sympathetic ear and one that they learned to trust.' Beatrice knew that she sounded rather prim and defensive and hoped that Troumeg wouldn't pick up on this, but she fancied he had. He changed the subject again and what he asked next she first interpreted as making up for his previous question.

'What are you. Five-ten, five-eleven?'

'Between the two,' she said, over her glass.

'I seem to remember that you had a boyfriend when we first met. Adrian, wasn't it, the chef? It didn't work out?'

'You've got a good memory,' she said, without committing herself any further.

'I don't suppose you're short of suitors,' he said, emptying the remains of the bottle into her glass. 'Good looking woman have such power. I've had the opportunity over the years to watch them at work.'

'That doesn't sound all that complimentary.'

'Oh, I meant no offence. But men can be such saps, don't you think? Give them a pretty face and they're done for.'

'I've had a couple of boyfriends since Adrian,' she said, omitting the fact that, as far as she was concerned, both fell into the category just defined by Troumeg.

'You must tell me more later,' he said, 'over dinner.'

She returned to her hotel, kicked off her shoes and lay on the bed aware that she had been both charmed and criticised by Troumeg but not quite certain in what proportion. She began to think about the evening and the approach she would take to get him to take part in the film, but she fell asleep before she could decide on a strategy.

She had not brought the clothes for a smart restaurant but she needn't have worried, for *l'Assiette* had none of the usual formal starchiness of a Michelin starred restaurant, the tables crowded together in a comfortable room with scuffed white floorboards. Troumeg, who had arrived before her, rose to his feet as she entered and he beckoned her to the table in the window which looked on to the canal basin. He gave her the chair with the view and even before they sat down a figure in whites appeared at their table.

'Ah, Jean-Paul, may I introduce one of the best film makers in England, Beatrice Palmenter.'

'*Enchanté.*'

'This is Jean-Paul's place and when you taste the food you'll want to come back.'

Beatrice looked up at the chef who gave a little bow towards her. 'If I might recommend "*Le Menu Gourmand*",' he said and smiled.

'You don't ignore his suggestions, Beatrice. They're really

orders dressed up to sound polite.'

And so it was that she ate one of the best meals she'd ever tasted and discovered that Joseph Troumeg didn't soften his approach to her at all.

'You're not here to talk about the series I want to make, are you?' he said as the *mousse de chèvre au miel et huile d'olive* was served.

She shook her head.

'Do you always get what you want?'

She thought about it, taking the soft cheese and rolling its sweetness around her mouth. 'I'm afraid not.'

'I was talking about your work.'

'So was I,' she said, but she knew that he could see that this wasn't the complete truth.

'You know I don't want to make a film of my life, not the way you want it, anyway.'

'Why not?'

'Boring. It's all in the past.'

'And...?'

'There's no "and". I want a series about me now, not some historical document for which I might just as well be dead.'

'Do you always get *your* own way?'

'Mostly, yes.'

'Mostly?'

'Yes, well people aren't quite as interested in me now as they used to be.'

'Surely my film will change that?'

'No. They'll just think I'm dead. Joseph Troumeg's obituary.'

'"I always look forward, never back,"' she quoted to him and he raised his eyebrows in agreement.

'Tell me,' he said, 'why the revival of interest? I thought you'd given up on the idea.'

'My boss thought that now's the time for the film.'

'Ah, Mr Graham Roth. I remember him from before. And do you?'

'That depends,' she said. 'Would you be interviewed for the programme I want to make?'

She knew he'd say yes because he could control what information he gave, but she could see in his face that he was weighing the significance of giving in to her.

'And when would this be?'

'Soon, but not too soon.'

'You want to find out more about me first.'

She nodded.

Jean-Paul materialised and Troumeg pulled out a chair for him to join them at the table.

'*Le filet de bar et mousse de fenouile ecumé à l'anis* was a triumph,' Troumeg said. 'A sublime meal.'

Jean-Paul nodded his head in acknowledgement and turned to Beatrice. She saw how his dark hair fell across his forehead, still sweaty from his efforts in the kitchen, his eyes betraying his intentions. He reached out and touched her forearm. 'And you, did you enjoy the meal, Beatrice?'

'Brilliant,' she said, moving her arm. She was concerned, not because she couldn't cope with the situation, for men coming on to her was part of life's daily pageant, but because of an alarm bell that was ringing somewhere in the back of her head. Jean-Paul had very white teeth and a smile that spoke of pleasure in his own good looks. How easy it would be to flirt back with this Frenchman but she checked herself knowing that he might well be another in the line of men that would simply take up her time and then become forgotten chapters in her life. She looked at Joseph Troumeg as if to say weren't we in the middle of talking about something important. Jean-Paul got the message and stood. 'I must see the other tables,' he said and then to her 'you know where I am the next time you're in town.'

'Well, you made quite an impression on him,' said Troumeg. 'As you do on many men, I'm sure.'

'Shall we continue discussing the film tomorrow morning?' she asked, ignoring him.

'Why not, my dear, why not.'

Later, as they walked back along the canal, she thanked him for the meal and he raised his arm dismissively before peeling off to his apartment without a backward glance. She watched him disappear into the night to end a day which, to all intents and purposes, might have been planned by Joseph Troumeg himself.

CHAPTER FOURTEEN

She knew it would come to this and when the moment arrives she isn't afraid, for she has absorbed the signs and already decided that whatever came next was right. They are to leave. She makes it easy when her mother tells her, for she can see that however concerned her mother is at giving this news, she is also happy. There is a certainty about her and although she doesn't talk about the sailor or her father she knows that her mother is doing what is best for them both. They are to go on the tide in two days time and there is much to be done. She has no time to think of the consequences and she finds it hard to imagine what the future will hold, but she trusts her mother and experience has taught her that her mother tells the truth.

Now she is running again, northwards beyond where she has been told the king sat at court and from where the City would always be ruled, towards the old garrison at the high stone wall. She hadn't known how to tell her friend about her father's death, but she now feels she can't leave without explaining. She sees her yellow hair in the distance and calls her name. She stops and they run towards each other. They have been friends since they fled from their homes up river, when they had escaped through the woods by what would become Russell Square and then eastwards to the old Roman city. Adversity had thrown them together and it was now to separate them, for she conveys to her friend the news that she is to leave on a ship with her mother. She can see the bewilderment in her friend's face and sees that it is fear of the unknown, of not being able to give dimension to the world beyond her established boundaries. For several years the two girls had marked out this territory, up river and down, playing along the foreshore and the Roman walls and then across the river, by the great bend, opposite the marshes where her father had once kept the cattle. She tells her friend of his death and the other girl, who has never known her own father, feels twice the sorrow. They vow always to be friends and to spend some part of the next day visiting the places they liked to go best. They arrange to meet by the bridge and go westwards to the old house where they have spent many times together.

Only when she is running back does she feel the sorrow of having to leave her friend, although when she stops, near the meat market, which is still a meat market, she thinks she might be crying for her father, the one cause of tears being the excuse for the other.

They are to travel a long distance across the sea, her mother tells her, to a place where the sun shone most of the time and where some people had dark skin. She watches her mother's face as she tells her this and sees that behind the happiness there is doubt, as the lines across her brow show. She kisses her mother as her father had done on the bridge, disguising her own fears and telling her mother that she has no idea what the sea will look like. She has heard stories about the storms and the waves but cannot really imagine a stretch of water wider than their river. She has never travelled far from the spot where she now holds her mother and the enormity of what they are about to do is like a chill wind behind her neck.

The next day she and her friend set off from the bridge and follow the river past the spot where the girl had watched for her father. They walk in silence, the events that are overtaking them too big to comprehend completely. They leave the shore and climb a short distance to a clump of ragged bushes growing just above the high water mark. The trees hide the remains of a stone and brick house whose roof had fallen on to the mosaic floors below. In places these patterns had also collapsed revealing a series of what they thought were stepping stones, small columns of brick that appeared once upon a time to have supported the floor. The bushes have pushed through and destroyed the building and when they first discovered the place they had climbed and sat on the highest of the remaining walls. On one such day, a year earlier, the blonde girl had dropped a small pewter brooch which had held the sweep of her costume. It would remain lost until discovered by a young Italian conservator working on the site nearly a thousand years later as the concrete supports of an office building were driven into the ground around the ancient site.

From the top of one of the remaining walls, through the bushes, she can see the opposite bank, although she tries to exclude the land from her view across the water. She wants to picture what it is like at sea, with no land in view. It is cold and the wind hurries towards her along the flat surface of the water and she imagines it would be even worse out at sea. The boat, she had seen, was open but for a small covered area at the front and she shivers at the thought of the journey. Her friend puts her hand on her shoulder and she can feel its warmth.

We are going to start a new life, her mother had told her and she knows that she refers to the sailor for whom she has made the necklace. Her mother is at ease with this man with the pale hair and eyes and natural authority. He has land in Provence, her mother says, a place many miles away in the south where he sells the produce he grows and what he bought at the ancient port, objects from fabulous lands across the Mediterranean sea. She accepts, with the plague all about and the Norseman threatening to attack again, that her mother is doing this for their best interests. She has faith that her judgement is for them all.

When she returns to the river she carries some her mother's wisdom with her and even though her friend is not about to leave on this journey, she is able to reassure and diminish her fears. She feels a woman to this girl.

CHAPTER FIFTEEN

In the morning there was a note waiting for her at reception, Jean-Paul inviting her to join him at the café where Joseph took his breakfast and where he would join them. She wondered if the chef had spoken to Joseph and organised this chaperone for himself, making it difficult for her to turn down the offer. She was walking up the quay when her phone rang and she saw that it was another possible suitor calling from London.

'Beattie? Hi, I hope I'm not interrupting anything?'

'Good morning, Harry. No, I was just on my way to breakfast. I'm in Paris.'

'I thought you might like a further update on young Flotsam.'

There was a businesslike tone to his voice and it was clear that Dr Harold Wesley wasn't about to make the same mistake as he had the last time he called.

'We've just had the DNA back from one of the other bones I picked at the site and by a complete miracle it matched the skull and belongs to the same skeleton. It was a middle finger and I won't bore you with technical details but it's all to do with epiphyses,' he rushed on, contradicting himself, 'and there is just the weeniest possibility that Flotsam is indeed a girl, although I would need far more evidence to go public on this. Other than to you, that is.'

It was strange to receive this information by the Bassin de la Villette in central Paris and for a moment Beatrice wished she was back in his laboratory so that she could share his enthusiasm. The idea of the small hand offering a clue across all these years made Flotsam even more real.

'Maybe we should go back to the Thames,' he continued. 'I'm keen to increase my area of search. Maybe the erosion on that side of the river released a grave. It happens. We've got a lot more Roman stuff coming to light now. The river changes the whole time. When will you be back?'

When would she be back? Beatrice had no idea. 'I'm not quite sure,' she told Harry. 'I may know later this morning. But you could go back to the site without me, couldn't you?'

'Of course, of course. But I know how attached you feel to Flotsam...'

'I do,' she confirmed and told him she would call later when there was more shape to her plans. She rang off just before entering the café where Jean-Paul waited on the terrace, a cigarette in his hand, his long hair freshly washed. She joined him at the table and he called over a waiter. He was clearly pleased to see her and she enjoyed his attentiveness as he fussed around making sure she got what she wanted.

'So you make films,' he said, leaning forward towards her. One of her earliest lovers was a Frenchman and she recalled him now, a young student she'd met on holiday in Brittany, who had the same instinctive confidence with women as Jean-Paul now exhibited. 'Tell me what about,' he said, leaning towards her.

Beatrice reacted to this familiarity and knew full well that this undoubtedly attractive man wasn't really interested in her films. 'Rape, for example, and the innate conservatism of the revolutionary French.'

He frowned and she softened a little and took pity. 'A series on a women's refuge – a place where women can go to escape their abusive men – and another about the fortieth anniversary of the 68 riots in Paris.'

'My father told me about that,' he said, picking up on the easier subject. 'He was a student at the Sorbonne, but he didn't take part.'

'Or he told you he didn't take part.'

Again the chef frowned, not quite following her.

'Many of the people I spoke to played down their part in what happened. They didn't want their sons and daughters to know that once upon a time they threw cobblestones and hurled tear gas canisters back at the police. Revisionist history at its most basic.'

'It's normal,' he said, but she could see he was not really interested. 'Are you here for much longer? I am free later this week, when one of my sous-chefs is standing in for me.'

'You make it sound as if we might be going away somewhere,' she said.

'If you like. I was thinking a club, or dinner somewhere else, perhaps?'

And so the process begins again, she thought and the new sense of uneasiness remained with her so she hesitated over her response, even though she knew exactly what it would be.

'Do you mind if I say no?' she said. 'I'm not sure of my plans and I won't be until I talk further with Joseph.' And then, as an afterthought, 'what do you make of him?'

'I've not known him for long, but he has a big reputation here in France. They see him as one of their own, which of course he is even though he made his fame abroad. He tells me that he was born here, in this *arrondissement*. Some years ago he had a restaurant in Paris, down on the Left Bank, and one in Provence, in Marseille, I think. He often goes to the south. Maybe that's where he's gone. Anyway, if you're free, just let me know,' he said as he stood. 'Now, I must go to the market. See you around.' And taking his leather jacket from the back of his chair, he was gone, unused, she thought, to being rebuffed.

Twenty minutes later, Troumeg still hadn't turned up so she called his apartment. There was no reply, not necessarily an indication, she knew, of whether he was there or not. When she went to pay, the waiter shook his head and said that it had been taken care of. She went round to Troumeg's apartment and rang the outer bell, again with no luck and for the first time that morning considered that he might have once again upped sticks and departed. She called in at *l'Assiette* to get Jean-Paul's mobile number.

'So soon.'

The response was what she expected and she ignored it. 'Did Joseph say that he would definitely be at breakfast this morning?'

There were a few beats before the chef replied. 'Well, I didn't actually speak to him but he always goes there for breakfast.'

Typical, Beatrice thought. She should have guessed. She was about to ring off with the briefest of goodbyes, when she stopped herself. 'Do you have any idea where he might have gone?'

'He's that sort of man,' the chef said. 'He never used to say goodbye. One day he would be here and the next day he'd be gone.'

Despite her initial disappointment at being back to square one, Beatrice was somewhat reassured with this behaviour for it conformed with her appraisal of Joseph Troumeg as not being quite as he seemed, an elusive man with an opaque past. She considered her options over a further cup of coffee on the terrace, but there seemed to be a collision of paths open to her and she was uncertain which to chose. She could stay in Paris, hoping that Troumeg might turn up, return to London on the assumption this is where he might have fled, or simply stop and take a rest, as Amanda had suggested. Instead, her mind slipped back to Flotsam, the young girl who had perhaps lived and played along the Thames a thousand years ago. She saw the shape of her skull, the arch of the eye sockets she had observed in the palm of her hand and tried to put flesh on the bones, to imagine her life. How quickly history escapes us, she thought again, the pieces of Flotsam's life open to interpretation and fantasy, just like the way Joseph Troumeg presented his own childhood.

Somehow this process of thought prompted a decision and finding a note she had made for herself on her phone, set off for the *mairie* of the 19th *arrondissement* where she hoped she might be able to bluff her way through the civil service procedures and find out more about the parents of Joseph Troumeg. Although Joseph had told Jean-Paul he had been born here, she remained sceptical, but it might just be that Troumeg had taken a flat in this part of Paris because he knew it well and felt sentimentally attached. For now, at least, it seemed to Beatrice the most logical of the paths to take.

The town hall was all that she might have expected of French bureaucracy, an elaborate building, majestic, with high windows and a pillared entrance above which two great stone figures stood guard, the perfect outward representation of the labyrinthine processes she expected to find inside. She wasn't disappointed, although during the walk across the *arrondissement* she had worked out an approach to help her through the expected red tape.

'I am trying to trace the parents of my godfather,' she told an efficient looking woman with spectacles that did justice to the ornate exterior of the building. She was one of a number of assistants providing help in a large room marked *Registres d'État Civil*.

'His name is Troumeg. He was born in 1935, so his parents would have been born in the first decade of the century, more than a hundred years ago.' Beatrice hoped this fact would allow her to do a search without producing a birth certificate and she was directed to a computer screen where, having waded through the necessary preambles, a screen message told her that she could study records up to April 1911, but not beyond.

There were no Troumegs born in the 19th *arrondissement* between 1900 and 1911. In fact, the name Troumeg didn't exist at all in the records that were available to her. She wasn't entirely surprised, since Joseph Troumeg's father could have been born anywhere in France, let alone this particular *arrondissement* in Paris. She tried Leval, Odile, but again drew a blank. Beatrice was keen to find out if there was a marriage certificate for the couple sometime around 1935. She looked back at the counter and assessed her chances. The woman who had helped initially was busy talking to someone else but either side of her were two colleagues, an older man in a blue cord suit and pale yellow knitted tie and a younger man with a crew neck sweater over a collar and tie. She chose chord over sweater.

'I've come to Paris,' she said leaning forward, to find out about my godfather's parents. He's too old to make the journey and is losing his memory. I want to try and find out when they were married and if, indeed, they lived in the 19th. I'm sorry if my French is poor. Please excuse me.'

'Your French is excellent, *madame*. Do you have any idea when they might have married?'

'Sometime in the mid-30s, I think.'

'Can you prove your connection to your godfather?'

'I'm awfully sorry, but I can't. Do I need to?' She looked him in the eye and held his gaze for a moment.

'Strictly speaking, yes, but since you have come this far let us see what we can do. What were the surnames?'

'Troumeg and Leval.'

'Let's say sometime in the 30s,' he said, smiling at her and she watched him access the files on his computer. 'This is very kind,' she told him and every so often he looked back at her as his machine chuntered through the marriages in the 19th *arrondissement* in the years before the war.

'I'm very sorry,' he said. 'There is no record here of such a marriage.'

He stared at her, not wanting this to be an end, willing, she knew to help this woman in front of him. Beatrice recalled the year that all this started, the long hot summer not long after her father's death, sometime in the middle of her first year as a teenager. For the first time in her life she was noticed, people would look twice at her, or boys more particularly, turning, talking, whispering. Already she looked older than her years and her long hair came down to her shoulders where the eyes of those onlookers would continue over her chest and down to her legs. It felt like an achievement, that she was being rewarded for being herself for the very first time. She revelled in it, this new power so suddenly and effortlessly handed to her and she used it indiscriminately. She frowned at the memory of the young girl who at first did not fully understand the consequences of the power she held. Later she did, but her path had been set. To be noticed, to be able to achieve it almost at will, became a necessity, almost a drug so that now, more than a quarter of a century later, the process of flirting with the man in front of her was a matter of almost habit, even though it was now justified as a useful tool of her trade. But here, in the grand *mairie* of the 19th *arrondissement*, beneath the elaborate stonework of the vaulted ceilings, she shook her head and the glimpse she had of her former self made her suddenly sad.

The man continued to regard her with admiration and when she focused on him again she smiled and made to turn away but stopped and decided to take another chance. 'Might Joseph Troumeg have been born here outside of marriage?' she asked, widening her eyes at him. Beatrice could do this, she knew, use her looks to get what she wanted.

The civil servant looked at her and smiled back, knowing that he was being manipulated but quite happy to play the part of puppet.

He began to look through the catalogue of births. 'We still have no record at all of a Troumeg on the larger register of names, but we have a number of Levals. What was the Christian name?'

'Odile.'

'Ah, here we are,' he said. 'This must be it.' He swung the screen towards her, clearly pleased with himself and suitably rewarded with a winning smile from Beatrice.

In front of her were the details of the birth of Joseph Leval on November 1, 1935; mother Odile Leval with her address, 23b Rue Manin in the 19th and her age, 20. There were two witnesses, Albert and Juliette Vaillard, Café Le Fin, on the rue d'Aubervilliers and the names of Odile's parents.

The space for the name of the father was blank.

The man in the cord suit beckoned her towards the screen. 'Look,' he said, tapping a finger against the glass, 'her parents are called Levy.' He dropped his glasses down his nose. 'Quite common between the wars for Jewish families to make their names more French. Levy to Leval is a small step, but significant. I expect she did it to protect the child.'

Beatrice made a note of these details and then leaned across the counter again to put her hand on the chord forearm, leaving it there as she said thank you to his face and, by his reaction, quite making his morning. Walking back to her hotel, somewhere down the hill before the canal, a line of young girls snaked out of a school ahead of her, two by two, holding hands to cross the road, their teacher arms outstreched to halt the traffic. Beatrice watched them talking excitedly, their high-pitched voices filling the street and she slowed to a halt and allowed them to pass. Where was she in this group? Which young girl would have her needs, for surely there would be one, if not more? In this small Paris street, which she'd never walked down before and might never do so again, she was being pushed to remember something. She stood still, hoping to give substance to this powerful feeling. The line of children had disappeared, but she remained motionless on the pavement, her head slightly raised, her eyes looking at nothing.

CHAPTER SIXTEEN

Life was about to turn again.

The sailor speaks to her as a grown woman, asking her to help her mother on the journey. He is very different from her father, but she feels just as safe with him and she watches the gentle way he escorts her mother on to the wooden deck. The river is still, the water at its highest and soon it would begin to ebb, tugging her away from the world that she has known all her life. On the quay stands her friend, her blond hair clear amongst the others gathered to stare in wonder and puzzlement at their departure. The group recedes and slips out of sight to become a memory as they drift down stream, pulled around the great bend where her father used to work and onwards to the wider river and territory she has never seen before. The wind takes the large sail above her and she hears the ropes straining as the men on the oars relax and break their rhythm. Slowly the flat land on either side becomes more distant and the line between it and the water harder to define. The boat rocks now and she holds on to the side, keen not to show her fear. The wind is behind them, the sailor says, and they are making good time.

It would be more difficult when they turn back on themselves around the coast where the oarsmen would be needed to push them through the waves.

Her mother sits in the stern, on the chest that contains their possessions, clothes, tools, precious stones and metals. She is staring out to sea. How much easier it is for me, the girl thinks. She trusts her mother and understands her anxiety, the burden of her decision to uproot her family and she realises that one day such responsibility will come to her.

The sailor joins them and begins to tell of the old port where they are heading, founded by the ancient Greeks. He speaks of its magnificent harbour and the ships that came from other lands to trade there and how the sea was so blue it almost hurt your eyes. The girl looks at the grey waters around them and tries to imagine such a blue sea, grateful to the sailor for making their destination so exciting and worth the difficulties of this voyage which, he says, might take twenty days to complete. He tells them he has a large house on the hill overlooking the harbour where he grows lemons and in summer the plants climb the walls to flower in bright orange and purple. The girl watches him take her mother's hand and tell her that his own father was from the north, a Norsemen and his mother from the south and that he had sailed with his father from an early age, learning a little of the language of many different lands. As the day wore on he tells more stories of his adventures, about the storms at sea and the treasures he had seen on land and she preserves these in her mind, layers of history. Each day he tells them more, sharing his life and in turn she listens to her mother speak of her husbands and how she had become a jeweller. And so the time passes, the women taking turns to wash behind a screen erected at the stern, the men scrupulous in their attention to their needs. When he confirms that they have finally turned southwards, the storm comes and the waves lift them so high that all they can see is sky one moment before being plunged deep into troughs where they are surrounded by green walls of water. At first the girl is afraid, but she notices the men around her are unconcerned and she marvels at the way the boat rides the seas so that before long she becomes exhilarated by the rise and fall of their progress. When she sleeps the movement is a comfort and after seven days the memory of the blond girl on the quay is recalled less and less and she gives herself up to the life ahead of her, beyond the swells.

CHAPTER SEVENTEEN

It was happening again, the tentative steps towards another person's life, the slow gathering of facts to help build the picture which would be presented as truth in the way that only television can. So, Joseph Troumeg was older than Beatrice thought, his mother younger and his father a mystery. Clearly there was a father, but was he an American journalist working in Spain who met his mother in Paris? For now, did it really matter? And was Troumeg merely an anagram of gourmet, as suggested in several articles she had read, just another part of the old man's playfulness with his past? Troumeg didn't want this intrusion into his life and Beatrice considered her motives for pursuing him and failed to come up with an answer. She'd had an uneasy feeling from the moment she left the *mairie*, perhaps a reaction to establishing a first finger-hold on to Joseph Troumeg's real past, a tiny crack from which to explore further. Wandering aimlessly back to the hotel, she decided to call Amanda.

'I thought you were in Paris,' her friend said.

'I am, but I wanted to speak to you.'

'Mmm, what's the problem?'

'Do I always call you when there's a problem?'

'Sometimes. And you know that Harper has his rest about now, so clearly you want a natter.'

Harper was Amanda's fourteen month old son, although Beatrice was sure she hadn't chosen this moment to call because she knew he might have been having his nap.

'It's about Joshua, isn't it?' Amanda said.

'Is it?'

'Or maybe Ben? Or what was the fellow before him? Chris, wasn't it? Or was it Anthony, the one your mother liked? There's a chef somewhere as well, isn't there? Adrian?'

'What about them?' Beatrice said. Amanda had this ability to put her on the defensive.

'Let me guess. You've plunged into another project and maybe you've met someone else and you're worried that the same old wheel is turning yet again.'

'Is that it?'

'Well, it usually is Beattie.'

'Except it feels different this time.'

'What, you've met someone you really love? I think I may have heard this before.'

'No, no. I haven't. I suppose that's the point. I don't want to get involved again, at least that's the way it feels.'

'But you've also said that in the past.'

'Have I?'

'C'mon, Beattie.'

'Joshua said that I was good at exploring other people's lives and not my own.'

'And...?'

'And I'm worried he might be right. Other people's lives are a good way of ignoring my own.'

Amanda softened. 'They're not necessarily mutually exclusive, you know. What are your symptoms?'

'Well, doctor, two men have show a modicum of interest in

me recently and this has made me, well, recoil. And I think I'm on to something with the next film project but I can't seem to get that excited about it either.'

Amanda Lodge was two years younger, but Beatrice accepted that in some ways she was wiser even if she often bridled at her direct approach.

'A couple of questions, Beattie. Do you want a permanent relationship or are you happy with the flings you have? And what's so special about Mr Joseph Troumeg in the first place?'

'In order. Yes. No. And I'm not sure.'

'Well, I'll tell you one thing, Beattie. This is the first time I can remember you hesitating before heading directly into another relationship destined to end up like the others.'

'Yes, I know. I suppose that's a plus, except it doesn't feel like one.'

'It is.'

'I don't know quite what to do. I have this feeling of dread, like something awful is going to happen just around the corner.'

'Change might be about to happen, Beattie and it might not be for the worse. In a way you do know what's going on, Beattie and you've done something about it. You called me. Look, I've got to go. Harper's just woken up. You must have worried him as well. Let me know what happens.'

Change is what I've been good at, Beatrice thought. I can do that easily, move from one project to the next, one man to another. It seemed to her that it was the staying that was more difficult, that demanded more attention. She recalled her journey back from the *mairie* and the moment when she'd stood still on the pavement trying to give shape to a feeling that was demanding attention somewhere just out of vision. And, as is the nature of these moments, she thought, some part of the answer came to her now. The old wheel is turning again, Amanda had said and it was true that she worried that the results would be the same without her knowing why. But now she was beginning to see the shadow of the reason why. The first part of the equation came easily, too easily, the being noticed, the attraction, the attracting. For so long, she glimpsed, this is all she needed for it appeared to justify herself, to satisfy her need to be liked, to give shape to her existence. The success as a film maker, a clever organiser of others, a clear, intelligent and creative thinker, was somehow relegated to second place behind her other, more primitive need. She stored this information, not quite sure she understood it, still not certain of its dimensions.

On one side of her she could hear the trains rattling in and out of the Gare de l'Est and on the other the cries of children in a school playground. She sat down on a bench outside a swimming pool and looked at the information she'd noted at the *mairie*. She had two choices: find rue Manin and the apartment where Joseph Troumeg may have spent the early years of his life, or the Café Le Fin, where the witnesses on the birth certificate had lived. She spread out her map and saw that she was close to the rue d'Aubervilliers, so she chose the second of the options and began walking northwards, the noise of the trains keeping her company as she went. Her pace was desultory, her mind distracted and so she was not really aware of her surroundings. It was only when she came upon the groups of people outside an old industrial building on her right did she focus. It was a handsome, restored red brick hall with a glass roof, now an arts' gallery but until late last century, she read on a board attached to the building, the centre for all funerals in Paris, with thousands of hearses sent out into the city each year. She looked again at her notes from the *mairie* and wondered if Café Le Fin was named for this very reason. She didn't expect it to be still there, but walking further up the road she saw the sign. The interior, with a zinc bar and dark, bent wood furniture and lace curtains on brass poles protecting the lower half of the windows, looked as it might have a hundred years earlier. She sat at a table in the window, the shadow of the lace making an elaborate pattern on her face. On the walls, black horses wearing ostrich feathers pulled glass-sided hearses accompanied by men in dark tails and top hats. The film maker part of her, the one that dealt in images and their meaning, saw the juxtaposition of life and death, the birth of Joseph Leval beginning nearby, the premature end of Flotsam a thousand years earlier and her own presence here, alone in this part of Paris so associated with death. She picked up a paper napkin from the table and wiped her eyes and would have liked to put it all down to her period, which was about to start, but knew that it wouldn't be true.

She ordered a hot chocolate and enjoyed the comfort of the sweetness, a taste that took her straight back to her childhood when the drink was rationed by her mother who saw it as an indulgent treat. It was no surprise to Beatrice to be drinking it here. Perhaps in a film about her own life she'd begin with hot chocolate, a symbol of sweetness to compensate for her mother. She smiled and applied the same logic to Joseph Leval, the camera returning to the place of his birth, the cries of a new born baby mixed over the sounds of horse and carriage on cobbles as a hearse sets out for another body.

It was four o'clock in the afternoon, the doldrums, when the café was caught between lunch service and the early evening drinkers. Beatrice sat alone in the dark room. Ahead of her a blackboard outlined the plats de jour: *Sandrine Vaillard propose*, it began but before she read the dishes, Beatrice fished out the paper from her pocket and realised it was the Vaillards who had been the witnesses at the registering of Joseph's birth. Was this their daughter, or grand-daughter? Beatrice had picked up the trail once more and when the waiter returned he confirmed that Sandrine was indeed the owner and she would be back around six.

When Beatrice wandered back down to the arts' centre her mood was quickly distracted by the vibrant mix of art under the restored glass roof of the magnificent building, the installations and digital works on display, so much life in a place once given over to death.

Sandrine Vaillard was a boisterous woman perhaps in her late fifties, with red cheeks and grey hair tucked in a bun behind her head. Beatrice told her she was making a film about Joseph Troumeg.

'Why?'

'He's famous and interesting,' Beatrice said, wondering why she asked the question.

'I'm named after him,' she said, pointing at her chest. 'My middle name is Josephine. My parents had me late and spoke of him often.' Her voice trailed away as if she was about to say something else but thought better of it.

'Did your parents ever speak of Joseph's father?'

'*Mais, non,*' Sandrine said, emphasising the negative. And then she stopped, again weighing what she should say. 'My parents told me that Odile was always very proud to be a single parent. Amazing in those days. She was ninety-two when she died.'

Beatrice paused, doing the sums in her head. 'So, she only died four years ago?'

'Yes. I went to the funeral.'

'But Joseph wasn't there?'

The *patronne* shook her head. 'I don't think they had seen each other for many years,' she said. 'Perhaps there was a reason for this, but things get lost in history, don't they?'

'Where did she live, exactly?'

'Over by Buttes Chaumont.'

'In the rue Manin?'

'You know it? She'd been there for years.'

'That was the address on the birth certificate.' Beatrice wanted to say more, but there were too many questions clambering for answers.

'Will you have supper here?' Sandrine asked. 'I can recommend the veal.'

Beatrice said that she would be delighted and would return at eight o'clock. She wanted to walk across and see where Odile used to live, the mother who Joseph used to describe in glowing terms but whose funeral he failed to attend.

She had to walk back over the canal to reach rue Manin before finally locating the apartment block where Odile had lived for so long. It was not what she expected, more Italian than French, an early concrete building with rounded, modernist balconies and metal framed windows. She sat in the park opposite and tried to imagine pre-war Paris and the young woman who lived here, strong and self-possessed enough to become a single parent and cope with what Beatrice could only imagine as the muttered disapproval of society. How different for Amanda, who had become pregnant with Harper after a short relationship and whose decision to keep the baby was applauded by all her friends and even by her parents. Half the children at his toddlers' group, she had told Beatrice, came from parents who weren't married and at least fifty percent of those were single parents. Society changes and history forgets.

Odile Leval lived opposite until she was ninety-two, her son a world famous figure but, it appears, estranged from her. What more would she discover about this strange man on the one hand so accommodating and on the other so evasive.? Beatrice imagined that Odile might have sat on this very bench, the Parc des Buttes Chaumont no different then from what it was now, in a city that would soon be invaded and Jews like her rounded up and shipped to the camps and exterminated. Odile had even changed her name to help protect him from deportation. How could Beatrice think of her own dissatisfactions when she had never been confronted with matters of life and death, merely the discontents of a rich, middle class child in the early years of the third millennium.

Later, as promised, the veal was good and her mood was restored even if Joseph Leval remained tantalisingly out of reach.

CHAPTER EIGHTEEN

It is hot and she seeks the shelter of the wooden seat. Her body aches from the long voyage and although she is thirsty she is allowed to drink only a small amount each day. After a week, just after the storm, they stop at a harbour to take on more supplies and when she stands on the stone pier her body continues to move with the sea. Their journey southwards has kept them close to the coast and the girl cannot understand how the sailor knows their position. The houses overlooking the harbour are of stone, strong and permanent.

They stay a short while but are soon continuing their journey towards the sun, the water becoming bluer by the day. After a further week they change direction again and she can see the excitement in the sailor's face. Now there is land on both sides and he points to the triangular mountain to the north and tells her that they are in a different sea and will be home in four more nights. She thinks about the home she has left behind and then the one she is sailing towards. The sea sparkles all about and it is warm on the deck and occasionally fish leap from the water and she remembers the ruined building she has left behind and her friend who might be playing there now. Who would be safer, she thinks? She hears the other men talking on the deck, sensing they are nearly home. She watches her mother, who has swapped one world for another and hopes that she will have the same strength to control her own destiny, for already she glimpses that this is the key.

When, finally, they come upon the white stone coastline, which makes the sea bluer than ever, the girl watches the boat turn towards the land rising on both sides, a tall hill to her right and a lower swell to her left. Then there are buildings and boats, more than she has seen together before until finally they are embraced by the natural harbour and can go no further. The sailor steps out of the boat first and then helps her mother and finally, with an elaborate bow, takes her hand and guides her ashore. She stares around her, squinting her eyes against the sun, the light quite different from what she has left behind. Some of the men carry their belongings up the hill and they follow the sailor through houses of stone and wood. They enter a fortified gate where servants greet them, bowing to the sailor. In a courtyard there is water splashing into a stone pool and the sailor gestures for them to drink. She is shown to a room with an arched window overlooking the harbour and a bed which, when she lies on it and shuts her eyes, seems to sway. She marks this moment, the stone walls around her, the bright light outside and a future she cannot guess. In her hand she holds the gold cloth which she unfolds to take out the brooch, her fingers tracing the round smoothness of the crimson stone. She holds it to her chest and for the first time in almost twenty days, drifts into a deep sleep undisturbed by the splash of the sea, the snores of the men and the flap of the sail pulling them along, the accompaniment to her dreams.

When she wakes it is dark and at first she is frightened, but the shape of the doorway is clear from the light from below and she follows it, down stone stairs to where a fire is burning in the courtyard. She looks at her mother and the sailor and takes the plate she is given. She tastes olives for the first time and the flesh of squid, new names that the sailor tells her and she sits down in the strange land and smiles.

CHAPTER NINETEEN

That Beatrice felt wretched was not solely down to her period, although she was prepared to use it as an excuse. There was no reply from Troumeg's phone yet again and she pressed off her mobile in irritation. Last night's meal had been good, but the carafe of red wine which Sandrine had offered on the house was now slowing her down and making her movements clumsy. She only had one place to go and set off for the rue Manin hoping to catch one or more of the residents as they left for work. How ridiculous not to be able to ask Troumeg about all this instead of having to act like a private detective and she asked herself again, was it worth it? She took a chance when she got there and rang on 23b, not expecting a response. When a female voice answered she told the truth, that she was making a film about Joseph Troumeg and believed he may have been born here. She was buzzed up to be met by a woman probably a few years younger than herself and certainly a lot more awake. The apartment was a perfect reflection of the period it was built, geometrically shaped black leather and chrome furniture with abstract paintings on the wall, circles and squares in primary colours.

'Do you like it?' the woman said, watching her visitor's eyes roam around the room.

'It's perfect. I can't imagine it was like this when Troumeg lived here.'

'Who knows. The woman we bought it from was very ill. She needed the money to afford a nursing home but she died shortly after the final *compromis* was signed.'

'Odile Leval?'

'Yes.'

'She was Troumeg's mother, but don't ask me where the surname came from. What was she like?'

'Frail but dignified. To tell you the truth, we felt bad buying from her but she insisted. She liked us. Or should I say, she liked my husband who deals in this sort of furniture. The old woman was comforted by the idea of the apartment retaining its originality.'

'How long did she live here?'

'Almost seventy years. At least that's what she told us and what the deeds indicate. Incredible isn't it?'

What Beatrice thought she kept to herself. How could Joseph Troumeg, clearly a very rich man, not help his mother by paying for the home? And, if she died soon after selling the flat, to whom did she leave the proceeds in the will, assuming she had one?

'The truth is,' the woman continued, 'she was so ill at the end that we let her stay on after we'd bought the place. She died about two weeks later, in that bedroom.' She pointed at a door. 'It seemed right and I'm glad we did.'

Beatrice stared at the door, wishing she been able to talk to the old woman, aware that she was lifting the curtain on a private family issue and now intrigued.

'Did she have any other family, do you know?'

The woman shook her head. 'I really don't know. There was a friend, a few years younger, who used to visit her. She lives in the block, down on the first floor. I'm afraid I don't know her name, or which apartment it is.'

Afterwards, Beatrice went across to the park and sat on the bench overlooking the lake, as she had the night before. She tried to imagine what it was like for Odile to live in the same home for seventy years and couldn't help speculate on whether it was pleasure or disappointment that kept her there so long.

Her mobile rang and, seeing that it was her mother, she let the phone pulse in her hand for a moment before answering. Eileen Palmenter had developed over the years the uncanny knack of phoning at just the wrong times.

'Darling, I think you're in France, aren't you?'

Beatrice was amazed that she had remembered.

'I'm phoning from Toulon,' she continued. 'Surrounded by sailors, let me tell you. Gorgeous uniforms.'

So Toulon was the Toulouse of their lunch at John Lewis. She waited for the point of the call, for a demand was surely not far behind.

'You said you might be able to join me here, since you were going to be in France.'

Beatrice had said no such thing but Eileen Palmenter had the ability to slightly alter the facts in her favour and her daughter had yet to decide whether she did this knowingly or not.

'It would be so nice if you could. Are you still there?'

'I'm sitting in a park in northern Paris. I'm working.'

'They do those nice fast trains, don't they darling? You could be here in a trice.'

And was the selective hearing part of the same set of skills her mother used to get her own way? It was now over twenty-five years since her husband had died and in that time, Beatrice had concluded, her mother had become expert in looking after no one but herself.

'How long are you there for, mother?'

'Well, that's the point. Slightly longer than we thought. There's something wrong with one of the ship's engines, we're told and they're putting us up for a week in a rather nice hotel.

It's the least they could do, of course, but there are worse places to be. I know you're not with anyone.'

Eileen Palmenter popped in this last sentence in what sounded like an afterthought, but Beatrice read it as code for it's not difficult for you to drop what you're doing and take the train.

'I'll need to phone you back.'

Even before she rang off, Beatrice could visualise the turn down in her mother's mouth, the disapproval at not having got what she wanted. A lone magpie landed on to the path in front of her and walked lopsidedly towards a rubbish bin.

Her phone rang again and she glanced at her watch. It was ten o'clock in Paris, an hour behind in London and Harry Wesley was about to start his day.

'How nice,' she said. 'I've just been talking to my mother.'

'Now, let me unpick this. Compared to speaking to my mother, it's nice to hear from you. Or, by the by, I've been talking to my mother and it's nice to hear from you.'

'Oh, the former. With a bit of the latter.'

'Well, I'll try and extract the best from both versions. The truth is, I'd like to see you.'

'You mean in relation to Flotsam?'

'No, I mean in relation to you. You didn't call me back so I thought I'd try again.'

Beatrice got up from the bench and turned around, shielding the phone for reasons that weren't clear since there was no wind. 'What did you have in mind?'

'Look,' he said, 'I can't really work out the impact you've had on me, but you have. I'm grateful that Flotsam has been acting as a go-between but it's a bit more than that. I don't want to use strontium isotopes to get to you anymore.'

'Is that an alco-pop?' Beatrice's flippancy was an instinctive reaction to protect herself, the trip of an overloaded fuse on a circuit board.

'We find them in teeth and they will help tell us where

Flotsam came from. I could come to Paris for the day.'

Many men flirted with Beatrice. Indeed, it was part of the process she found easy but at this moment she thought of Amanda's observation about the repeated pattern of unsuccessful relationships. Clearly, she was saying, that discernment was necessary at this stage and here her judgement was uncertain. If it's possible to entertain a series of important thoughts in less than two seconds, this is what Beatrice did now.

'I'm not sure.'

'You're not sure about me coming to Paris? You're not sure about me?'

'I'm simply not sure.'

'You mean you're usually sure but now you're not?'

'I think that's it exactly,' she said.

She could hear him thinking before he replied. 'And that might not be to do with me, *per se*? I least I hope that's true.'

'I think that's partly true.'

'Partly. So there's a little hope, then.'

She didn't say anything.

'How is Mr Troumeg?'

'I can't find him. Well, I did have supper with him and now he's disappeared.'

'Do you always have this effect on men?'

The question, although asked lightly, made her think, for the truth was quite the opposite: she usually disappeared first.

'Can I call you back, Harry? I haven't decided what my plans are.'

'Don't leave it too long, Beattie, because I'll only call again.'

For the second time this morning she was procrastinating, uncertain of her own reactions, in need of a route map to show her the links and distances between the disparate strands of her life. She was pushing away the decisions, not committing herself but perhaps this was the very point Amanda was making to her the day before. Had she set out for Paris and the pursuit of Joseph Troumeg to deliberately isolate herself so that she could gain some perspective? The thought cheered her up and for the first time that morning she felt better. The single magpie had now been joined by another and she took this as an omen.

She was about to get off the bench when her phone rang for the third time.

'It's me, Amanda. I hope you didn't mind what I said to you yesterday?' She didn't give Beatrice time to answer. 'The thing is, I got a call this morning from that archaeologist fellow, Harold Wesley. He wanted to know more about you.'

'What did you tell him?'

'Well, that's the funny thing. It wasn't so much what I told him, more what he told me.'

'Go on.'

'Well, he started by saying how brilliant you are. He'd made a point of seeing your Bafta films. They showed the final one again the other night, by the way, and he picked up the others on iPlay. Then he said you'd been worried that you didn't use your forensic – that's the word he used – forensic skills on your own life. He was taken by this since he'd been told the same thing about himself.'

'And...?

'And he sounded different from the others. Joshua, Ben, Chris, Anthony...the others.'

'You've been warning me not to keep repeating my mistakes. Now you're phoning to encourage me.'

'Not quite, Beattie. I'm just saying he sounded different. He was asking the right questions. He was certainly very interested in you. Anyway, I thought you'd like to know. Enjoy Paris.'

The gardens of Buttes Chaumont, with a folly perched on the hill to one side and a lake in front with the sound of a waterfall, were a fantasy gardens to release Parisiennes from their daily grind. She took the bridge across to the island and climbed to what she discovered was a faux temple and looked down on the northern flank of the city and the sweep of the road where Odile Leval had lived for so long. She must have known this park intimately and had no doubt stood on this very spot, perhaps even with her son.

She took the mobile out of her pocket, knowing that she had two calls to complete, but almost immediately slipped it back for she realised she still had no answers for her mother, or Dr Harold Wesley.

CHAPTER TWENTY

She watches the fishing boats unload on the long stone quay. She is brown now and when she stands in the sun it no longer bites into her neck and shoulders as it had in the beginning. The fishermen know her and she is learning to understand them and use their words. In front of her the iridescent blues of a thousand tiny fish wriggle in a wooden box and next to it, in line and glistening, larger fish with names she is beginning to recognise. The sailor had been right. The sea is almost too blue and bright to look at, flashing repeatedly in the morning sun. In the market the colours continue, reds and yellows on fruits she has never seen before. She wonders why everyone doesn't live here. Occasionally she remembers her friend, her blond hair like the sun but accepts they will never meet again. Like the old grey river, she belongs to another life. Here she has long stopped looking towards the mouth of the harbour in fear of the Norsemen.

In a town of many races, she is still regarded as a curiosity. This suits her for she enjoys being an outsider and it matches her increasingly independent life. She spends most her days outside and although she has made friends along the waterfront she is happy in her own company. Her mother continues to make jewellery and the sailor is often away for weeks at a time, so she enjoys a singular existence, sometimes accompanying the fishermen on trips to markets inland but more often climbing the white hills to the east of the port to look out over the sea. Here she can see forever and when the wind blows she stands with her arms outstretched, her body leaning forward, perfectly balanced, free and untouchable.

CHAPTER TWENTY-ONE

By midday, Beatrice had still not returned the calls and another piece of unfinished business awaited her when she got back to the hotel. Jean-Paul, still in pursuit, had left a note asking if he could take her to dinner that evening. She screwed the paper into her pocket to rest against her phone. She went to her room, set up her computer and for the time being at least, decided to postpone her responses, hoping that the answers would become clear during the course of the afternoon. She registered the fact that there were at least forty-five million references to Joseph Troumeg on Google and limited her search to verifying the name of his early restaurant in Provence. She found out that it had been situated along the north side of the old port in Marseille. It had a short life, no longer than two years and since Troumeg had opened it before he became a celebrity, did not bear his name, but that of the old city, Massilia. "These were my years of learning," she read over and over again in different articles, "when the fishermen and the market people would define what I would cook that day, the best that land and sea could provide. It was my apprenticeship.

I owe a lot to Marseille." The restaurant opened in 1957 "at a time when garlic had yet to be invented in Britain," continued the quotation in typical Troumeg style. He was twenty-three years old and clearly however much Marseille had given him, it wasn't enough to keep him there long.

But might he have gone back now? And if not there, why not any of the other places over the world where he'd had restaurants, shops and homes? Once again, she sought a logic for his disappearance, hard when the man appeared to move by instinct rather than reason. She doubted that amongst the avalanche of references on her computer there would be one that would make her task any the easier.

She did see, however, on a map of the south of France that Marseille was not too far from Toulon and that single fact confirmed her plans for the next three days. She intended to please everyone else by pleasing herself. She phoned Jean-Paul and told him she would be happy to be taken to dinner that evening. He didn't sound surprised, but that was to be expected, although he might have thought differently if he'd known why she'd agreed to his invitation.

She approached calling Harry quite differently.

'I'm sorry it has taken me so long to get back to you.'

'I'm just glad that you have.'

'I'm going to be in France slightly longer than I thought. I've got to make a trip to the south in a couple of days time. Were you serious about taking me to lunch in Paris?'

'Of course. Has Amanda spoken to you?' He didn't wait for an answer. 'I hope you didn't mind?'

'No, not at all. I think you've made quite an impression on her.'

'That's what I was hoping. Well, what I mean is, I was hoping she would give a positive report about me.'

'I think I've probably got that already, but it's always nice to have another point of reference.'

'Like in our jobs, really. Checking our sources.'

'If you like.'

'What about tomorrow?'

'That's what I was going to suggest. It's an expensive lunch.'

'All in the interests of research, you understand. We need to discuss our child Flotsam.'

'You sound as though you might be able to claim it on expenses.'

'It's an investment in the on-going project,' he said.

'Could you get here for coffee?' Beatrice was going to suggest the café where Troumeg took his breakfast, but remembered that Jean-Paul might be lurking there and changed her mind. 'I'll see you at the Terminus Nord, just opposite the station. Eleven?'

'Perfect.'

The last piece in the jigsaw was her mother and Beatrice knew that however much she wanted her daughter to see her in Toulon, she would make it appear that she was doing Beatrice a favour. And so it was.

'The day after tomorrow? Well, I suppose that's ok. Let me just check with Jean.'

Beatrice resisted being drawn into this game and held back from mentioning that she would be doing some work in Marseille. She knew that her mother would assume that she was merely being accommodated, and in that she would have been correct. Having laid the paving stones of the next three days, Beatrice set off back to the rue Manin with renewed energy, crossing the increasingly familiar 19th *arrondissement*. She was preoccupied with Joseph Troumeg's history of himself, the gap between fact and fiction, the impreciseness of history. She couldn't account for it but she carried with her the sense that her actions were being governed from elsewhere and a new energy surged through her and she broke into a run and was whistled at by construction workers on the avenue Jean Jaurès

It was late afternoon and people were returning from work and she waited outside the block, getting her breath back, before following a man in a dark overcoat through the outside door with a smile and a thank you. She went up to the first floor in the hope that, because of her age, the woman she had been told about would more than likely be at home. At the third apartment she was greeted by a suspicious voice.

'Who is it?'

'I was visiting *Madame* Leval's old apartment this morning and I was told you knew her well. My name is Beatrice Palmenter and I'm researching a film.'

'About Odile?'

'Well, not directly. About her son.'

The door opened and a chain was slipped off its berth. A tall woman, elegantly dressed, allowed her to enter.

'I'm sorry to disturb you,' Beatrice said, but her apology was met by a shake of the head.

'I'm Marguerite Fourcas. I'm only too happy to talk about Odile. I miss her. A whisky, perhaps?'

Beatrice noticed from the small brass clock on the mantelpiece that it was just after five o'clock and imagined a drink about this time was a regular routine for the woman.

'Here's to Odile,' the older woman said. 'But it is Joseph you want to know about, I think.'

'I want to know about both.'

The old woman laughed. 'I was a few years younger than Odile, but I knew her for almost sixty years. She barely mentioned Joseph, except once in the early days, when we first met. You know the story?'

Beatrice shook her head. 'Only that she was a single parent and that Joseph didn't come to her funeral.'

Marguerite looked at her. 'That's about it. I don't want to waste your time, but the truth is Odile told me very little, only that she never saw her son. When I asked why she remained silent.'

'Did something happen between them?'

'Who knows. You must understand that Odile was a very

active woman. She didn't appear to regret not seeing him, far from it. She used this place as a base and was often gone for weeks, especially in the early days.'

'Did she ever talk about the war?'

'Never.'

'Wasn't that strange for someone of her age?'

The woman smiled sympathetically towards her. 'The answer to your question is no. And yes. Many French people refused to talk about it, but, then again, many did. I could understand both. But she barely referred to it.'

'But didn't Odile change her surname in the 30s?'

The woman shrugged. 'That's the first I've heard. Many did. I knew she was Jewish and, believe me, many Jews did not want to be reminded about what took place. I respected that.'

'You met Joseph?'

'Alas, no. By the time Odile and I became friends, he was gone.'

'Did she say when he left?'

'No. As I say, it was not something she talked about.'

'Strange, though?'

'Families,' she said, taking a sip of whisky.

'Joseph has often spoken of his mother to the press. Don't you think that's odd?'

'We all like to create our own histories.' There was a finality about her statement and Beatrice looked at Marguerite Fourcas and knew that, at another time, in different circumstances, the old woman would tell of her own history, real or imagined. Beatrice took her telephone number and promised to be in touch and on the way back to the hotel tried to imagine what it would be like to be a mother and never talk about your child, particularly one as famous as Joseph Troumeg.

She had just enough time to shower and change in order to be suitably late for Jean-Paul who was waiting in the hotel bar downstairs. She paused on the stairs to watch him, leaning on the counter with a glass of Ricard, a dark blue shirt under his leather jacket, quite unconcerned at her tardiness. He kissed her on the cheek, but didn't offer her a drink and beckoned her to follow him through the door. Outside a cab was waiting. Inside, he made no attempt to tell her where they were going and she didn't ask. The journey was short, no more than fifteen minutes, and they pulled up in a street of ill-lit office buildings, an unlikely place to find a restaurant. Once again she followed him down a much narrower street towards a beacon of light and in through doors to the bustle of diners crammed into a small room. Jean-Paul was greeted with bear hugs and rapid French, with barely a glance towards her, and finally they were escorted to a table in the corner, pressed tight by diners on other tables close by.

'Cosy,' she said, almost her first word of the evening.

'The best table,' he said.

The maitre d', who she could now see had a walrus moustache, approached them, beaming. He spoke to Jean-Paul and told him what he thought best on the menu. Finally she was asked what she would like to drink and chose another whisky.

'He says the *ecrevisses* are delicious,' Jean-Paul told her.

'Yes, I heard,' she said.

'This is one of the hardest restaurants in Paris to get a table,' Jean-Paul explained.

'I'm not surprised at this size.'

They ordered, but not before Jean-Paul had gone into a detailed conversation with the walrus about the other dishes. She looked around and it was true that the restaurant was all that you might expect from an old fashioned bistro, apart from the enormous prices. Jean-Paul began to explain that everything was original, the restaurant having been bought by a group of enthusiasts to stop it falling into the hands of a chain. He spoke vividly about the erosion of the old Paris and the demands of tourism and commerce.

'What do you think?'

'It's charming,' she said. 'Do you bring your girlfriend here?'

'I have done, yes.' He smiled at her.

'And she knows I am here tonight, I expect.'

He opened his hands. 'Why do you want to know about my girlfriend?'

'Tell me about your parents, then.'

'My father was a butcher and my mother used to help him.'

'And how did you get on with them?'

'Fine. My father could be a bit of a bully but so can most fathers.'

'Did he bully his wife?'

Jean-Paul tilted his head one way then the other, which probably meant yes and certainly what did it matter. She waited.

'He loved dogs.'

'He loved dogs but bullied his wife and son. He sounds almost English.'

Their main courses arrived and for a while they ate in silence and she thought of meals with Joshua, where he'd spoken endlessly about his passion for the designs of Charles Eames, of Ben's obsession with founding his own company, of Anthony and his flirtations with her mother, of Adrian, another obsessive chef and all the other men who had performed in front of her as if she hadn't really existed.

'I said, what are you thinking?'

She looked at him. 'My boyfriends.'

'You have more than one?'

'I have had more than one, yes.'

'And now?'

'And now, no.'

He moved a little closer to her and she was amused to see that he had not registered the tone of her responses, or had chosen to ignore it.

'My friend Amanda says I always choose the same sort of man, that I repeat my mistakes.'

Jean-Paul was clearly pleased to hear this information, probably thinking he could be the exception.

'And what sort of man is that?'

'That's a good question, Jean-Paul. If I knew, it might save me a great deal of trouble.'

He placed his hand over one of hers. 'But you could have any man you wanted, Beatrice.' He squeezed lightly as he said her name.

'Perhaps that's the problem, Jean-Paul,' she said, gently removing her hand. From the look on his face, he clearly enjoyed this game but the process of flirtation was entirely one sided.

'Tell me about your girlfriend.'

'What is there to say?'

'I suppose that is why I am asking.'

'She's just someone I'm seeing.'

Something had taken hold of Beatrice and she was reminded of the tide pressing against her boots in the Thames, a gentle but insistent weight conveying a message that she had yet to decode.

'I'm sure she wouldn't want to be so lightly dismissed. What does she do, where does she live, how does she get on with her parents, is she moody? That sort of thing.'

When Jean-Paul frowned she knew it was not simply because he didn't have the answers. He was irritated and blew air between his lips which said "I am wasting my time and my precious night off."

The evening trailed away and Beatrice filled the silence with talk of her films, her father and her mother in Toulon, but she was talking to herself, as she knew only too well. She had rattled back to the 19th alone in the cab, but quite happy. The clouds had parted and a gibbous moon gave enough light to define them but not enough to dim the stars beyond. The street lights flashed by at intervals, the frames of a film, a familiar sequence she had used several times, her face flickering in and out of darkness.

CHAPTER TWENTY-TWO

They were taking fish inland to the big town by the bald mountain. The path led northwards, climbing all the time so that when she looked behind the sea became wider and the shape of the coast more defined. When she does this, she can see that the boy is watching her, as he had done before, and she takes pleasure in this. It was not the look of mocking curiosity that some gave, that told her she was an outsider, but more focused and direct. He is the son of the merchant who organises these trips to the interior, an olive skinned boy whose hair is tight packed and shiny. She knew it was his father who had asked her mother if her daughter might accompany the group, since they would be away several days and he would not want her to worry. In turn, her mother had explained this to her with a gentle smile and she thought more was contained in this exchange than mere approval for her absence. She can see her mother more completely now and each day register her beauty so that she might contrast it with her own.

As she climbs the path she feels the smooth surface of the crimson stone at the centre of her brooch, a token of safety and a confirmation of her as a woman.

It is winter and the wind blows hard in their faces. This pleases the men because it will keep the fish cool and helps the donkeys who carry the packs with sad eyes and small steps. The path weaves on through the bleached hills and she thinks of the sailor and her mother and what she had seen. He had come back from the sea and she had watched from the stairs unseen as he took her mother in the way that had been explained to her in the grey town. It was clear that her mother wanted what was taking place as much as the man and from time to time she shouted encouragement. The girl knew that she could not share this moment with her mother, that it belonged only to her and the sailor, but it was not a shock to see what they were doing. She had tried to imagine the act of sex, but until now she had been unable to describe its extremes.Somewhere on the path, which is now the *autoroute* 7, at the brow of the long climb, when the sea began to disappear behind them, she understands some of the elements that make her who she is, that her mother had helped create, directly and also without knowing. Her breasts are clear on her lean frame and the legs that run so fast and carry her up the pitted hills have taken a new shape in proportion to her fuller body. She is still tall and slim but she notices that men look at her differently and she comprehends why.

They come to the monastery an hour before dusk, the remains of which can still be seen close to the white stilted viaduct which supports the high speed trains to the sea. They are fed by the nuns in a long room with high windows open to the wind and in return give some of their fish. Water is brought for them to wash and she imagines the boy's body. Later he approaches and speaks to her and she sees that they are being watched by the others, playing out a part that is expected of them. He tells her that his father had come from another land to the east, along the sea and that his mother had died giving birth to him. In return she offers her stories of the grey town and describes how the Norsemen had killed her father, a warrior who had fallen in to the river to be carried off by the gods. They swap what they know, trading their pasts, offering up the details for investigation. The girl understands this barter and knows that it is part of the negotiation. Even in her excitement and the closeness of their heads, another sensation is clear, one which will keep her awake in the long room with the wind howling above. That part of her which could climb alone to the hills, that everyday would relish her singularity and independence, might be lost in this exchange, and this tempers her joy. But then she thinks of her mother, the jeweller, with two husbands and now the sailor, who still maintains her identity, who could give herself and yet remain herself. She looks up at the curved moon and at the stars, brighter than ever in the sharp clear sky and sleeps, her body lifting upwards into that very sky, the same then as it is now.

CHAPTER TWENTY-THREE

Beatrice could see that Harry Wesley had come fully armed with excuses, for she imagined that, in the cold light of day, he might have regarded this trip as a folly and therefore rather exposing. He was already installed when she arrived, a lap top in front of him with an array of papers and folders to one side so that there was barely room for his coffee cup, let alone hers. He was nervous when he rose to greet her, only the third time they had met and he was unsure whether to kiss her on the cheek or shake her hand and in the end did neither. He turned to his computer for support, for on the screen was the familiar skull and he pointed at it, declaring that he'd brought their daughter, Flotsam. Even before she sat down, he swung the screen in her direction.

'Watch,' he said.

Beatrice did as she was told and in front of her Flotsam came to life as skin, lips, hair and then eyes were added to the skull in a slowly animated sequence which finished with the face turning to look at her and, disconcertingly, blinking. Beatrice could feel her breathing change, grow shallower, the image almost as shocking as the bare skull had been when it was first in her hands.

'I meant to save this up, but I simply had to show you.' He pressed the return key again and the head began to turn and the perspective widen to reveal a slim figure standing, naked, with small breasts, her hands placed modestly across the top of her legs.

Beatrice shook her head at Flotsam made real and she reached out and followed the shape of the girl's face with her forefinger.

'From the basic geometry the head gave us, we came up with this. We can't be certain, of course and we'll never be able to prove anything, but I think this is a pretty good stab of what the young girl might have looked like.'

'You've decided that she is a she, then?'

He looked uneasy. 'Well, actually, I did this for you. We really can't establish one hundred percent that Flotsam is feminine, but I know you're sure that she is, so for the purposes of today...'

Beatrice could see that he was slightly embarrassed, as though he had not only transgressed the strict disciplines of his science but declared his hand too early. She was still taking in the shape of Flotsam, which continued to rotate before her so realistically that she expected it to walk from the screen at any minute.

'We've made her a teenager, just.'

The face that looked back at Beatrice had a small, firm mouth and wide brown eyes with short dark hair giving her an almost boyish appearance.

'Did you decide that she should look like this?'

'Don't you like her?' Harry Wesley sounded concerned and retreated into his professional manner. 'Some things we can be sure of, the basic shape of the face, the hair-line, the size of the eyes...'

'...but not the colour?'

'No, that's artistic licence.'

'May I have a cup of coffee now, please?'

'Oh, gosh, sorry.'

She watched him order and in those few seconds tried to decide whether he had done all this work for her or would have done it anyway, as part of his job. What she then asked rather took her by surprise.

'Why did you make her naked?' She remembered her awkwardness at that age and knew that she would never, ever have wanted to be seen naked.

'We often do,' he said. 'We're interested in the physiognomy and we're speculating on body shapes and type.' He was still in osteoarchaeologist mode.

'I was thinking of her...' She thought for a moment '... dignity. Or perhaps *pudeur* would be a better word.'

'Her modesty,' he added. 'I think you're right. I'm sorry.'

As far as romantic lunches in Paris were concerned, she thought this was a strange opening exchange, a discussion on the sensibilities of a thousand year old pubescent girl.

'I didn't think it would be like this,' he said

'What did you imagine?'

'I always intended to show you the computer realisations, but I wanted to do that later. To tell you the truth, I wasn't sure how I was going to kick off, so Flotsam sort of saved the day.'

'A thousand year old go between...'

There was a commotion around them, two large Americans with appropriately sized bags were attempting to get into the brasserie to the distain of the waiters. The distraction, Beatrice noted, allowed Harry Wesley to revert to the script he had originally prepared.

'Have you found what you wanted in Paris?'

'No. Troumeg's gone to ground again. He could be anywhere so I'm at a bit of a loss. Tomorrow I go down to Toulon to see my mother and I shall pay a visit to Marseille to see where his first restaurant used to be.'

'Do you think he's deliberately avoiding you?'

'Well, I suppose I do.'

'So, he must have something he doesn't want you to find out.'

'Or he couldn't care a damn, one way or the other.'

'Is he like that?'

'He's charming but wilful, would be the best way of putting it, I think.'

Outside it began to rain heavily, scattering people for the cover of doorways and back to the entrance to the station opposite.

'Where was it you were going to take me to lunch?'

'To tell you the truth, I hadn't booked anywhere.'

She looked at him and then at the rain teaming down outside. 'I think the decision's been made for you,' she said. 'Chances are you'll come all this way to Paris to travel no further than a hundred metres from the Eurostar terminal.'

'It would have been worth it, though.'

This was the first declaration outside the safe territory of Flotsam and she wasn't quite sure how to react. Perhaps taken aback by his own forwardness, Harry was now negotiating with a waiter for a table for lunch and so Beatrice was relieved of having to make a response.

'So, what's so fascinating about Joseph Troumeg?' he asked and Beatrice could hear that the question was not a challenge, but a genuine request for information. So she told him about the famous food writer and restaurateur and what she'd learned in Paris, describing the two old women and the visit to the town hall and he listened as the rain continued to beat down.

'What do you think happened between Joseph and his mother?' he asked, responding to the story and just as curious as Beatrice at the information she'd unearthed. They discussed the possibilities and, looking back on the lunch afterwards, Beatrice remembered how easy it had been to talk to him, how well he listened. The phone call changed all that and she cursed herself for having answered it, but there was no way of telling it was Jean-Paul. As it was, she left the table and took the phone to stand under the awnings outside.

'It's me.'

'I'm in the middle of lunch. I need to get back.' She was annoyed and was about to end the conversation.

'So you don't want to know where your *Monsieur* Troumeg is at the moment? If you're free, I'll tell you this evening over a drink.'

And with that he'd gone. When she returned to the table Harry could see something had happened and she ended up telling him about Jean-Paul.

'You mean you had dinner with him last night?'

'He's boring and self-absorbed,' she'd told Harry but she could see he wasn't convinced.

'When did you arrange this?'

'Why is that important?' Now she was irritated at his reaction. 'Yesterday, a few moments before I called you, if that makes any difference.'

'Well it does.'

So for the second time in less than twenty-four hours, a meal began to go downhill and she was cross with both Jean-Paul for having caused it and with Harry for making claims on her which she believed were unjustified and presumptuous. The prediction she had made that Harry would see very little of Paris turned out to be true because he returned to the station after lunch with a nod of the head and a tight smile not far distant from a grimace.

By the time she saw Jean-Paul in the evening she was in no mood for his usual antics and point blank refused his offer to go clubbing later that night in return for the information about Troumeg.

'Look, Jean-Paul, get it into that French head of yours, I'm not interested in going out with you. Got it?'

In the end, he'd given her the piece of paper in disgust, not the least troubled by her reaction to him but convinced that she was stuck up English girl, not worth the trouble.

And so, here she was, still in the bar two hours and several whiskies later, tracking over the ruins of the day. When she fished her phone out of her bag, she had a missed call and when she played it back she could tell he was still on Eurostar and she struggled to hear all he said.

'Look, I'm sorry. That was very pathetic of me. I had built this Paris thing into something larger than it was and I have no right to be cross that you had dinner with someone else. I've spoilt what started out really well and I could kick myself. Sorry. Harry.'

How strange to be caught between two extremes of male behaviour, she thought, comparing the arrogance of Jean-Paul with the jealous indignation of Harry but, on further examination over another whisky, she realised their similarities. Both men had made a series of assumptions about her, Jean-Paul that his good looks would cause her to fall into his arms and Harry that because he had shown interest in her she should put the rest of her life with men on hold. Another whisky had her examining the doomed relationships with Joshua, Ben and Anthony, not to mention other, briefer flings. She couldn't quite put her finger on it but somewhere in her slightly drunk state she understood that in here was an equation she had to understand for failure to do so would finally undermine her and no matter how cleverly she was able to stack these disastrous relationships on some dusty shelf at the back of her mind she couldn't forget them or her failure to make them work.

Was it wise to try and call Harry now? Had she been insensitive to tell him about Jean-Paul? Would it seem that she was protesting too much if she said that she'd only decided to see the chef so that she could contrast his behaviour with that of Harry's and to get a free meal? She tried to focus on the piece of paper that Jean-Paul had tossed at her when he realised he wasn't going to have his way: 12 rue de Petit Puits, Marseille, it told her, road of the little well. She would go there after she had seen her mother and the very thought of that meeting brought further gloom to a day that had promised so much more.

She got unsteadily off the bar stool and her phone chirruped. It was a text from Dr Harry Wesley. 'I'm sorry about the naked Flotsam. She deserved better. Harry.'

CHAPTER TWENTY-FOUR

The arms of the great trees are bare and gaunt, black fingers against the blue sky. She is distracted by the gurgling water of the fountain and the sounds of bartering in the market. When she hears the horses and screams she is suddenly back in the grey town looking down on the old river, a spectator to the death of her father. The memory makes her as incapable of movement as the tree whose bulk she rests against. The horsemen come closer and they are silent because her mind will not accept their presence. Even the screaming women now have no sound, just their distorted faces and they run past her without looking. She could see the men with stakes and swords silhouetted against the pale dust of the square broken apart by the bulk of the dashing horses, scattered and thrown to the side. The very thought that she had left this behind makes her reluctant to accept the evidence of her eyes and she stands by the tree in denial. She would resist the destruction of her happiness. The first horse comes by and the foam from its mouth flecks into the air and drops on her bare arm. Behind six more horses bear down on her, still in silence, for she continues not to acknowledge them, allow them entry into her life. Even when the boy tackles her and bundles her to the other side of the flaking tree she is not of the moment and does not feel the gravel bite into her arms and face nor hear her own scream. The boy covers her with his cape and she retreats further into its blackness, his hot breath on her face.

When he pulls her to her feet, the first thing she sees are the fish covered in grit, their blank eyes looking upwards at the trees. He drags her away, across the stony ground and into the alleyways beyond the open space. She watches him go back to the square and scoop up food that had been abandoned before sprinting back to her with it bundled on his back. More horsemen come through and they wait until the dust from their hooves has settled before slipping out of the town. She is angry now and when she recognises the path which had brought them in the day before, she shakes her head and points eastwards, along the banks of the river. They follow the valley before turning southwards into the hills. It would take them three days to return to the port, but they would be quicker without the donkeys. She is restored, in charge of her senses again and they follow the contours of the hills towards the sun which moves across their horizon as the day unfolds. Only then does she wonder if, in the larger scheme of things, this was destined to happen, that some good was meant to follow the evil, that somehow she had been blessed.

In amongst the low trees and the rough white stones of the hills, they find a recess which gives them shelter and they lay together, his cloak once again covering her but this time for warmth, his breath calm on her neck and they sleep, the fall of his arm over her stomach and soon she is beyond even the strange cries of the night. When dawn wakes them, stiff limbed and cold, she knows the trust between them was made real. They stand and point southwards, each in slightly different directions, waiting for the sun to come over the horizon and tell which of them is closest to guessing the route they should take. She has no fear now, if indeed she'd had fear at all. The hills, over which one day the metal arms of pylons would link to carry power down to the great city, rise before them and they move onwards, the boy taking her hand as she steps off the limestone ridge into the meagre warmth of the sun. Behind them they can see the bald mountain, its bare outline pink in the sun but soon it is swallowed by the hills that are carrying them southwards. They stop finally in the northern shadows of what would become the Chaîne de l'Étoile and rest at the abbey. When she lies alone that night she feels in her cloak for the brooch and the sudden chill that runs through her when she cannot find it is greater than her concern about the charging horsemen of the day before. She goes to the stone window and looks out to the countryside and knows that somewhere in that dark landscape she has dropped the crimson stone. She does not cry for a part of her believes it was meant.

CHAPTER TWENTY-FIVE

The train swooped down over the broad valley carried on what seemed an endless bridge. Beneath her she could see the pattern of habitation, the zigzag of linking roads and paths, the isolated farms and, fleetingly, the outline of an old building, the stone foundations revealing that it was probably of some importance. The grass around it was carefully tended and Beatrice imagined it was an ancient monument, perhaps an abbey. It was gone almost as soon as it arrived. The journey wasn't quite long enough for her to finish Joseph Troumeg's book about Provence in which he extolled its virtues, paid homage to the region's influence on his life and described how to cook a series of typical dishes, each illustrated in glorious colour. Real life, of course, was absent from these pages; Joseph Troumeg, with his undoubted skills, was presenting an ideal, almost fantastic world, to seduce the aspiring reader.

The journey was a comfort and she had switched off her mobile, leaving behind the haughty Jean-Paul and, for the time being at least, the remorseful Harry. Even though she was heading towards a mother who exhibited a range of behaviour that would put these two men in the shade, she was happy with the fact that purpose had been restored to this journey. She was changing at Marseille, where she would be returning the following day to continue her pursuit of Troumeg, and today she wanted to walk down to the port to familiarise herself before going on to Toulon. La Canabière in all its faded grandeur, took her straight down to the old port which lay snug between the hills, watched over by the all-seeing figure of the Virgin Mary standing on top of the Basilica. She saw another opening for her film, with a panorama of old, black and white footage taken from the church – she was sure some must exist – mixed with a closer sequence down here by the port, continuing in monochrome before bleeding into colour as Troumeg walks into shot surveying a scene hardly changed in the fifty years since he'd opened his first restaurant. Somewhere over to the right it had been, but she wanted to save that investigation until tomorrow and turned to retrace her steps to the station and her less than all-seeing mother.

It took just under an hour for the train to follow a tortuous route around to Toulon, time enough for her to list the questions she wanted to put to her mother. She hoped these would complete a sequence with those she'd asked Jean-Paul – and meant to put to Harry – and if she already knew the task was incomplete she expected it to get worse with a form of extreme obfuscation from her mother. Every so often she saw the Mediterranean in cracks through the hills, in the same way she saw herself, never long enough to draw a conclusion or to be certain that it wasn't simply a mirage.

The cruise ship was disproportionately large in the harbour, its white bulk a brash contrast to the old buildings which it dwarfed. At least the aircraft carrier, larger still, had the grace to be painted grey and was absorbed by the background. Her mother's hotel was modern, modest but with a marvellous position on the quay. Quite what Beatrice expected from the meeting she wasn't quite clear except to know that she would be made to feel that she was doing her mother a favour rather than responding to an invitation. And so it was, Eileen Palmenter in the pink, blue and white flowered dress which she had shown Beatrice in John Lewis, appearing surprised when she saw her daughter in the foyer.

'Darling,' she exclaimed, 'is everything alright?'

'Fine, mother. You invited me down, don't you remember?'

'Did I? Oh, well, what does it matter. I'm afraid I'm wearing the dress you didn't like when I showed it to you.'

'No, that's not quite true. You thought I wouldn't like it, but I think it suits you perfectly.'

'How long can you spare for me?' she said, as if she hadn't heard, once again opening a new arena for dispute, into which Beatrice refused to enter.

'Have you found somewhere nice for us to have supper? My treat.'

It was hard to imagine Eileen Palmenter as a child of the 60s. Even though she had been a teenager for seven years of this iconic decade, the events that made it famous appeared to have passed her by. She never referred to her childhood and what few photographs existed of her during that time might just as well have been taken in the 50s. They showed a pretty girl, more often than not in a dark cardigan above a calf length skirt. She had grown into the age she appeared to be in these pictures.

'I imagine you'll be going tomorrow,' her mother persisted.

'Which gives us both supper and breakfast. Show me where we're going.'

There was a strong wind and the rigging on the aluminium masts were sending out a high pitched percussion and the plastic flaps on the waterfront cafés were breathing hard in response. The hills behind were already pink tinged with the late afternoon sun and Beatrice watched her mother hold her hair in place as though it might snap.

'I'm sure you haven't just come to see me,' Eileen Palmenter shouted as they made their way along the waterfront. Beatrice thought about lying, but changed her mind.

'I've got some work to do in Marseille tomorrow.'

This information seemed to satisfy her mother who took her arm. 'So you thought you'd fit me in.'

This is the way it always is, thought Beatrice who, over the years, had become used to this game and had learned not to take it too seriously, regarding it as part of the friction generated by entering the gravitational pull of her mother's world. She waited until they had arrived at the restaurant before speaking again. It was on the corner of the front, with beautiful views over the jumble of yachts.

'I'm going to see where Joseph Troumeg had his first restaurant,' she said. 'Did you ever eat in any of his places?'

'Well, there's a question,' she said. 'You may not remember, but your father didn't really do that sort of thing.'

Beatrice didn't. 'But what about you? You must have had some suitors since who've taken you out?' She watched her mother turn her head as though she was averting her eyes from an unpleasant sight.

'I don't know about that. I seem to recall going to the place he had in Mayfair. It was rather good, as far as my memory serves me.'

'And were you taken?'

'Why does that matter?'

'It's something you've never talked about. Dad, that is and what happened afterwards.' The conversation had moved more quickly than Beatrice had expected, or indeed planned and she could see that her mother was glad of the distraction of ordering. Her friends' mothers seemed to fall into two categories, those who confided in their daughters and those who competed but she felt her mother, whilst certainly not the first, was not really the latter either.

'It's all in the past, anyway,' her mother said, folding the napkin over her knees, clearly wanting to change the subject.

'Have you had a serious relationship since Dad?'

'Heavens, what is this, an interrogation?'

'It's just something you've never talked about and I was interested.'

'And some things should remain private.'

'Why? Lots of my friends have conversations like this with their mothers.'

'So you're criticising me now, are you?'

'No, I don't suppose there is a correct way of being a mother. Anyway, how would I know?'

It was the crack that her mother had been waiting for. 'Indeed. The chances of you becoming a mother seem to be receding by the day, even though I can't keep pace with your changing boyfriends.'

'Yes, there have been rather a lot,' conceded Beatrice. 'But these are modern times, mother. That's what happens.'

'Is it? Doesn't seem to make you any the happier.'

'Were you happy with Dad?'

'Really, darling. Of course I was.'

'Tell me about him.'

Eileen Palmenter broke off to instruct the waiter on how to fillet her fish and Beatrice was once again reminded of the steeliness of her mother. It was clear she wanted the subject dropped, but Beatrice pushed her further.

'Where did you meet, for example?'

'I must have told you, surely?'

Beatrice shook her head and wondered if her mother would continue.

'Why this interest, anyway?'

What Beatrice would like to have said, as the masts of a large yacht moved gracefully across the windows, was because it might help me understand where I get my attitude to men from, but she didn't. 'I'm just surprised that I don't know, that's all. Was it love at first sight?'

'What an old fashioned thought. No wonder you still can't

find a man, if that's your criterion. I took some persuading. There's your answer.'

'And what about sex?'

'Really, darling, we're about to eat.'

'I thought the sixties brought sexual liberation for your generation of women.'

'I'm not sure we should be talking like this. It doesn't seem right.'

'I can't remember you or Dad telling me the facts of life, but maybe you did.'

'You didn't need telling. The boys were queuing up from the start and as I've told you many times before, I've lost count of the men in your life.'

Beatrice had interviewed many people in her role as a television director and had learned the most important rule was to listen to answers instead of planning the next question. What she was hearing from her mother, apart from evasion, was implied criticism, her inability to find a husband, her sexual precocity, the inappropriateness of her queries. This was all familiar territory, but Beatrice had never before sat her mother down with the intention of interviewing her.

'And who told you the facts of life?'

'Certainly not my parents.'

'Were you a virgin when you married?'

Eileen Palmenter stopped eating and regarded her daughter coldly. 'I don't think I should answer that question. Suffice to say, you certainly won't be. I think you should pay more attention to your life than ask impertinent questions about mine.'

'That's why I'm asking.'

'You were always difficult, Beatrice. From the start. At school you wouldn't conform and I had no one to help me once your father had gone. We expected a lot more of you.'

Beatrice, who had heard this before, kept her counsel, fascinated that her mother had evaded answering any of her questions, merely deflecting them and criticising her instead.

Beatrice knew, of course, that she could never change her mother but it saddened her that there was so little real interest in her life, that the valve only operated one way and that was in favour of her mother. It had grown dark by the time they had finished the meal and the wind had dropped so that the boats had stopped agitating at their moorings. She told her mother that she had checked into a somewhat cheaper hotel nearby and they air kissed before Beatrice wandered off to find such accommodation. It was only now that she turned her mobile back on to see four missed calls from Harry Wesley and a text. She sat in a square opposite an enormous fountain and listened to the hypnotic sound of the water and considered that her mother might be disappointed and angry that her life hadn't been like her daughter's. Perhaps Eileen Palmenter's relationships with men had been unremarkable and her envy had been converted to poisonous and undermining criticism. Sometimes Beatrice thought that her mother was talking about a different child when referring to her, an imaginary creation that bore no relation at all to Beatrice.

She took out her phone and considered listening to the messages and reading the text but for now she had no energy and slipped it back into her pocket and went over to the fountain where she flicked in a euro and watched it sink to the bottom and join the other coins.

CHAPTER TWENTY-SIX

When they begin the descent from the hills they can see the port below them and the tiny figure on the dock, although the distance in between takes several hours to complete. He holds her hand as they come nearer, for both now recognise the woman who is waiting.

She watches her mother come alive and begin to run towards her, her face caught between tears and joy. She holds her in her arms and the boy looks on and her mother sees this and embraces him too, telling him that his father has returned safely but feared both of them had been lost. When her mother has recovered and dried her tears, she takes the boy's hand again to affirm the reality of their new status. That night a feast is prepared with the boy's father and they talk of the incident in the distant town and how they had survived, the days and nights on the hills and both parents can see that there is a bond between their children. She eats the lamb flavoured with herbs but her worry of what she has to say means the food settles badly on her stomach. She sees her mother looking at her, knowing there is a problem and she waits for her to ask, dreading the moment when she has to admit that she has lost the brooch. When the time comes something strange and wonderful happens, for on hearing the admission her mother simply throws back her head and laughs. Once again, she takes her hands and tells her that it is she who is really precious, more important than gold and garnet, who could not be replaced and that although the brooch could never die, it could also never live. She could see that the boy is watching, the boy who'd known no mother. He is older and she feels that his face tells all there is to know about him, that in its various shapes, the forehead with its single line, the eyes that look without blinking and seem always about to ask a question, the mouth and the chin that signal both strength and sympathy, she can gauge him.

The next day her mother declares to her that she would make another brooch to replace the one that had been lost on the hills. She shakes her head and explains that perhaps there was a reason why the brooch had been left behind. That night she had dreamed of the beautiful stone set in the round, silver shield, lying in a crack between the dry, white rocks, ignored by the animals, impervious to the storms which in summer and winter shrouded the hills and made them the loneliest place in the world. In the dream she saw the spring flowers grow up and around the red stone so that above it there waved stems of deep chalky blue and vivid yellow amidst the thick smell of thyme. She had moved on from what the brooch represented, the dream told her and she sees that her mother understands.

The horsemen who had destroyed the market remind her of the impermanence of things, that life can change in the short time between a father's hug and his lifeless body falling in the river. And with this comes the awareness that her mother had embraced this uncertainty and not allowed it to crush her spirit. The older she becomes the clearer her mother appears, as though she is walking away from her shadow and can more easily perceive her shape.

CHAPTER TWENTY-SEVEN

Beatrice woke to the sound of her mobile vibrating on the bedside table. She unwound herself from the sheets thinking that she was outside and brought her hands to her face expecting it to be cold to the touch before moving them down to the ache in her back. She fought hard to recapture the dream which she knew had taken place in the open and was tantalisingly close to her. She was conscious that she was feeling positive, that something pleasant had taken place even though she didn't know what. She looked at her phone to confirm that the sender was Harry. In the midst of her dislocation, she ran through the four messages he left, the first three reiterating his apologies for his behaviour. The fourth had her leaning forward on the edge of the bed.

'Oh, I've just been thinking,' the message ran, the voice quite different from that of the penitent apologies, 'that it's hardly likely that the old woman – Marguerite I think you told me her name was – would not have asked Troumeg's mother more about the war and her son. Women aren't like that, are they? I have a hunch you should check again.'

She lay back on the bed and extended her right leg which she examined in detail, bending it towards her before extending it again. It was an involuntary gesture and after flexing the leg a couple of times more, decided to respond to the message.

'Thank goodness,' were his first words on hearing her voice. 'Can we start again?'

'I wasn't aware we'd started in the first place.'

'You're right, of course you're right.'

'So what's this about women and what they talk about?'

Happy to get on to safer ground, she could hear his tone change.

'Wouldn't you have thought that if Marguerite and Odile had known each other for more than half a century that two things of such importance as children and the war would have cropped up more than once?'

'It's possible,' Beatrice said. She lay back on the bed and straightened her other leg, pointing her toes forward as she used to at ballet classes when she was six. 'Do you have any other insights for me?'

'Only that you fascinate me.'

She thought about this for a moment. 'How can you say that when you hardly know me?'

'I'm not sure that's true...'

'What, a couple of muddy afternoons on the Thames and a less than successful lunch in Paris,' she interrupted.

'I wonder I needed that much,' he said.

This caused her to hesitate before replying, because it opened an arena of debate which had troubled her for a long time.

'What do you mean?'

'Well, I thought I could tell a lot about you from the very start.'

'How?'

'I don't really know and I don't really care,' he said. 'It's not something I want to examine too much. Something about the shape of your face. I just want to be given the chance to find out if I'm right.'

Beatrice had heard versions of this from several men, but there was an ingenuous quality to Harry Wesley's approach which was quite different, not arch or suggestive and for some reason it made her place her legs together, toes in line and raise them above the bed.

'What did you have in mind? Lunch in Marseille might not be a great idea.'

'Is that where you are?'

'No, I've just gone ten rounds with my mother in Toulon and I'm about to have more of the same over breakfast.'

'You must tell me more,' he said and Beatrice thought that he sounded as though he meant it.

'Thank you for your suggestion about Marguerite. I will certainly speak to her again. Later today I'm off to Marseille to continue my pursuit of Mr Troumeg.'

'I'm glad we're talking again. Call me and let me know how you get on. And I'll think about a safe venue for us to meet.'

Afterwards, whilst showering and then padding around the small bedroom getting dressed, Beatrice weighed up the call trying to assess what she thought about Harry Wesley and whether he really was unlike the other men who had come and gone in her life. She couldn't give her thoughts any shape but she was conscious, like an animal is of a another creature hidden in the undergrowth, that something was moving just out of sight.

'Did you sleep well, mother?' she asked in the breakfast room, bright in the morning sun.

'As much as one ever does, these days. I'm a light sleeper and those wretched gulls don't help. When are you off?'

'I'm in no hurry. Did you think on about what we were talking about last night?'

Her mother picked up her napkin and spread it on her lap. 'I suppose you have to be like this in your work. Never taking no for an answer.'

'Yes, that's true, I do have to be like that. Some people call it a skill.'

'Or a very bad character trait. Anyway, the answer is no.'

'I just wondered how you knew that Jim Palmenter was the right man for you. Was it his looks? Or his sense of humour? I mean, what did you think when you first saw him?' Beatrice asked this whilst taking a croissant and layering it with jam.

'He appeared perfectly ordinary to me, if you must know. He was a serious man.' She wiped her mouth as if to zip it shut.

'It's not a lot to go on, is it? I mean, did you kiss on the first date?' Beatrice felt disengaged, the impersonal interviewer that her mother had earlier scorned. 'How does one know these things?'

'Well, you clearly don't. Your father proposed to me on holiday in the Cotswolds.'

This much Beatrice knew, having been told the story several times. 'But how long after you met was that?'

'Several months. In some ways he was quite romantic.'

'Quite romantic is rather damning him with faint praise, isn't it? You must have slept together before you got married?'

'You're doing this deliberately, aren't you? Is it something you're working on? The sex lives of our parents, or some such nonsense.'

'It's a good title. I must remember that. No, it's more personal.' Beatrice waited, for here was another opening for her mother to pursue, if she'd heard.

'Your father was a good man and let's leave it at that. Now, wasn't it Joshua you were currently going out with?'

Beatrice was surprised that she remembered, although experience had taught her that her failure to remember, or her misremembering, was nothing more than an act.

'Yes. Joshua. You're right.'

'Well, how's it going?'

'It's gone.'

'Not again. I can't say I'm surprised. What do you do wrong?'

'I can tell you what he did wrong, if you like?'

'It's always someone else's fault, isn't it?'

Beatrice had expected this. 'He never used to listen to me.'

'And they were all the same, were they?'

Eileen Palmenter's defence was impenetrable, as Beatrice knew and full frontal attacks were rebuffed with ease and so she tried a lateral approach, conceding ground whilst she regrouped her forces. 'Maybe that's the problem. I always choose the same sort of man.'

'I hardly think so dear. You can't have two men more different than a classic car expert and – what did Joshua do, something in design, wasn't it?'

The wrong-headedness of the response didn't deter Beatrice. 'Was Dad like other men you'd been out with, then?' It was a final attempt to come in under her mother's radar but, like the others, it failed.

'I wasn't that sort of girl, Beatrice, as I've told you before. Now I have to go and meet Joan. We're going to the market, the one by the fountain. Are you going to join us?'

It was an indifferent offer, take it or leave it, but nevertheless Beatrice walked alongside her mother to the market where she met Jean, who, in a matelot top and chinos, looked more the part for a Provençal market than her mother who was in another floral print dress.

'What do you do?' Joan asked, as Eileen busied herself buying an olive wood spoon.

'I make films.'

'Really. Your mother never mentioned that.'

They strolled on between the colourful baskets and bolts of cloth patterned with cigalas. 'She said you were in television, but I got the impression that you might be some sort of assistant.'

'My mother doesn't fully understand what I do.'

'I don't suppose many people know how to make films.'

'That's true, Joan. I'm trying to make one about Joseph Troumeg and I'm getting nowhere at the moment.'

'Such a charming man,' Joan said. 'I believe he saved my

marriage. I couldn't cook a thing until he came along. Made it all so simple and yet glamorous. He was like one of those characters in a pantomime, sort of unbelievable and yet adorable.'

'That's very well put and quite true. So you'd want to see my film?'

'Oh, of course.'

'Even if it showed you another side of his life, one that we might not know?'

'Do you think there is one? I can't imagine it.'

Why couldn't I have had even this brief conversation with my mother, Beatrice thought and wondered yet again at the culs-de-sac that most of their exchanges produced. And later, on the train, she was left with the dissatisfaction of having even attempted a more direct conversation with her mother, the vague feeling that she was still expecting to find an answer when all she would reaffirm was her mother's rigidity.

****

Marseille was a city to match her mood, restless and vaguely uneasy, the dark shadows of the narrow streets and the blinding light of the sun in the open spaces a challenge to her senses, an assault continued in the unblinking stares of the Arab traders and the noise of the traffic. She could feel the eyes on her, scanning her body and once of twice she felt the brush of a stray hand across the top of her legs and when she turned to look or challenge was met by those same eyes, now innocent. She climbed the long gloomy steps underneath the lines of washing, towards the old town, pulled deeper into the maze of lanes and alleys where the Greeks and Romans had traded. Kids in trainers slapped past her and old men in doorways watched. Graffiti covered the lower walls and she began to lose her sense of direction, the alleyways constantly in the shade beyond the slant of the sun, her map unable to keep pace with this latticework of passages. She tried to picture a young

Joseph Troumeg in these streets, knowing his way, speaking the patois, in the early years of his career before money lifted him from the city and gave him to the world. Having twice got hopelessly lost, retracing her steps and almost starting again, she stumbled on rue de Petit Puits at the sharp angle where it joined the rue de Panier. Bread and water, a happy conjunction for a man who, over the years, had been elevated to the status of god in the world of food. She looked for number 12, but not all the doors were marked. She estimated that it might be a plain restaurant with old metal chairs and tables on the uneven road outside. Two men were eating what looked like couscous with chicken and preserved lemon, shovelling the food into their mouths, looking over their forks at her breasts and legs. A thin Arab stood stock still behind the counter, almost lost in the dark and she went in to ask him if this was number twelve. With a gesture of his thumb upwards he indicated where she should look. To the right of the restaurant was an arched doorway with the head of a cherub in the centre. The eyes of the two men were still on her as she pressed the buzzer and when she didn't get an answer, she walked over to the table to ask them if they knew when Joseph Troumeg would be back. They shook their heads and continued eating. She didn't want to sit and wait although she knew that both men and the thin face watching from inside, would have known about the comings and goings of Joseph Troumeg.

Further along another café offered a less threatening arena and she sat outside and drank a beer and watched the shadow creep across the road until it touched the opposite curb. She had a view of both approaches to the doorway so she just sat nursing one beer and then another until the sun had left completely and an appropriate gloom had closed around the ancient streets of old Marseille. Perhaps the men had told him on his return, or had relayed a message, for it was obvious from the way he approached that he knew she was waiting. He drew alongside and the look he gave her was quite different from the coldly suspicious eyes of the diners, or the greedy gaze of the sexual predators.

'Christ,' he said. 'Haven't you got anything better to do than follow me around?'

And with that he shuffled along the street to disappear into his doorway. She followed to find the door open. She hesitated just a moment before stepping into the blackness of the interior.

CHAPTER TWENTY-EIGHT

She is walking over the bleached white rocks to the south of the town, where the water in the coves seems lit from beneath making the sea the most brilliant of pale blues, like the stones in her mother's jewellery. She sits alone in the shade of a tree and watches the distorted outlines of the fish in the translucent water.

Her mother said that the boy's father had asked her to make a ring of gold and she knows that her response to this information would decide whether she would make it or not. The way her mother spoke told her that she could decide one way or the other. She sees the ring as a natural successor to the brooch, the first a symbol of her becoming a woman, the second of her arrival at marriage. Although she feels no hesitation in her heart, she still wants some time to carry the information with her before giving her mother an answer. She takes off her clothes and from the edge of a rock she had swum from many times before, raises her arms above her head, feeling the shape of her body, the tautness of her stomach and thighs, before diving into the sea, pushing herself underwater, enjoying its coldness, widening her legs, completely free. The wind, which had been blowing hard from the north for five days, has now dwindled to the breeze which brushes her face as she breaches the surface. She can feel the dimensions of her body, its extremities and she has ownership of it all. She pulls herself on to a flat rock and lies back in the sun, the sea water running between her legs and glistening on her breasts. She shuts her eyes and although she was expecting to think about the boy, it is her father that first comes into her mind, his face on the bridge and the wind that had blown up the river and made them both turn away. She sees in his eyes the trust and pride he had in her, a belief that she would carry on after he had gone. And then she sees her mother's eyes, different and more rebellious, but conveying the same message of belief in her daughter, that no matter what her spirit would not be broken. Behind her she can hear the chatter of the small birds she often sees here, their beautiful heads of gold and red, moving in groups in the shade of the branches high above, just out of reach.

Her body had now dried and the breeze is beginning to chill her but the decision had been made, or at least confirmed. She returns to her mother and sees her at work amongst the silver and gold, the clasps and pendants. She approaches her side and stands with her, slightly taller now and sees a line of three rings on a plain dark cloth. They are all gold, the first and largest with a raised top and the pattern of a cross, the second a plain band and the third a thick strand of gold evenly twisted, which she picks up. It is too large, but nevertheless she slips it onto her finger and then holds her hand out to her mother who takes it and kisses its back.

The decision had been made.

Later she sees the boy and tells him. They walk together, up the hill to where the basilica would one day be built and sit looking down at the port. He puts his arm around her and they stay until the sun has disappeared behind the old town.

CHAPTER TWENTY-NINE

The darkness of the hallway swallowed her and she stopped, suddenly unable to see, her arms feeling for the walls. And then ahead of her the outline of a partly opened door and she moved cautiously forward assuming that Troumeg had expected her to follow. She entered a large kitchen with a central unit of light grey marble into which had been set a range and a sink. On top lay the bags that Troumeg had been carrying. Beyond was an elaborate conservatory, painted dark green and hung with two wire chandeliers. She looked behind her where the red tiled floor led to a seating area with a day bed of bright cushions and a handsome open stone fireplace. The restaurateur was nowhere to be seen so she wandered through to the conservatory and its long wooden table at the centre of which was a large bowl full of different fruits. In the distance she heard a door click open.

'Enchanting, isn't it?' he said, drying his hands as he approached, once again acting as though she had been expected.

'Do you have somewhere like this in every city?

He appeared to ignore her. 'I don't own this. I do my photo shoots here and the odd programme. Those television people wreck everything in their path, as you know.'

She did. 'Very sensible.' Beatrice noticed the sheets of lighting gels rolled up in one corner secured by a large clip. It was an excellent place for filming, she could see and deduced that it must face north so that the sun would be less of a problem. Troumeg came past her and sat at the long table.

'So what are we going to do with you?'

She looked at him but he had turned away and was in the process of taking plates from a cupboard and wiping them with the towel he had brought from the bathroom.

'In a way,' he continued, 'I quite admire you but I do wonder if you haven't got something better to do with your time.'

'What's wrong with this?'

'How old are you?' he asked.

'Is that important?'

He wandered through to the kitchen and from the fridge he brought some cheese and cold meats on a yellow plate and laid it on the table.

'Let's see, about thirty-six, I guess.' Again, he wasn't looking at her, but continued to shuffle between the kitchen and the conservatory collecting two glasses and a bottle of pink wine.

'Almost thirty-seven.'

'And you want to chase around after me.' It wasn't so much a question as a statement.

'Is there anything you want to hide?' she said.

'We've all got something to hide, my dear. Even you.' A further shuffle and a pair of linen napkins were tossed on to the table. 'Especially you, perhaps.'

She frowned. 'How do you mean?' Once again Troumeg had turned the process of interrogation on its head.

He shrugged. 'How'd you feel about someone wanting to make a film about you?'

'It's different,' she said. 'I'm not famous.'

'But you don't want to make a film about my fame, do you?' He was looking at her now and she shook her head. 'But it wouldn't be interesting unless you were famous.'

'To you, maybe. To you.' He sat opposite her and opened his hands towards her. '*Bon appetit*.' He poured her a glass of pink wine.

She cut a corner of cheese and took a sip of the wine.

'You're not really interested in food, are you?' he asked, looking at her. He got up to return with two sticks of celery in a glass and salt and black pepper in small bowls.

'I'm interested in you in the same way I was interested in the women in the refuge.'

'I don't doubt it.'

Joseph Troumeg, she saw, remained entirely in charge, able to move the conversation wherever he wanted. 'You made up the name Troumeg.'

'Of course I did.'

'Why?'

'It sounded better than Leval.'

'Or Levy?'

Not missing a beat, he cut another slice of cheese and took a sip of wine. 'Not the best sort of surname to have in Paris between the wars, wouldn't you say?'

'But you've never talked about this,' she said, betraying slightly more eagerness than she'd wanted.

'I've told you,' he said, wiping his mouth, 'I don't do the past, not in that way at least.'

'Just as a series of dishes dressed up, in a beautiful setting, so you can perpetuate the well polished story of your life.'

'Something like that. But I expect you do exactly the same thing.'

'Except that I've never had to. I've never been famous.'

'What difference does that make? I would guess that you didn't want people to know about your boyfriends and how you got to thirty-seven without one of them. Am I right?' The way he spoke made her feel that he knew about her and so she looked away and stared at the bowl of fruit before she answered.

'Something like that.'

'*Voilà*,' he said, getting up again and shuffling towards the kitchen to take a large frying pan off the wall. From the fridge he took a bowl and poured its contents into the pan and flicked on the gas ring. Beatrice watched through the glass and then joined him to spectate. Troumeg took a bowl of strawberries, hulled them whilst the liquid was warming and then tossed them in, followed by a handful of pink peppercorns. She watched as the sauce began to bubble and the strawberries soften, releasing a sweet smell which filled the kitchen. Troumeg shook the pan gently before spooning some of the contents on to two green plates. He leant across to the freezer to bring out a carton of ice-cream, adding a dollop to one. 'I imagine with a figure like yours, you're happy to have a little ice cream? The strawberries have been sautéed in a reduction of lemon and lime juice so may be a little tart even with the castor sugar.'

They sat and ate. 'Do you cook?' he asked.

She shook her head.

'So how long are you going to do this television business?'

'That's the sort of question my mother might ask.'

'And you would resist answering, I imagine. Children?'

'Who knows?' she said, the tables fully turned once again. 'What about you? Do you have children?'

'What do you think?'

'Did you want them?'

'Heavens, no. Looking after me is a full time occupation.'

She laughed at this easy admission.

'You didn't think much of the chef in Paris?'

'He's rather pleased with himself and not that interested in me. Apart from one thing, of course.'

'What about the others?' Troumeg said, standing again to put a kettle on the stove.

'Oh, they all want that as well.'

Now it was Troumeg's turn to laugh. 'So do you think your luck will change? Before it's too late, I mean.'

Beatrice didn't know how to answer and in the pause Troumeg continued.

'I gather I'm sounding like your mother again.' Outside a pair of brightly coloured birds landed on a fig tree. 'What does she think, anyway?'

'She gave up on me a long time ago,' Beatrice said. 'Doesn't understand my work or my boyfriends.'

'And you want to persuade her otherwise?'

'I thought I did.'

Troumeg pushed a small but heavy cup towards her and half filled it with coffee. 'You're going to persist, aren't you?'

At first Beatrice wasn't sure to what he was referring, although the answer she imagined would have been the same whatever. 'Yes, I guess so. Why didn't you go to your mother's funeral?'

Again there was no hesitation in Troumeg's reply. 'Because we didn't see eye to eye and I chose to do something about it.'

'What did you fall out over?'

'What did you fall out with your mother about? Everything and nothing.'

'But I'll go to my mother's funeral.'

'So you say,' Troumeg said, taking the plates back into the kitchen and leaving them on the marble top by the sink. 'So you say.'

'What happened to your father?' Beatrice was looking at his back as he rinsed the plates.

'I can't put these in the dishwasher,' he said. 'They're early Wedgwood and I've had them since I first came to Marseille. No dishwashers back then.' He laid them carefully on the grey surface. 'That you'll have to find out,' he said, responding to her question.

'Who was he?'

'Who was he, indeed.' Troumeg dried the plates and stacked them in a cupboard. 'And your father? What can you tell me about him?'

'He died when I was twelve. Heart attack. He was an actuary. He worked a lot and I didn't see much of him. So you're part

Jewish?' Beatrice wrenched the conversation back to Troumeg.

'That's a fair deduction,' he said.

'But your father wasn't Jewish?'

'Indeed not.'

Troumeg was silent and he walked over to the day bed where he adjusted the cushions and sat down.

Beatrice followed. 'I'm not sure if my father or my mother really liked children. I was an only child and sometimes, listening to my mother, I wonder whether she didn't consider me a mistake from the start.'

'Not a nice feeling to have. No wonder you haven't had children.' And he laughed.

Beatrice began to smile too, partly promoted by his mirth but also at the idea she might not want children.

'Are you going to disappear again?'

'I might, I might. But I imagine you'd find me. You're that sort of girl. You're likely to wash up anywhere. Like flotsam.'

Beatrice stared at him. 'Flotsam? Why do you say that?'

'There's a rootlessness about you. A sort of impermanence. A drifting quality, shall we say. Little girl lost.' He looked over to her. 'We never like to hear about ourselves, do we? Unless it's positive, of course. That's why I like my pretty pictures of the past. So much nicer.'

Flotsam. She found herself unable to tell him of the coincidence, although why she wasn't sure. She thought of the skull washed up by the Thames, the shape that Harry had put on the bones and she could see the brown eyes looking at her. Somehow this stare was not that of a restless girl unsure of herself.

'Cat got your tongue?'

'Sort of.'

'Well, I have some errands to run. No doubt I will see you later. Just click the door shut when you go.'

'How are we going to leave things?'

'Well, I guess that's entirely up to you.'

And he was gone.

CHAPTER THIRTY

She wakes early to the screams of the birds. The sun has yet to appear over the hills and the blue sky is veiled with grey. The water in the harbour barely moves and the boats are still at their moorings. She has time before her mother begins to prepare her for the day. She smoothes her hands down her body to confirm her ownership which she knows is about to be exchanged, not just for the gold and the property, but for a partnership which she could not yet describe. It was a barter she was prepared to accept, although she is uncertain of its dimensions. Today the boy would enter her in every sense and there is fear and excitement in her apprehension. She runs down the hill, steeper than the one in the grey town, but the exhilaration is the same, her long legs extending beneath her, the easy strides carrying her downwards to the harbour. She sees a fish break the water and she takes this as a welcome for her and for the day. The air is warm, edged with the smell of the sea, interlaced with all the perfumes of the land. It was easy to forget in this stillness that the sea and the land could be so harsh, could rise up and destroy as easily as they could delight.

They have arranged to meet just before sunrise and when he joins her they both point to the exact same spot where the sun would soon roar out from behind the rocks. He kisses her and she can feel him against her, pressing and obvious, but he would wait, they would wait, until later. This was a moment alone with him, before their families surrounded them and they became changed, plural and not singular. If they had wanted it to be different, she had told him, they could decide at this meeting. He had not completely understood but she knew that if her legs had decided to carry her away, to the hills and beyond, she could and that it would be understood, if not by the boy, then by her mother. But this is not what she wants and she embraces the boy one last time before these embraces became official.

Her mother braides her hair and holds it in place with two gold clips each heavily patterned. She enjoys the sensation of the hands on her, working towards making her look perfect and she remains quite still until directed to move by the gentle push this way or that. The sweep of her pale green silk costume is secured by a brooch of gilded bronze, nothing like as beautiful as the one that she had lost, but this was deliberate; it could not and should not be replaced. Around her waist her mother has made gold chains which hang in two sweeps, which she explains showed her position in the household. Finally, around her neck she places a silver pendant, a clear round rock held with delicate silver fingers, so that she could see clearly, her mother says, her future. She does not reveal the gold ring.

At the ceremony the two families come together, important in their different ways, the girl notes, in dress and look, the boy's parents dark haired and short, her mother tall and more angular. When the boy looks at her they both smile for they know that they have a bond beyond the reach of those around them, to which only they have access. This separateness is finalised by the ring, the most delicately twisted band of gold, bright against her brown hand, which fits perfectly on to her finger. At this moment, there was no past or future, only the present and she places her other hand over the ring and feels the gold take its warmth and spread through her. This feeling intensifies later, when she watches him approach her, naked and unembarrassed. All that existed of time was in the seconds before she touches him and the moment he enters her, the brief stab of pain and then the overwhelming sensation of only being in that moment, of nothing else existing. She clings to this instant, this capsule which is not marked by the seasons' passing, or recorded by the pen, but exists just for itself and would never change.

CHAPTER THIRTY-ONE

Beatrice sat in Joseph Troumeg's kitchen and watched the red and gold birds in the garden cluster and chatter in the trees. She thought she might be like one of those birds, but with a useless wing, turning helplessly in circles in the dust on the ground, unable to defend itself or take off. The old restaurateur, who always gave the impression of being one step ahead of her, a meal prepared, the wine chilled, was also able to talk to her in a way that she found disturbing, to wing her and bring her to the ground. Some people call me a witch, he had said and she now knew what he meant. She considered that her resolve to find more about his background was also to do with a need to shed some light on her own, personal histories which each owner seemed determined not to examine.

It was almost dark when she left his apartment and clicked shut the door beneath the cherub's head. The restaurant was lit with a pale yellow light and the tall thin man behind the bar watched her as he wiped a glass. Somewhere in the streets up above her the noise of a party filtered down through the dark alleys, shouts of celebration and happy laughter. She walked back the way she had come and stopped to look down on the harbour, the rectangle of water reflecting the lights along the quays. She was startled by a noise behind her and began to hurry, taking a long, wide flight of steps between high walls of houses, on to another street which appeared to lead downwards to the sea. She broke into a run and was not entirely sure why. She had left her suitcase at the station and she returned to claim it before finding a hotel nearby. An orange fluorescent light burned just outside her window, sucking all but its colour out of the room, but it was quiet and she lay on the bed. She asked herself whether, having found Troumeg, it was worth staying in Marseille to talk with him further, but she decided that he would continue to block her progress. Troumeg was determined to write his own history, one which appeared to obfuscate his past and this made her more determined than ever to discover the facts about his childhood and early life. She could just hear the trains clanking in and out of the station and the distinct ring of the public address.

Troumeg was quite right. She would not want a film made of her own life and to the accompaniment of the sounds outside, she imagined what it might be like to interview herself and she began with a question that had been posed, or gently lobbed in her direction, by Troumeg: how come she was in a her late thirties, unmarried and without a boyfriend? And she knew the question was one she'd often asked but never answered, or if she had, in a most flippant way, saying this was the path she had chosen and that men were impossible. So how would she answer it now? She found the answer elusive, as distant as the noise of the trains, a background with little or no definition, a succession of men who, like the trains, came and went. Would she have dared ask herself why, pushed for a more specific response? Why did she chose the men in the first place and what was it they did wrong? And would she have dared ask what was it she had done wrong? What pictures would she have put to these sequences? How would she have visualised failure and repeated patterns of behaviour? She closed her eyes and thought of the shelves in her bedroom back in London which had altered with each arrival, some subtle changes, some more abrupt, photographs propped up, ticket stubs discarded, books stacked, mementos paraded to be cleared with each failure, only to gradually accumulate again and she saw in her mind a locked-off shot of the shelves with the clustering and clearing of each man's presence. The thought made her sad and she heard the music behind the sequence which at first was slow and melancholy but the more she stared at the imaginary pictures, the more staccato and mad the accompaniment became, perhaps a hectic piece of solo harpsichord. Even as she knew that this would be an effective way of describing the arrival and departure of Joshua, Ben, Adrian, Anthony and the others, it would be merely slick, a surface representation of what had occurred. It would fail to address why and she knew she would have to interview her old boyfriends for this and she wondered if she could, if she was clever enough, or brave enough, to find the clues to what had gone wrong. Behind this lurked the larger question, the one that threw the others into sharp relief: did she want children? If her immediate reply was 'yes' and 'there's no rush', which it had been on many occasions, why had nothing happened? Was Troumeg right; did the experience of her mother prejudice her view of having a family? As she had done many times before, Beatrice asked these questions in her head but the replies were faint and unspoken and so she could not be certain of the answers. Perhaps she had always wanted others to give her the clues but she had neither the parents nor siblings to help and perhaps she was too intolerant to listen to Amanda.

She was wide awake and stood by the window looking down on the patterned tiles of the pedestrian zone, black and white lozenges marching in line either way. She had been away for nearly a week, lost in a limbo of her own making, deliberately procrastinating about the Troumeg project. Soon she would have to commit herself and tell Graham Roth her decision and justify her not inconsiderable salary. But she wasn't quite there yet and her hesitation was unfamiliar and, again, imprecise. Both Joshua and Ben had told her she was obsessed with her work and both had been uncomfortable about accommodating her work in their lives. That clarity had now deserted her.

Her mobile rang and she didn't recognise the number. She answered cautiously and was surprised to hear Troumeg's voice and puzzled because she couldn't remember ever having given him her number.

'I couldn't bear the thought of you having supper alone in this big, wicked city. May I take you out?'

It was a moment before she could summon a reply. 'That's kind. But I'll pay.'

'As you like. There's a place you can't miss along the north side of the harbour. Painted yellow ochre with Bouillabaisse in large blue neon lights. Half an hour?'

Joseph Troumeg had done it again, made her feel that all this was planned, that taking her to supper had always been on the cards. There was always a method behind his decisions, as she was beginning to discover and as she approached the restaurant she was fairly certain that this might be the site of his first venture as a restaurateur.

'You've probably already worked out that this used to be mine, once upon a time a million years ago.' He kissed her hand and moved the chair out for her to sit down. 'Mind you, it was a bit prettier in my day. Then,' he said with a laugh, 'so was I. They do, however, some excellent fish.'

'Massalia.'

'Indeed. Not the first restaurant here to be called that, and not the last I should think.'

'Do you have any pictures of it in those days?'

'Alas, no. Filing is not my hot point. We had some, but you know how it is. Let me describe it, though.'

For the next few minutes Joseph Troumeg painted a picture of the restaurant he created over fifty years earlier. He reminded

Beatrice of a man who saw everything but pretended to know nothing, or was it the other way round? His position as owner and maitre'd afforded him unparalleled access to the gossip, slurs, rows and rivalries of the town, information he absorbed, balancing different accounts of the same incident, comparing versions of someone's bad behaviour, remembering prices paid for local properties and the grievances that followed, never allowing his knowledge to show, never betraying his confidences, showing incredulity when called for, shock or sympathy, laughter and concern, when appropriate like an actor on a stage, wonderfully concealing his real reactions and deductions to which very few, if any, gained access. It was a technique that had carried him through life and was keeping Beatrice at bay now.

'Were you talking to your mother in those days?' Beatrice felt a little rude cutting across his colourful account of the restaurant.

'Ah, Beatrice, nose to the grindstone again. As a matter of fact, I wasn't. The die had been cast, so to speak and I was on my own.'

'Why Marseille?'

'Why not Marseille? I knew a woman down here and used to come a lot.'

'A girl friend?'

'Sort of.' He was smiling, quite happy, it seemed, to release this information. 'She was the mother of a boy I was seeing. She had a small café up the back there and she was a great cook. I sometimes used to help her.'

If the first part of the sentence was new to Beatrice, the end was familiar. 'And this boy was your lover?'

'Oh, I wouldn't put it as dramatically as that. A friend, shall we say.'

Beatrice wasn't sure which direction to follow. 'Did you ever have a long term partner in your life?' Troumeg had ordered bouillabaisse for them and the soup was delivered before he answered.

'Of course,' he said, spooning the *rouille* into her plate. 'Not to be missed,' he said. 'Hot, hot.'

'You've never talked about that.'

'Neither have you,' he said.

'Well, that's probably because I've never had a long term partner.'

''Bout time you started, isn't it?'

'Who was he?'

'He died. But enough about me. I'm sure you'll dig it all up in the end. It'll stop you thinking about yourself. Now, have some more sauce.' He scooped some more into her dish, his remark apparently incidental. 'For such a public man I've always had a private life and I would like to keep it that way.'

'Are well known people allowed to do that?'

'This well known person is, especially since I've got this far. People like me for my books and restaurants and my TV programmes. They don't care who my partner was, or is.'

'You know that's not true.'

'It is for me.'

'I'm sorry,' she said. 'I should be more grateful. It's kind of you to take me out tonight and I shouldn't be questioning you like this.' Even as she said this, she wondered if she meant it.

The fish arrived on a trolley pushed by two waiters and what followed was quite clearly a well rehearsed tradition. A great white dish was put on the table at the centre of which was a large, heated stone. Around this the fish were carefully arranged before great ladles of saffron broth and potato were cascaded over the tableau to much delight from Troumeg.

'Fabulous. A bouillabaisse such as you have never seen before. *Rascasses, dorade, becaisse de la mer*, heaven.'

Beatrice wanted to laugh at this dramatic presentation and couldn't help see it as another sequence in the film, Troumeg delighting in the food being served in his old restaurant and she watched him animatedly discussing the fish with the two waiters.

For a while they ate, variously spooning the fish directly from the large plate on to their own, or, better still, straight into their mouths. Troumeg told her how he had learned to cook, all drawn from familiar material and for a while she was happy to sit and listen. He ordered some more wine and after it had been poured she leaned forward to speak to her host.

'It seems to me,' she said, 'that a succession of men have wasted my time.'

'That's quite an admission coming from you,' Troumeg said, sitting back in his chair. 'But I think true. But why can't you spot them coming?'

She shrug. 'There's the rub, I guess.'

'Listen,' he said, 'stop looking and it'll happen.'

'I have,' she said.

'Well, let's see, shall we.'

They chatted on and he began to tire. They left not long later, the old man escorted to the door by the restaurant staff like a movie star. Outside he turned and began to climb the hill to the old town and he waved a good night to her without turning round. She waited until he had disappeared from view before taking a final look at the harbour and the fortified entrance through which ships had sailed for three thousand years and more.

CHAPTER THIRTY-TWO

She lies naked on the bed. No wind blows through the room and the heat presses down on her. The hills absorb the sun and hurl it back on the town. It has been like this for many days and life is lived in the shade. She puts her hands on the rise of her stomach and then slowly downwards to rest between her legs. It would happen soon. The families had celebrated the news and she felt part of the order of things. Her mother had told her she had been the same age when her first child, her sister, was born. She described the birth and explained the baby's death a year later in a way that did not frightened her. Life goes on, she had said and you were my gift and soon there will be another. This morning the heat makes it impossible to think of the effort of birth. She watches beads of sweat coalesce and travel down her body. Even the birds are quiet. There is no energy left to be wasted. She remains still and heat rises from the white rocks. Time is compressed and expanded. There has been no gap between the young girl who ran down the hill in the grey town and the one who lies motionless in the heat and yet there seems an eternity between the two.

The heat increases and the air changes colour. The clouds arrive like a silent army and midday becomes dusk. The clouds are bloated like her, dark grey bellies fused with yellow. It was all meant to be, the storm and the baby. Her mother had said the sign would be the rush of water and as the thunder crashes above and the first great drops of rain fall to disappear in the hot dust, she knows she is beginning. Her mother arrives at the door and her face smiles and shows no fear. And then time is lost again. The flashing light accompanies the pain and the rain keeps beat with her heart. She can smell the hot wet stone. She knows the woman from the town who had delivered many babies is there as well. Her face and hair are wet but this is not the rain. Now the thunder and lightening came together, hammer blows on the roof of the house. Rain water snakes across the floor. Or was this pool her own water? She cries out and her mother encourages her, shouting along with her. With the rain comes the wind and she feels it cross her body. Her mother wipes her face and squeezes water into her mouth. Then she calls out, not for the baby, but for her husband. Was he at sea? And her mother kisses her and tells her he is waiting nearby for a beautiful baby. She is swallowed into time once again and hours are seconds and seconds hours. The flashing lights have stopped and the rumble is distant when she feels her body empty. In this moment of exhaustion comes a baby's cry and then on her stomach is placed a life which charges her own. She sees it is a girl. Her dark hair is flattened to her skull but on her face is a smile, she is certain. Slowly the room resumes its dimensions and her husband is there, stooping to kiss his daughter. The air is clear and clean and a sheet is placed over her and the baby. The child's warmth was her warmth and they are fused outside the stomach as they had been within. Her mother and the other woman step back into the shadow of the door and she is left with the baby and her husband and time starts again. The mountains have retreated to release the town and somewhere a bird begins to sing. And the baby sleeps.

CHAPTER THIRTY-THREE

Somewhere, in a distant room a long way away, a baby was crying and she listened to its demands, more articulate than words.

Did it take her by surprise that as she lay in the orange-washed room she, too, began to cry, not with the purpose of the child, but a gentle weeping that seemed to appear out of nowhere? She was unable to decide whether the tears were of joy or sadness, self-pity or relief, but they came and wouldn't stop. Eventually, some time after two in the morning, they ceased and she experienced the curious relief that crying can bring and she knew at once that it had been her admission that had produced the tears. She had never before declared that a succession of often foolish men had wasted her time. She'd sensed it, yes, but never put voice to the observation and the very act of speaking the words to Troumeg had loosened her defences. Perhaps the process had begun earlier, when he had referred to her as flotsam, triggering the image of the fragile skull in her hand. Whilst Joseph Troumeg appeared master of his own history, had created a hinterland for himself and perpetuated his own myths, she was merely a victim of the tides, unable to control the direction of her life. It was with this thought that she fell into a deep and untroubled sleep that not even the brightest of Provençal mornings could disturb until almost eleven. When she woke, she laughed at this untypical indulgence.

Beatrice decided to see if Troumeg wanted a late breakfast but she sensed as she walked around the lip of the old port he wouldn't be there. She rang his bell and then asked the thin man behind the bar if he'd seen him but he was almost as silent as the cherub above the door. In a way, she was happy that Troumeg had disappeared again further confirming that mysterious quality around which she would be able to build a film. She felt lighter this morning and his absence was a release for her to continue her search. She checked out of the hotel and caught the early afternoon train to Paris and in the three hours and twenty minutes it took to speed up the spine of France she was re-energized

Beatrice was a producer, paid to bring order out of chaos, to compress a story into exactly fifty two minutes, a television hour. Production periods were established, budgets created, crews hired and the story researched so that it had a beginning, a middle and an end. It was what she was good at, she knew. She was used to making things happen, giving shape to ideas, persuading and cajoling and not taking no for an answer. She knew, then, that it was not beyond her to find Joseph Troumeg's father and to discover the truth about the rift with his mother.

Somewhere just south of Lyon, not far from the great cooling towers that spoiled the views of the Rhône valley and the dry hills through which the river flowed, she arranged her laptop in front of her and placed her mobile alongside, as though she was starting a day at the office. When the phone rang to disturb this temporary order, she jumped in surprise.

'I've thought about a place we could meet in relative safety,' Harry Wesley announced directly. 'You sound as though you're on a train.'

'I am. Just south of Lyon. Doing about two hundred miles an hour.'

'Are you coming back here, or stopping off at Paris?'

'Paris.'

'Ah, risky territory, then.'

'I'm going to be there at least one, possibly two nights.'

'Is that an invitation?'

She had to admit that it might have been construed as one, although she didn't quite know how to respond to his question. A field of cows came and went before the train plunged into a tunnel and the connection was broken. She instinctively switched off the mobile but as soon as the train emerged into the bright day, felt guilty and pressed it back into action. She waited for it to ring again and then wondered if he might think that she'd deliberately cut him off so she called him back.

'Tunnel.'

'I thought you might have cut me off.'

'I thought you might think that, but I didn't.'

'In that case, what about the British Museum?'

'What about it?' Below her she could see the *autoroute* run alongside the track, the train effortlessly leaving behind the glinting cars as it dashed northwards.

'There's something I want to show you.'

The *autoroute* began to peel away and a man stood by his car beating its roof in frustration at having broken down. She craned her neck to watch him but in a matter of seconds he was gone.

'Hello. Are you still there?'

'Sorry,' she said. 'I was distracted by something out of the window.'

'Well, as I was saying, it seems a safe enough environment, lots of other people about. And I could show you some of the Anglo-Saxon stuff that Flotsam might have grown up with.'

'So this is more like work, rather than a date?' The train

rushed through a station too fast for Beatrice to register its name.

'As you wish,' he said.

'When were you thinking?'

'What about Saturday morning?'

That would give her two clear days in Paris and Beatrice warmed to the idea of having a sort of deadline to limit her time in France. 'Eleven at in the café under the new dome?'

'See you then.' And he rang off, part of a story that demanded further explanation, like the man on the motorway, but in a way just as out of reach, a single frame from a film.

By five o'clock Beatrice was back at the canal having reserved a room at the same hotel from the train. She wasted no time and with Harry's voicemail observation in mind, walked over to the apartment block by the park to see if she could find out more from Marguerite Fourcas. Perhaps the old woman would be on her second whisky which might help her cause.

'*Madame* Fourcas? This is Beatrice Palmenter. I came to see you the other day about *Monsieur* Troumeg.'

She could hear the woman absorb the information and re-orientate herself around the surprise visit before the buzzer clicked open the door.

'You must excuse me for coming unannounced,' Beatrice said in her most precise French.

'Any visit is a treat for me, *madame*.'

Beatrice accepted the drink that Marguerite must have poured for her in the time it took to climb the stairs to the first floor. It was the old woman who started proceedings.

'You want to know more from me.'

Beatrice smiled. 'Yes. Please.'

'I wondered if you would come back.'

She sounded almost pleased and the thought occurred to Beatrice that she might have something to get off her chest, so she came straight to the point.

'I suppose I thought it was unlikely that you could have

a friendship over such a long period without knowing more.'

The old woman laughed, a laugh which was much younger than her years. 'Of course. But I'm not such a lonely old woman as to tell a complete stranger the story of my life, or that of Odile Leval for that matter.' Although she got up slowly she walked easily over to the corner of the room where, unseen by Beatrice at first, she had a small lap top computer.

'I looked you up,' she said. 'I like your work.' She moved the screen around so that Beatrice could see an image of herself from her own website. 'What made you interested in Joseph?'

Beatrice smiled at the woman. 'I met him a couple of years ago and he seemed an interesting and amusing man so I began to read up on him but the stories were all the same. I just decided to find out if there was a reason for this and if I could find out more. Which, in a round about way, brings me here.'

'The internet is not merely the province of the young,' the old woman said, perhaps in response to Beatrice's smile.

'It is to both our advantage,' Beatrice said, with a small bow of her head.

Marguerite returned to her seat and picked up her whisky. 'It is true what I told you. Odile spoke very little about the war. When I met her, you must understand, we were still coming to terms with what had happened, what we, the French, had done during the war. Sometimes it takes a long time to gain perspective.' She paused and took a sip of whisky, holding it in her mouth before she swallowed. 'She told me that her son had never seen his father, that he had left her as soon as she became pregnant, sometime in the winter of 1934. She told me only that he was an American journalist.'

Beatrice slowly absorbed this information, replaying in her mind the number of times she had read Troumeg's repeated account of his father, the romantic spin put on this absent man, the glamorous war correspondent.

'Troumeg says he was in Europe covering the Spanish Civil War, but the dates don't match. Did she say any more?'

'She was very philosophical about it. I think she liked the man, but what do I know, really.'

'But I don't think I would find a Donald Troumeg if I looked for ever, would I? This is a name that Joseph made up.'

'She never told me his name. Maybe she wanted to preserve a myth, like you say her son has done. Perhaps that's where he gets it from.'

'But something did go wrong and he stopped seeing his mother, although he's never spoken publicly about it and has given us the typical airbrushed version, another fantasy.' She couldn't think of the French for airbrush, but Marguerite understood what she was trying to say and offered the word herself: *aèrograph.*

'But I don't understand how she could talk so little of her son and his growing fame, let alone respond to the stories he was making up about his childhood.'

'But perhaps, when he was young, it *was* perfect. Certainly she spoke to me about how they would cook together and how he often used to help the maid, I can't remember her name...'

'Monique.'

'That's right, I remember now. Monique was the housekeeper and Odile would tell me how she would leave them together and return to sumptuous meals that they had prepared between them.'

'So at least that part is true. I wonder if Monique is still alive?' Beatrice frowned and tried hard to remember if she'd ever seen a surname mentioned in the hundreds of on-line clippings she'd read. It was a long shot since she would probably be in her nineties.

'The boy was only five when the war started and the Germans came to the city. Can you imagine how frightened Odile must have been, a single parent in a place where even the French hated the Jews? I don't know how she – they – survived.' She shook the ice in the bottom of her glass and it rang like an alarm in the small room, the echo filling the silence that followed her statement.

'But you must have asked her?'

'Of course. You must remember I didn't know her during those years. I had my own battles to fight elsewhere.' She pushed her glass towards Beatrice who added a splash of whisky to the melting ice. Marguerite nodded and looked at the other glass and Beatrice poured a measure into her own. 'Until you have a child you simply can't understand how far you would go to protect it. My son died from the flu before the war started and sometimes I saw this as a blessing, that I didn't have to fear for him during those dark years.'

Beatrice was about to offer her sympathies but the women held up a hand to stop her. 'It was a long time ago and I have many memories of him. I mention it to show you how much I understood what Odile had to live through.'

'Do you think she had something to hide?'

'Once upon a time, many years ago, you lived under an invader, first the Romans, then the Danes and finally the French, but it was so long ago that you've turned it to your advantage. The English have no idea what it was like to be humiliated by the Germans. So close and yet so far away.'

Beatrice acted as she would have done if a camera had been recording this interview and remained quiet. Somewhere the traffic flowed up and down the rue Manin and the ambient hum of time passing filled the moment and if it had been on tape she would have let this telling atmospheric silence continue, the old woman's eyes staring ahead as the years peeled away.

'She didn't speak, but I heard stories. After the war the French tore themselves apart. We hated each other even more than we hated the Germans, if that is possible. Can you imagine, I saw a woman running naked down the boulevard St Michel. Her head was shaved.' The old woman held her glass but she was not drinking. 'Her body was shaved and between her breasts she was tattooed with a swastika. They were beating her like an animal. Seventy years ago. It's not long. I still walk by the spot, in front of the cafés where people now sit and chat, and

I can see her, the red marks across her buttocks, the terror on her face. The shame.'

Beatrice waited again, perhaps five seconds, or was it five minutes?

'But this was not Odile Leval?'

The old woman shook her head. 'No, but it might have been. It is what they said, but I think I understood differently. There was another quality in Odile, a dignity beyond this.' The old woman refocused and looked directly at Beatrice. 'Who knows? What was the truth and what were lies flowed into each other. What Odile did, I don't know. But she survived when many, many Jews did not. I miss her.' She pushed her whisky glass forward again.

CHAPTER THIRTY-FOUR

The baby's head is so soft it frightens her. She looks down on the tufted crown and feels the heat of her small face pressing against her breast. Her hand traces the warm outline and her fingers spread across the dome in protection. On the baby's tiny wrist is a bracelet of thin silver wire through which has been threaded three amber beads. Her mother said the beads represented the three generations of women who now remain silently together in the room, grandmother at her bench under the window, the child asleep in her arms. She sees her mother differently again, understands the fierce animal qualities that had made her survive and which binds them together. Now it is her duty to do the same for the life that lies across her lap. Everything has changed and her body is alert in a way that it has never been before. It frightens her to think of the horsemen who had attacked them in the market and she shuts her eyes and feels even more keenly the helplessness of the baby on her knee. The long hot summer is over and dull grey clouds have taken the colour from the landscape. A fire burns and gives off the sweet smell of wood and the very perfection of the scene causes her to worry, to hug the baby closer, to realise how easily this could be taken from her.

And so it was.

The sailor is killed on a day of thick snow which lies on the town like a cold glove to transform their lives. The rigging that collapses and brings his life to a sudden end starts a succession of events which merely confirmed her sense of dread. Her mother takes the blow with the stoicism she has come to expect but she is regarded as cursed, with three husbands and two children dead. She observes that people become more formal with her, unable to place this thrice-widowed woman within the pattern of life. For the first time, during that strange winter, the southern port appears alien. Perhaps it is the birth of her child which provokes the sensation of being separated from her natural environment, the realisation that this is not their true home. And she weighs the dilemma in her mind, the wish for the child to see the grey town and the old river, with the fear of the long and dangerous journey back. Her mother is troubled with the same impossible equation and from time to time she sees her staring out over the port, lines creasing her forehead. She never stops supporting her daughter and grandchild and declares that the answer will come in the fullness of time. She ministers to her mother, to return what she herself has been given. When the summer comes around again and the hills appear too hot to touch, she raises with her husband the prospect of making the long voyage back to the grey town, of changing the colours of his life. The baby is now just taking her first steps and soon she would be speaking the language of the south, her father's own tongue. The girl knows the mantle of responsibility is passing to her and she tells her husband. He picks up the child, who has the same brown skin as him, both made for the sun. When life offers so many dangers why would they impose a treacherous voyage on themselves and the child? And she knows he is right and she accepts the decision. But her apprehensions persist, her body constantly tense for a blow which she expects to come at any minute, so much so that she can barely let her child out of her sight. Never before has the future so preoccupied her, seemed so uncertain, so hard to peer into.

CHAPTER THIRTY-FIVE

Beatrice took the Metro to the junction of the boulevard St Germain and boulevard St Michel and stood at the busy crossroads before ordering a coffee at one of the cafés that Marguerite had described, sitting with the tourists, watching the flow of people, smartly dressed, comfortable, intent on their lives, pass in front of her and she imagined the naked woman running between them, unseen, a ghost from the past but indelibly present and deliberately ignored.

It was what Marguerite hadn't said which haunted her swaying passage on the Metro. She had been given the incomplete elements of a crossword puzzle clue, with neither the question nor the answer entirely clear. The old woman might just as well have been talking about herself as Odile and Beatrice was unable to make a judgement. Marguerite was suggesting that to survive the war in Paris, particularly as a Jew, some element of collaboration might have been necessary. Had Joseph discovered this or perhaps even witnessed the humiliation of his mother? Was it shame that had driven the young boy away and out of his mother's life for ever? Her assessment of Troumeg changed and a shadow fell across the proposed film so that in her mind the music changed, the style of filming altered and its purpose became all the more serious. It was cool sitting out on the pavement and she could feel the first hint of winter not far away. She wandered along the boulevard St Michel in the direction of the river and could not shake the image of the naked woman out of her mind. It appalled Beatrice that Marguerite had seen such an ugly and violent act in a street of such beauty. This was history witnessed by someone still living and yet somehow it was still not entirely clear, the truth still just beyond her grasp, partially obscured, uncorroborated.

In the end, she walked all the way back to the hotel, across the Île de la Cité, up the straight line of Sebastopol to the Gare de l'Est, where she picked up the canal that guided her back. She was impatient for the next day to begin for what the old woman had said haunted her and she needed to know more, wanted, she realised, to protect Odile Leval and, in turn, her son. And to do this she needed facts.

So, as she arrived at the hotel and although her feet ached, she turned back across the 19th *arrondissement* towards the Café Le Fin. It was too late to visit Marguerite again but she hoped that Sandrine Vaillard might offer her some more clues. With the luck she believed comes from persistence, Beatrice found the *patronne* installed in the kitchen and arranged to talk to her after service was finished. When eventually she emerged to slump in the chair opposite, blowing the hair from her eyes, Sandrine called for a drink.

'How are your searches going?' she asked, raising a glass of red wine before drinking it down in one. 'The kitchen seemed hotter tonight, for some reason. So?'

'Well, I'm getting there. I saw Odile's friend, Marguerite and I went to see Troumeg in Marseille. In fact, we ate at his first restaurant, not that it's the same, of course. I was wondering if you might have any photographs of Odile, say a picture of her with your parents?'

'There's one over there, with all those other pictures by the door. I should have shown you before.' She got up and lifted it from the wall and brought it over and placed it in front of Beatrice like a plate of food. The black and white photograph showed three people in dark overcoats taken in front of a church.

'Odile's in the middle and those are my parents either side.'

Beatrice held up the framed photograph and stared at a woman whose hair was worn in the style of the day, a series of controlled waves over a long face in which she could see traces of Joseph Troumeg, or at least thought she could.

'That must have been taken in the early 50s,' Sandrine said, 'so she would have been in maybe her late thirties.'

Troumeg was right in calling her a beauty, for she stood centimetres taller than even Sandrine's father and she struck the pose of a model, with one leg slightly in front of the other and one hand on her hip.

'Why do you think Joseph didn't come to his mother's funeral?' Beatrice hoped Sandrine wouldn't mind the direct question.

'My parents, when they were alive, told me that it was to do with a disagreement they'd had many years before, but I can't tell you much more than that.'

'And they named you Josephine after him. I don't think they would have done that if they thought Odile would have been offended. Did your parents talk about Odile and the war?'

'Do you have a reason for asking?'

Beatrice weighed up what to say in reply. 'I was wondering if something happened during the war, or immediately afterwards, that might have caused a rift between mother and son.'

'Well, something must have happened. Curiously, he must have left around the time of that picture, although I've never thought of that before. Here, let's have a look.' She took the frame and turned it over, running her fingers along the tape before releasing the photograph. She examined the back where in pencil was the date, *'Mai 1953'* and the words *'avec Odile'*.

'May I make a copy of this and return it to you?'

'But of course.'

'I don't want to say more at the moment, but I will when I'm certain about what I've been learning.'

'Sounds a bit serious...'

'Who knows?'

Every so often on the way back to the hotel, her feet stinging and hot, she stopped under a light to look at the photograph and the handsome woman posed at its centre. This was not the face of a woman whose son had fled, or one locked in the misery of some personal drama. Perhaps it had yet to happen and she was ignorant of the events that were about to overtake her. Or perhaps she was never to know the reason why he left. How infuriating that a history so recent should be so tantalisingly out of her reach. She had two days in Paris before she left for London, forty-eight hours to try and discover the truth of events that occurred around these very streets seventy years earlier. Time leaves its clues, but also covers its traces, she thought and that night, perhaps not surprisingly, she dreamed of the skull and the life it represented, one whose details had been lost almost completely.

The next morning Beatrice was concerned that Marguerite might be resistant to seeing her again, so she phoned in advance to ask if they could take coffee together.

'I think you might have misunderstood what I said last time,' Marguerite said quickly, only too glad to see Beatrice again and straighten her account. And so it was later that morning Beatrice made her way up rue Manin, the sun lighting the Buttes Chaumont park to her right and several copies of the photograph in her bag. Perhaps it was the sharp morning light, or the aftermath of last night's whisky, that left its mark on the old woman's pale face at the door. Or was it the memories that Beatrice was disturbing, the carefully settled alluvium in the layers of her memory. When they had their coffees in front of them, Beatrice showed her the photograph.

'She was a handsome woman, wasn't she?'

'Always. I used to be slightly jealous that she had to do so little to look so good. I had to work much harder. When was this taken?'

'1953.'

'I don't know whether it feels like an eternity ago, or yesterday.' She stopped and stared, as she had done the day before and Beatrice wished that she was recording these conversations for what was happening was not rehearsed and she was witnessing as memories and connections joined and came to life. The old woman nodded to herself, piecing together the events and chronology of those distant days. Beatrice waited and looked at the watery eyes in front of her, the face so much more fragile than the day before. 'I didn't tell her about the death of my son for a long time, either. In the end, we both had things to forget.'

Again Beatrice allowed the silence to unfurl. 'Do you have your own photographs of her?'

She pointed at a brown envelope on the sideboard and Beatrice reached out to get it and with the encouragement of Marguerite, carefully tipped the contents on to her lap.

'I knew you would want to see these. My husband took many of them. He was a good photographer. He died ten years ago and I find it difficult looking at them. But I did, for you. And Odile, of course.'

Beatrice sifted through the dozen or so pictures and watched Odile Leval grow old and yet never lose the looks that distinguished her. In two of the photographs she was with a man, leaning into him on one and holding his hand in another.

'That is Elliot. An artist. American. She was with him for a long time. A nice man.'

Beatrice looked up at her and had no need to ask the question.

'Yes, he's still alive, but he's in a home. He has declined since her death. The address I have written on the back of one of the photographs. Take them.'

'Thank you. Is there anyone else alive who knew her in the early days?'

The old woman was shaking her head even before Beatrice finished her question. 'They're all gone. And I will be soon. The chapter will close.'

'How did you survive the war, Marguerite?'

'I did what I had to, like Odile. We were blamed, you know. We were blamed for surviving. But, enough.' She placed the palms of her hands flat on her thighs. 'Go and see Elliot. She will have told him more. Perhaps you should make a film about Odile and not her son.'

And she laughed the girlish laugh Beatrice heard the day before.

In the park afterwards, returning to the now familiar seat beneath the hill, she looked at the photographs again, shuffling through the snapshots of a life unknown and it occurred to Beatrice just how quickly she had immersed herself in this project, how it had taken her over and how, once again, it had enabled her to put everything else on hold. How much easier it was to pick at the corners of Odile's past, chase the shadows cast by Joseph and she felt a moment's guilt, an uneasiness which arrived like the cold wind in the boulevard café. In one of the photographs, taken when Odile was perhaps fifty, her hair cut short in a black plastic mac, she looked almost modern and her smile revealed white teeth, made more so by the dark lipstick, a woman clearly happy, not encumbered with a past or dreading a future. Beatrice could point to photographs of herself which appeared to tell the same story, particularly if you are a woman who people regard as beautiful.

What do we know, Marguerite had said. What, indeed?

CHAPTER THIRTY-SIX

The child runs with a freedom she can recall but not recapture, for now the drop from the harbour wall, the clatter of the horses on the quay and the sea itself conspire to give boundary to her fears. She can share the joy of the child but now it arrives with an awareness that it could be taken at any minute. She was in joy, but outside it, observing it, aware of its dimensions. She thinks of her own legs carrying her down the hill to the old river, her long strides seemingly effortless, lengthening with her speed towards her father on the bridge. Now his memory is sadder, because it too comes with an extra shadow. He would never see his granddaughter, never be able to compare mother and child. But this day she knows clearly why he stood on the bridge and why he hid his fears from her. As with her mother, she sees her father differently and in her new knowledge there is loss and gain. Like her observation of her daughter running, her memory of him is now tempered with her new understanding of him as a parent. Her memory has been given depth and this brings its own rewards and penalties, for the simplicity has been lost.

The plague arrives as it had in the old town, slowly and silently. On the hill she hopes they will be safe and she keeps the child indoors. When she sees the bodies, their legs disfigured, their sores open and weeping, she is frightened. There seems no end to the dangers laying claim to her daughter. Trapped in the room, they attempt to carry on as before. Her mother shows her how to widen the bracelet for the child's wrist and begins to teach the elements of her craft, to show how patterns could be gently beaten into soft metal, how gemstones could be polished and shaped. She gives purpose to their imprisonment. She has helped her mother before and has learned by looking, but this is different. Afterwards she wonders if she had deliberately decided to pass on her skills, if she knew what was coming. They work on a simple necklace that too could be expanded as the child grew, twisting strands of gold with a single pendant of yellow stone, its surface shiny and smooth, in a mount of gold so that the colours would merge with the olive brown skin of the child. It would be the last piece of jewellery she makes for even before it is finished, the symptoms of the plague show on her mother's body. She is frightened to touch her, to wipe her face and wounds, not for herself, but for the child. Her husband takes their daughter to the hills to live amongst the trees and she is caught between the anguish for her mother and the child. And then it is over almost before it begins. In two days a life that has given so much disappears in front of her and she is left looking at a face too still to be living, holding a hand too cold to shape gold again. She feels her dimensions extend again, to bring in territory she has not known before. The responsibility of wisdom has been transferred to her and its weight rests on her shoulders. It is not a duty, but a succession and she receives it with the generosity it is given. Her mother's body is to be taken to a grave outside the town where she can be buried in safety along with the others. Her granddaughter will never remember her. She will live on in a series of stories and in her jewellery which would be passed on until the connection was broken and merely a thing of beauty remained.

CHAPTER THIRTY-SEVEN

'Have you abandoned us all?' Amanda's simple question managed to combine indignation with displeasure.

'I'm still in France, on my way to a *maison de retraite*, if you must know,' Beatrice said, negotiating yet another set of Metro barriers on her way across Paris to Charenton.

'Well, that's all very well, but I've seen you do this before,' she continued, eager to get her point across, 'sort of disappear into a tunnel and ignore life for a few months and then emerge thinking you can just carry on.'

'Well, yes, that's sort of the nature of my work, Amanda and it is going to be a tunnel because I'm heading to the underground now. I'll call you when I come out the other side.'

She just heard Amanda say '...if you come out the other side...' before the link was broken.

La Maison Clemenceau was by the Bois de Vincennes, on the other side of Paris, at least sixteen stops and two changes and when she phoned to arrange a visit to see Elliot Honeywell she told reception she would be there in a hour. She looked at the spaghetti of colours that defined the system and wondered if she'd left enough time. Once she'd made the changes and settled herself for the final leg, she considered Amanda's call. How easy it was to operate in this vacuum, she thought, as St-Sebastian Froissart came and went, with no allegiance except to my work. By Reuilly-Diderot she imagined Amanda must have read her mind, given her doubts in Buttes Chaumont earlier and by Charenton-Écoles she was looking forward to agreeing with her friend.

'About time too,' Amanda said and Beatrice sat in front of the church opposite the station, noticing from the clock on its tower that she had about ten minutes before she was due at the home. 'He's called me again.'

It took Beatrice a moment to think what she was talking about.

'And it's clear that you've no intention of seeing him, at least in that sense. That's what he tells me. Why?'

'Not true, Amanda. Well, not completely true, at least. I am seeing him the day after tomorrow, when I get back from here. What did he have to say this time?'

'I don't know why I have ended up being your broker in this strange relationship, but he thinks you are entirely uninterested in him.'

'I'm uninterested in all men at the moment, Amanda.'

'What a time to start, Beattie.'

'But it is true what you say about my work. I can see it. It's a displacement activity, I realise that. I was thinking on the Metro that I get it from my father. His real world was dealing with future trends and improbabilities whilst the life he was living at home, with me and my hopes and disappointments, was a fantasy he didn't recognise or understand.'

'Goodness, Amanda. Where did that come from?'

'I've been thinking about it for a while now. How is it possible not to know your father, I asked myself and that's the answer I got. Joseph Troumeg never knew his father at all and maybe that prompted my thinking.'

'So, what are you going to do about it?'

'I don't know. I'm meeting Harry at the British Museum on Saturday. He wants to show me some Anglo-Saxon relics.'

'Doesn't sound like a typical first-date scenario. He asked me what you were like.'

'And what did you say?' Beatrice saw the big, black hand of the clock click forward. She knew the home was no more than two streets away and she began to walk in that direction, waiting for Amanda's response.

'I said I couldn't believe you'd got this far without finding what you want.'

'Not you as well. Troumeg said the same thing. I'm surrounded by people acting on behalf of my mother.' She laughed, partly in relief, but of what, exactly, she couldn't say. 'I'll come and see you when I get back. What about Sunday? I can give you a full report then.'

'Sunday lunch. Don't be late. You can hold Harper while I make the lunch. James is working.'

La Maison Clemenceau was a smaller version of the *mairie* of the 19th *arrondissement*, elaborate and showy, a deliberate display of wealth. The building was now reduced in the ranks and served as a nursing home. If Elliot Honeywell said on the phone that he would be happy to see her, he'd forgotten who she was by the time she arrived at his side in the large sitting room with views on the Bois de Vincennes. He was a handsome man who had clearly been dressed for the occasion, a jacket with crimson handkerchief in the top pocket, a clean white shirt and black shoes. Beatrice explained again who she was and that she wanted to talk about Odile Leval and at the mention of her name he smiled, nodded his head and repeated her name. She told him about the film and when she asked if he would mind answering some questions he agreed with another smile.

Beatrice, unsure of her ground, began too quickly. 'Did Odile ever talk about her son?' The question appeared to bewilder him and he frowned and stared at her and for one awful moment

Beatrice thought he might not have known about the child.

'Sometimes she showed me articles about him, but no, she spoke very little about him. She said it was in another life that he happened.'

'Weren't you curious about that life?'

'I had Odile and that was enough.' Again he looked directly at her with an expression that said surely you must be able to understand this.

'And what about the war? Her friend Marguerite said she didn't want to speak about that either.' Again the stare. Beatrice had been told that he suffered from mild Alzheimer's and she wondered if he couldn't remember, or didn't want to remember or perhaps remember and not want to tell her.

'She said she couldn't talk about the war.'

'And how did you feel about that?'

He narrowed his lips before replying. 'Bad things happened. I know. I, too, find it difficult to talk about the war.'

'But did you tell her about your own experiences?'

'Of course. She was the only one I ever did tell. With her I was able to be intimate.'

'But not the other way round?'

He shook his head. He had artist's hands, long and distinguished, practical and yet fine and he placed one on the other and rubbed over the liver spots and knuckles. He seemed to drift off into another space where the fragments of his life were collected like a kit waiting to be reassembled.

'I was glad she was mysterious,' he said out of nowhere. 'It was what she always remained to me.'

'Do you have any idea why she remained mysterious about the war and Joseph?'

'Perhaps she didn't want to hurt me?' And, then, as an afterthought. 'Or maybe she didn't want to hurt herself?'

He had said that Odile couldn't speak about the war and Beatrice considered the various interpretations of the word: that she physically and psychologically couldn't, that she had been traumatised to the point of silence; or that she was forbidden to do so for some unknown reason; or that she couldn't because she didn't want to. And then it dawned on Beatrice that all three could be true, that the act of describing those years might simply be too difficult, that the repercussions would be too great and so, ultimately she couldn't and had consigned her experiences to a vault inside her and locked the door and thrown away the key. Since Joseph, she assumed, was the only living family survivor the sole reason she would have done this was to protect him.

'Elliot?' she asked and he seemed to wake back into the present. 'When Odile died, what happened to her possessions?'

He appeared puzzled at the question. It was four years since she had died and according to the nurse at reception, he'd been at the home for almost a year.

'I couldn't look at anything,' he said after a long pause. 'She was a careful women, ordered and she knew she was going to die. It all went somewhere when I came here. Somewhere...'

Beatrice could see that he was finding it difficult to cope with the recent chronology of his life. 'Do you know where?' Even as she asked the question she knew that answer was lost somewhere in his dislocated memory.

'It doesn't matter now.'

Beatrice felt a hand on her shoulder and the nurse who smiled down on her did not have to use words to tell her she should stop and leave Elliot Honeywell to his thoughts. She said goodbye to the old man and as she was leaving asked the nurse on reception who now looked after the affairs of *Monsieur* Honeywell. She went into her files and wrote some details on a piece of paper. 'I think he's a nephew,' she said, handing it to Beatrice.

Outside Beatrice made a note of the address on the sheet she had been given and sat for a while in front of the church. Simon Honeywell, rue du Bac. 37, flat 3, she read. She was dissatisfied and felt caught in a loop of repeating events, as much to do with herself as Joseph Troumeg. She had just over a day left in Paris so she decided to continue her pursuit and tackle the other issue when she got back to London. She descended in to the Metro yet again and trundled north-westwards and having made a considerable loop and one change, got out at St Germain des Prés and walked along to rue du Bac. It was four in the afternoon so she wasn't surprised there was no reply from the address she had been given, so she meandered across the street looking at the shops. A couple of hours later she tried again and an impatient voice answered the intercom. Beatrice felt odd standing on the busy street shouting into the speaker her reasons for wanting to speak to a man who she had never met about a woman she had never known. He clicked her in and she took a small lift to the second floor where he met her at the gate.

'Simon Honeywell. *Enchanté.*'

He was a tall man in an immaculate blue suit and an open necked pale pink shirt. He guided her into his apartment and Beatrice had the sense of ricocheting into the lives of other people and barely glimpsing what was going on, a pinball out of control.

'I've just been to see your uncle,' she explained, although she had already shouted this into the intercom, 'because I'm making a film about Joseph Troumeg and I need to find out more about his mother, Odile.'

'Yes, you mentioned,' he said in perfect English. He was a handsome man in his mid-forties and Beatrice could see that he found her attractive, his smile warmer than it might have been if he'd invited a strange man up from the street. 'Please.' He offered her a place on the sofa and made her tell him the story of her interest in Joseph Troumeg.

'He always spoke so warmly about his mother,' she said, omitting the fact that he had disowned her, wondering if Simon Honeywell would notice or indeed if he knew of their estrangement. He offered her a kir in a long glass, adding a twist of lemon. 'It would be good to discover more.'

'It's all vague shadows to me,' he said, sitting on the arm of the sofa. 'My father was Elliot's only family and he died about ten years ago. I came to work in Paris and when he became, shall we say disorientated after Odile died, it sort of fell to me to help out, more by default really. I helped sell his apartment and took some of the precious stuff he wanted kept. Have you seen his paintings?' He gestured to the wall behind him where two colourful landscapes hung. 'He really was quite good and made a reasonable living.'

Beatrice got up to look at the paintings and he came to stand by her side, rather too close and she stepped away, pretending to look at a detail. 'You see,' she said while leaning forward, 'I'm trying to trace Joseph Troumeg's father.'

It was clear that Simon Honeywell knew little about the family history and right now was more intent on discovering more about her.

'There is a box marked Odile, which came from his apartment. Do you suppose I could allow you to look at it?'

The remark was deliberately teasing and she knew at once that she recognised this man, for she had met him in several guises before, thoroughly pleased with himself and not the least interested in her except sexually. But she could play this game as well. 'That depends if you'd be prepared to trust me,' she said, making her eyes wide and innocent as she had done to the man in the *mairie*. He got up and went in to another room to return with a black lacquered box with gold handles, placing it on the coffee table. She gave him a coquettish look whilst registering that this was a man without scruples.

'I have one or two calls to make. Why don't you see if there is anything of interest in there.'

She felt uneasy and considered that his own lack of respect should not be compounded by her own. She looked at the box, a life distilled into an area no bigger than a small suitcase and hesitated before lifting the lid. Inside were bundles of letters tied with ribbon, several objects, a larger folder of photographs and a framed photo of a boy wearing a white shirt and knickerbockers, his hair neatly parted, his face serious. It was Joseph Troumeg. She lifted the portrait and knew that she had been right: how could Odile Leval have accepted the separation from her son? She could hear Simon Honeywell talking rapidly in French in the other room. Beatrice was uncomfortable about looking at the letters and so she began examining the various objects, a small doll, a gold pocket watch, a round frame containing a lock of blond hair and what looked like a ring box in worn brown crocodile skin. She lifted this and pressed the gold pin to release the lid. Inside was a gold ring and Beatrice looked behind to be sure she was still alone before picking it up and turning it in her hands. There were words inscribed on the inside and she read *Seb T Toujours. 1935.* She replaced the ring and clicked the box closed and felt a mix of excitement and shame, as though she had furtively lifted the lid on someone's life in circumstances that were forbidden.

Beatrice experienced physical discomfort, made worse when Simon Honeywell came back into the room and offered her another drink. 'No thank you,' she said. 'I think I should be going.'

'But you've hardly started.'

'I know,' she said. 'Let me take your mobile number and I'll call to fix another time.'

'Can't I take you to dinner?'

'Do you mind,' she said, 'I really can't.'

And she left, descending in the old lift, like an intruder not wishing to be seen.

CHAPTER THIRTY-EIGHT

She had been told to stay behind with her daughter but she refuses. It is her husband who remains while she climbs the hill with the carts, far enough away to be safe, close enough to see the shrouds covering the bodies. She cannot allow her mother to go alone on this final journey. The day mocks their passage, clear and warm and full of birdsong.

The open pit makes no concession to rank and is without dignity. She watches from the trees as the bodies are lowered into the stony ground to lie together in a silent chorus, anonymous behind their white cloaks. She cries as the earth is shovelled on top, the scrape of tools hiding her sobs, each slap confirming her desolation. The flow of wisdom she has received from her mother will now cease and on the bleak hillside she already feels its loss. She looks down over the town and knows that she is not able to embrace it like her mother. A pink and grey bird with a white crest lands on the ground near her and performs a crooked dance. She cannot trust her thoughts for her head is full of sadness and there is no room for logic. Her mother told her to have faith in her instincts, that she would feel what was right and so she would wait.

She comes down the slope not to the town but to the sea where she removes her clothes and dives into the clear water. The dust of the hillside is lost, but not the pain. With her clenched fists she rubs her body until it is marked red, cleaning it for the return to her daughter. The child would not understand the loss nor would she remember the death and for this she is glad. Her grief is different, her loss permanent.

At first she is frightened to embrace the girl, frightened of the disease, frightened that her tears might alert her daughter. She plays by her grandmother's empty bench and stands at the window wanting to be outside. Life is a series of survivals which arrived like lines of waves, to be dealt with one by one with sometimes barely a gap between the blows.

She takes her daughter out along the sea, running with her across the bleached white rock, leaving the town behind. Where later great rusting ships will dock and unload and the city stretch in a great long finger towards the setting sun, at a place where the famous artists would come to record the beauty of these scenes, she hugs the girl towards her, covers her body as much as she can and tells her of the death. There would be no reply but there is a message in the way the words are said, the power of their conveyance, that the child would understand, the first of many messages that she would give, just as her mother had given her. When the great black fish leaps from the water not once but many times she knows that it has been received and above her the birds scream and swoop.

CHAPTER THIRTY-NINE

To eat in a restaurant alone, Beatrice had realised a long time ago, was to invite interest and so, as she had done in the past, she sandbagged her isolation with activity, open notebooks, a novel and a mobile phone in the hope that these would prevent inquiry from men keen to engage her in conversation.

By now she knew that looking into the box of Odile's possessions was a step too far, an intrusion into privacy and the only reason she had been allowed to do so was Simon Honeywell's hope that she would be grateful one way or the other. Well, one way really. She doodled 'Sebastian' and assumed this was the Christian name of 'Seb', the man who had given the ring to Odile. She added the 'T' and followed it with 'Troumeg' and a query. Too simple, surely? Joseph had changed his surname and she had failed to find any Troumegs at the *mairie*. She imagined the thousands of Americans, or Frenchmen who were called Sebastian or Sebastien. If she had looked at the letters she might have found the answer, she was sure but at that moment her hesitation had been correct and confirmed her feeling that she had no right to go further.

She looked at the number Simon Honeywell had given her and tapped it into her phone.

'Let me take you to dinner instead,' she said and when he protested that it was he who had invited her, she said there was a condition. 'I want you to look in Odile's box and find if there are any letters from a man called Seb, or Sebastian, or Sebastien. I don't want to see the letters, or know what's in them. I don't think it would be correct. And you'll find me at the Brasserie Île St. Louis. I'll be the one surrounded by notebooks.' And she rang off. She considered it was a small price to pay although she had second thoughts when, half an hour later, he sat down opposite her with the smile of a man who thinks he has won a battle. The brasserie was noisy and cramped and not what she would call intimate, the perfect place, then, for such an evening.

'How did you know about this place?' he asked and although it was a perfectly reasonable query she couldn't help but take the question the wrong way.

'Well, it's quite well known, isn't it? And we girls can be quite resourceful you know.'

'I used to come here on Sundays when I first came to Paris. It's a bit too noisy for me.'

But perfect for me, thought Beatrice. 'And what is it that brought you to Paris in the first place?' she volunteered.

'I work for Paribas, mergers and acquisitions. I'm from New York, like Elliot, but he left a little earlier than me. He liked it over here, I'm not so sure.'

'Why's that?'

'It's the French and all that red tape. They're different and I haven't quite got used to them. I'm not sure I will. It must be a nightmare to live here.'

'It has some attractions, though?'

'It certainly does,' he said, looking at her.

She chose not to respond and waited for him to ask some questions about her. They ordered and he told her, at inordinate length, what his job involved and the bonus he received the year before and how that had meant he had been able to buy the apartment in the rue du Bac without a mortgage. On his wrist he had a watch that was too big, no doubt bought with the very same bonus and he had the irritating habit of looking around every so often to see who had come in, or, more likely, who might be watching him. She knew he was deliberately keeping the Odile information to himself, wanting her to ask for it, but she carried on listening, amused at his self-absorption. Now that she felt distanced from this pantomime, stepped one pace back from the theatre of boy meets girl, she was more in control and could see the wheels and pulleys and special effects at work. He asked for another *picher* of wine but she shook her head when he went to fill her glass. He had yet to ask about the film, or refer to Odile.

'I think I have the information you want,' he said, taking an envelope from his inside pocket.

Beatrice was shocked to see what must have been one of the letters from the box. 'Do you think you should have removed it?'

'What's the difference? If it helps you, who's to know? Odile is dead and Elliot's on the way to being gaga. What would happen to it otherwise?'

She looked at him and saw how the smoothness of his skin, the lack of lines around his eyes and mouth, the very blandness of his features spoke of his inability to experience any of the feelings associated with delving in to the past of a member of his family. As in business, as in life, this was a means to an end. And she was party to this, shared a responsibility and she accepted at that moment she had a duty to the information she was about to receive, in what way she wasn't sure, but she couldn't treat the process as lightly as the man sitting opposite.

'Do you want to know his name?'

She refused to play this game and remained still.

'Yes, his name was Sebastian, with an 'a' and not an 'e'.' He paused.

'So he wasn't French,' Beatrice said, but wished she hadn't.

'Exactly. But he writes in French.'

He made to push the letter across the table but she shook her head. 'I don't feel that it is right to look at the letters without Elliot's permission.'

'But you don't mind if I do?'

'You're family. It's your decision.'

'And his surname? You'll want that, won't you?'

What a tedious man, she thought, catching a faint whiff of his after shave which clashed with the smell of food in the room.

'He was called Traugott.'

Beatrice wondered if she had misheard. 'Traugott and not Troumeg?'

She saw him nod. 'Two tees at the end,' he added, as she jotted the name in her notebook, still trying to assimilate the information. 'I've only read a couple of the letters and there's very little information in them beyond the usual endearments. The name sounds a bit German, or maybe English.'

Beatrice thought of Marguerite sitting in her apartment overlooking the park making her bleak observation of what some women had been forced to do during the war to survive. But Joseph was born four years before it started.

'Thank you for looking for me. This is most helpful.'

'Why don't you read through the letters. You have my permission.'

'I think I would need Elliot to approve it as well.' Beatrice asked for a coffee and hoped she could bring the evening to a close as soon as possible, but Simon had other ideas.

'Do you think he was Joseph's father?'

How she wished she was having this conversation with someone else more sympathetic. 'When were the letters you read dated?'

'One was 1933 and the other 1937.'

'So before and after the birth of Joseph,' and then, to herself, noted that Joseph was a Christian name that could be French or German, or even English or American for that matter.

'I thought we might go on to a bar I know not far from here in the Marais.'

Her reply was immediate and prepared. 'Would you mind, it's rather late and I have a lot to do tomorrow.'

He looked at the large dial on his wrist and showed her its face. 'It's ten-fifteen, nine-fifteen in England. You must have a very heavy day tomorrow.'

'OK, I'm just not interested in going to a club.'

'Another time, then?'

'Sure, another time.' She knew he wouldn't give up and that she would receive calls at odd times in the coming weeks, but she considered that he might be useful again and that Odile's letters could be vital for the film. They parted awkwardly, Beatrice not allowing even the most innocuous physical contact. After he'd gone she waited on the Pont St Louis, staring at Notre Dame, lit up like a stately liner. She intended to walk up through the Marais back to the 19th but if this was his intended route to the nightclub she was keen not to bump into him again.

Twenty minutes later she was underneath the cloistered pavements of the Place des Vosges when he materialised by her side. He had quite clearly been watching her since she left the Île St Louis, although he said differently.

'I thought you'd have to come through the Marais on your way back to your hotel and it's my luck to run into you again. Come to the club.'

She tried hard to remember whether she had let slip where she was staying and thought that she may have mentioned the Metro journey to see Elliot, but couldn't be sure. He put his arm around her and so she stopped.

'I told you why I didn't want to go to the club. What more can I say? Thank you for your help, but I've only known you five minutes and I really am tired.'

'Not too tired to walk all the way up to the nineteenth and

I can't imagine that a girl in television hasn't had quite a few flings in her time.'

'You're right in both assumptions, Mr Honeywell, but the former decision should lead you to understand the latter.' She was angry and walked away from him along the arcade, in and out of the shadows and she heard him shout at her back.

'What's wrong with you anyway?'

It was Place de la République before she had recovered her composure and expelled the indignation that had ballooned inside her at his remark. She felt a victim of herself and that made his verbal assault all the more painful and she saw how, in a slightly different scenario, she might have gone to the club with him and it was this thought that made her both sad and then enormously happy to be walking alone along the Canal St Martin. Then she stopped, caught again in the cycle of repeated events, first Jean-Paul and now Simon, both making assumptions about her, that she was available no matter what she was, or who she was.

She sat on a bench and looked at the dark water of the canal and it was Harry Wesley who came to mind, his face when she had told him she had been at dinner with Jean-Paul the night before. When she met Harry at the British Museum the day after tomorrow, would she be able to talk to him about her experience tonight? She put her head in hands in frustration.

Back at the hotel she slumped on to her bed and kicked off her shoes. Troumeg, Traugott. The two names blurred into one and re-emerged differently, the words changing position as she had imagined before for a title sequence. But now the names had a different significance and tomorrow she would attempt to find out what, to continue her journey into the life of Joseph Troumeg, or perhaps the life of Joseph Traugott.

CHAPTER FORTY

At first she is unable to stand at her mother's table because the image of her in the same position is too real, the succession too soon. In time, though, she begins to work with the tools and the metals that have been left behind and finds that when she does time disappears, mornings come and go, afternoons slip into evenings. She has one intention and as the long summer days unfold she works with purpose and the tools, precious metals and stones became familiar to her fingers and sometimes, when she has been working for many hours, her fingers appear to be her mother's, the nails dirtied and the whorls and patterns ingrained in a way she had once observed at her mother's side. There is an importance to this self-imposed commission which develops through the days but about which she remains silent. Routines begin to repeat themselves and her daughter now watches, her face no higher than the bench so that, in the fullness of time, her fingers too will replace those of her mother and grandmother. When she is certain that she is producing something of merit, she shows her husband who holds the ring to the light before fitting it on to her finger. The gold has been reworked from an earlier ring, part of the black bag that the sailor had given in the old town and she has now mounted one of a pair of crimson stones which she has rounded and polished. It is only when she sees the ring on her own hand that she decides to make a copy. It will not be exactly the same, but it would be a companion, which, as soon as she thinks of it, seems exactly appropriate and becomes precisely her aim.

And the summer arrives and departs. One evening, with the smell of fish cooking on the open fire in the courtyard, she shows both rings to her husband and their child. The flames intensify the colours and when she turns the rings against the light the stones seem to absorb the intense reds and yellows.

The next morning, before sunrise, she climbs the hill and repeats the final journey in the life of her mother to the spot where the bodies had been buried, difficult now to see except for a faint outline where the ground had been disturbed. She is still frightened of the disease and has left the child behind. At the far end of the grave, where she remembers her mother being placed, she stands and looks down at the soil, summoning her resolve. She begins to dig into the surface with a wooden spade, scooping the loosened top soil away with her hands. After a while she has created a hole deep enough to reach half way to her elbow. She rises from her knees and brushes the dust from her clothes. She takes one of the rings from the black bag and holds it to her lips, kissing the smooth stone before placing it at the bottom of the hole and covering it with spoil which she presses down with the palm of her hand, slowly and gently. Rising to her feet again she takes out the other ring and once again kisses it, placing it on the fourth finger of her right hand. As she had done before, she goes down to the sea and swims and cleans herself. Afterwards, she walks back to the town in the face of the rising sun which warms her skin and prepares her for what she has to do next.

She sees them from a distance, father and child, playing in front of the house, chasing, turning, touching and her daughter's laughter carries up the hill. They stop and he lifts her in the air and she embraces his neck and they wheel on the spot. He sets her down and she puts her hand in his and they walk down to the port, the swing of their arms in time with their steps. When they have disappeared, she sits on the slope and looks out to the sea. How could she ask them to return to the grey town, to leave behind a life that was natural to them both? She looks back to where her mother's body lies under the dry earth. At first her death had made her want to flee, to return to her roots but now she knows she could not dislocate the life of her child, nor that of her husband. And, for now at least, she could not leave her mother behind. She rubs the stone of the ring and once again kisses its smoothness.

They sit together and both husband and daughter see that she is wearing the ring and she tells them what she has done and why. Does she detect in her daughter's young eyes that she knows the true reason for having done this, so that in the future, when they leave, she will always remain connected? There is a force within her that seems beyond logic, moving against her like a current, but for now it is wiser to remain. Fate, she knows, will decide the future, as it had before. She looks at her daughter, sitting on her father's lap, who returns a shadow of a smile and she sees that she has been right and the young girl knows what is in her heart.

CHAPTER FORTY-ONE

It took Beatrice less than an hour and a half to find Sebastian Traugott.

Joseph Troumeg had been born Joseph Leval, Odile having changed her surname to disguise its Jewishness. Later, Joseph Leval, adopting the habits of his mother, had in turn changed his name to Joseph Troumeg, an anagram of 'gourmet'. But was it more than that, a further reflection of Joseph's playfulness with his past, the name so similar to Traugott, the surname of the man who may or may not have been his father? Beatrice had gone to sleep thinking about this equation and had woken with a continued determination to resolve it. She opened the blinds in her bedroom to reveal the glimpse of the canal between the buildings, called for coffee, set up her computer and trawled the internet for Sebastian Traugott and was immediately swamped by thousands of German connections. She had to be cleverer and tried 'Traugott 1935' and 'Traugott Paris' without luck and then, after her second cup of coffee and with the remains of a croissant scattered on the small table, decided on an even more logical approach than the computer and called the German Embassy in Paris. She was hoping that German nationals might have been registered with the embassy during that period. She spoke to an efficient information officer who promised to call her back. At ten-thirty the phone rang and the answer took her by surprise, and she froze halfway between standing and sitting.

'Sebastian Traugott was a cultural attaché at the embassy here between 1932 and 1938 when he returned to Germany. He was killed in 1940.'

There were so many questions that Beatrice wanted to ask that at first her response was silence. 'Where was he from?' she asked finally and learned that he has been born in Freiberg, close to the French border in southern Germany. Her mind ran quickly now, registering the improbability of a German official having a relationship with a Jewish women during that time and so she asked if there were any other Sebastian Traugotts listed. No, this was the only one, she was told. 'Do you have a photo of this Sebastian Traugott?' she asked, staring out of the window. The answer was yes and five minutes later she received an email on her computer with an attachment which, when she opened it, bridged almost eighty years and answered one question conclusively. Sebastian Traugott was a handsome man in the style of his times, his dark hair slicked down, his tie neat in his collar, his eyes looking off to the left and his face unmistakeably that of the young Joseph Troumeg. Beatrice could scarcely believe the similarity and the shock of seeing the black and white photograph and recognising the familiar features made tears gather behind her eyes to drop slowly on to the keyboard. She was stunned into inaction, unsure of what to do next and she absentmindedly ran her fingers over the wet keys.

One big question had been answered but many others gathered and hustled just behind, clamouring for attention. The first to emerge had an immediate answer. At some point Joseph must have realised, or been told, of his mother's relationship with a German. This must have been forbidden on so many levels that Beatrice found it hard to measure the consequences. Well, one was clear, for it produced a fissure between mother and child which would last a lifetime. And yet, at some future stage, Joseph changed his surname to a version close to that of his father. Why? The hotel room seem to press in on her and she left to walk along the canal and smell the tang of the water and imagine the same scene during the war, when the city was full of fear and hatred. The recollection was black and white, the canal a working waterway and she stopped and saw a sequence from her film, as she had done in Marseille, then and now moving from monochrome to colour, the face of Sebastian Traugott, the father, becoming that of Joseph Troumeg, the son. Lurking behind these images, though, loomed a more sinister face which happened to be beautiful as well as shocking, that of a woman with a shaved head and bewildered and frightened eyes, the face of Odile Levy, now Leval.

When Beatrice returned to the hotel room, she found the copy of Marguerite's photograph of Odile and first with her hand and then with a simple mask of white paper, tried to picture what she would look like without hair. She traced the line of where she imagined the dome of her head would be and then with nail scissors cut out the shape, a white skull cap. And then, for some unaccountable reason, she threw the scissors across the room, stood up and swore, ugly words that came out of her unbidden. She picked up the cushions on her bed and hurled them at the wall, snatched her key and left the room and slammed the door. She returned to the canal, walking quickly and without thought, moving northwards. Ahead of her a train rattled noisily over a rusting bridge and people strolled arm in arm and she broke into a run, as close to the side of the canal as she dared, getting faster, not really seeing what was around her, faster still, her feet slapping on the grey cobbles, beyond the moored boats until, exhausted, she stopped in the shade of a concrete flyover. She was bent over panting, her hands on her knees and she stayed like this until her breathing became normal and her heart stopped beating against her chest. When she raised her head she was surrounded by grafitti, vivid crimsons and electric blues, the face and body of woman outlined in black, thrusting her breasts towards the canal, pushing her body, in skin-tight shorts, to one side so that the shape of her was unmistakeably revealed. The image seemed to shout at her, but she could hear nothing and she covered her ears with her hands and tucked her elbows to the sides of her face.

Slowly she was aware of the sound of cars above her and she walked back into the sunlight and realised that she had come as far as the Périférique circling Paris in an endless loop. With this roaring soundtrack she slumped on to a bench and shut her eyes and waited until she understood what had happened. She heard a pair of ducks land noisily in front of her and a siren arrive and disappear above and then a dog bark on the opposite bank. It was several minutes, or was it more, before she opened her eyes and then stood and began the long walk back. By now she knew she wasn't angry on behalf of Odile Levy, nor in sympathy for her son, Joseph Levy, born Leval, probably of Sebastian Traugott and now named Joseph Troumeg but Beatrice Emily Palmenter whose history remained unexplored because no one had the remotest interest in the events that had produced her, to search and consider the forces that had shaped who she was, who was interested enough to give up something of themselves for her. She felt alone and knew that, if she had no one to blame but herself, she had no one to tell her this either.

Back in the hotel room, Odile with her white cap looked back at her and Beatrice resumed where she'd left off, lightly shading in the paper dome to produce a crude image of the woman with her head shaved. She then photographed it from various angles, adjusting the overlay, until she had a passable digital image. She then packed carefully, folding her few clothes into her small bag, laying her computer on top. She washed her face and applied some make up, brushed her hair and when she was ready to leave, sat on the bed and called the Imperial War Museum in London and via the press office and an archivist of the photographic collection, arranged a viewing for later in the day. She shut the door, paid and walked to the Gare du Nord and boarded Eurostar for London, a day sooner than she had planned. She slept most of the journey, an easy untroubled sleep and having gained an hour along the way, had a good part of the afternoon left when she walked under the great guns fronting the Museum. She had not only regained her composure but donned the professional cloak which had brought her so much success. She did so with a different purpose, however and one which she had only just begun to perceive. She had been quite specific to the picture archivist and although there were several hundred images waiting for her to view, the task was manageable. She had the detachment for what lay ahead, at least she thought so when she started. She placed her camera on the bench to the right of the computer and began to look at the black and white photographs, every so often picking up the camera and holding it near the screen. Not all the women were naked, but many were, stripped of their dignity, hopelessly vulnerable. The faces that surrounded them, French men and women, were ugly and taunting, some pointing, some in the act of slapping or punching. In one, a woman sat wearing a beautifully tailored jacket and skirt, looking down at the ground, her head perfectly shaved. In another, a woman naked from the waist, twisted away from the grasping, pinching hands that chased her, a line of blood dripping from her nose. After a while Beatrice could see that the women were a symbol of collaboration, that they carried the blame for everyone who had not resisted the occupiers, or who had gone as far as to help. Of these there were many, although it was the women they chose to blame, humiliate and kill, to distract attention from themselves. Wounding the prostitute, or the woman who had slept with the enemy to feed her children, was better than beating yourself. The more she looked at the women, pushed, pulled, pointed at, spat at, manhandled and shamed, the more she realised the haunting fact that most of the women with their heads shaved were beautiful.

It was late in the afternoon before Beatrice stumbled on the picture she wanted but, in many ways, hoped she'd never find. At first she almost missed it, because the figure was not the main focus of the photograph which showed a woman in the process of having her head shaved, with two women who had gone through the process standing to one side. One of them brought Beatrice's eyes to a standstill. There she was, the long face, the high forehead, the tall woman who was unmistakeably Odile Leval. Beatrice had no need even to compare the image with the one on the camera although when she did it was clear they were one and the same person. There was no shame in Odile's face and she was looking beyond the shaving that was taking place in front of her, not so much in defiance but as though her mind was elsewhere, or that she was searching for someone in the distance. The look touched a chord in Beatrice and for the second time that day she wept at the sheer sadness of the picture of the woman who she felt she could reach out across time and touch.

She signed a contract to reproduce the photograph, a copy of which would be sent to her and she left the museum with the image fixed in her mind. The legend to the photograph told her that the women had been sent to Fresnes prison where Beatrice could only too clearly imagine the treatment Odile must have received. She had seen images and read about its reputation and she shivered at the unfairness of the punishment that had taken a woman from her nine year old son and destroyed their relationship forever.

CHAPTER FORTY-TWO

The wind blows again, hot, clear and dry from the north and the sky returns to the ominous acid blue she knows so well. The dust whirls in eddies across the parched earth and the tips of the tall thin trees are bent so far they almost kiss the ground. The sea, a yet darker blue, is scarred with white and, like the sky, too intense to watch. This was the seventh day of disturbance and the wind rushes through the rooms and seeks out even the most sheltered corners. Nothing is still and it makes her feel uneasy, that in the roaring of the trees and the mad patterns of the dust, there is a message wanting to be heard but unable to escape. It is a year since her mother's death and this same dust has been laid and displaced many times on her grave, layering and eroding by turn. She is too distracted to work and even the child seems subdued and she watches her looking out to sea, her eyes squinting at the glare. It is a remorseless, unforgiving day which makes no concessions. She puts down her tools, rewinding the gold thread. The wind would continue to make it impossible for her husband to return to the harbour, so fiercely is it blowing from the shore. Her daughter is missing her father and later she will run down to the harbour in the hope that he has escaped the perverse winds and made landfall.

When eventually the wind dies down and the sea resumes its sly disguise the silence brings its own threat. Some boats come wearily back into the peace of the harbour, but not her husband's. The child now spends all day on the quay and every so often receives the reassuring touch of a returning sailor or sympathetic mother. Everyone knows the boat is missing but all say that it will appear soon. Perhaps he has been blown along the coast and taken shelter. They speak hopefully but their thoughts are darker and on the hill she knows the absence of the wind has brought no relief and the quietness has failed to sooth her. She had been unable to stop the wind, now it is impossible to dispel the calm and so she returns to work. The significance of the piece she is making is not lost on her and she thinks it yet another sign. The two sweeps of gold chain are linked by a garnet, also mounted in gold, with finely decorated clasps at either end. It is to be worn by a woman in the town whose husband had died during the winter. She would wear the jewellery around her waist to mark her position as the head of the household for his land, in one of the fertile valleys to the north of the town, is now in her charge. She holds the girdle hanger in her hands and weighs its significance and knows that she has to give it to the woman immediately. She takes her daughter with her, holding her hand on the quay and gently leading her away. Together they present the precious chain to the woman and what passes between them needs no words. It is a transaction that would have been more difficult if her husband was confirmed lost, or dead. Now it is possible to hope, to pretend, that he would return. She carries her daughter back up the hill, her long body too big but both have need for the comfort of each other's warmth.

The days go by and what was inevitable hovers just this side of truth, so that she cannot quite say that her husband is dead. Perhaps, she thinks, she will never be able to do this, that like her father he has been taken away by the water and may exist somewhere else. In this limbo it is hard to mourn and impossible to plan. For the moment she can only wait with her child and with each empty day departing feel their hopes become weaker. She wonders if the child will ever decide that he is dead, or become content not to know in order to keep alive the hope that at any given moment he might appear around the corner and sweep her up in his arms. As for her, she has made the decision quickly, for she knows about death and has learnt its ways. Now she must help the child do the same.

CHAPTER FORTY-THREE

Beatrice climbed the steps to the imposing entrance of another London museum, her mind still full of the images of Odile Leval, to be greeted by the slightly uncertain smile of Dr Harold Wesley. She could see that once again he wasn't sure whether to take her hands, or kiss her, so she offered first one cheek then the other, French style and by the time they were through the big doors he was in full flow.

'I'm so glad to see you,' he said, taking the top of her arm and guiding through the great rooms. 'How have you been? And were you successful in your searches? I'm so keen to hear more.'

There was barely a cigarette paper between his questions and she smiled at his almost schoolboy excitement. He looked different, but she couldn't quite define why although she could see that he was now wearing a pale linen jacket over his familiar chinos and trainers and in place of the usual T shirt was a white searsucker shirt with faint mauve and yellow stripes.

'You seem very thoughtful this morning,' he continued, yet to receive a response from her.

'You appear different as well,' she said, still amused.

'It must be the shirt,' he said, smoothing his front. 'I bought it specially.'

'It suits you,' she said and meant it. 'And, to answer some of your questions, I had a very successful time, although the word doesn't seem quite right.'

'What do you mean?'

'It's a bit of a story.'

'We've got all day. Haven't we?' He glanced at her for confirmation.

They arrived under the new dome and discussed its merits as they organised coffee.

'Weren't we meant to meet in here?' she said.

'I was too impatient to see you.'

They sat in the diffused light and she told him about the man she believed to be Joseph Troumeg's father and the photograph of Odile with her head shaved. She spoke in a flat, matter of fact way, as she might have done during a production meeting. He touched her on the arm again, resting his hand on her forearm now.

'Strange and difficult stuff,' he said. 'You must have found it quite upsetting.'

'I did. I am.' She looked at him and could see that his concern was genuine and that he was sharing some of her dilemmas.

'Can you be sure that he's the father?'

She shrugged. 'I don't have to tell you how hard it is to put your finger on history. My mind could be deceiving me, but Joseph looks like Sebastian Trougott and I'm pretty certain that in the archive picture of the women being shaved I saw yesterday, one of them is Odile.' She fished out her camera and showed him her montage of Odile with the shaven head. 'They're sending me the photo and when they do, I'll show you.'

Harry took the camera and stared at the picture. She watched him pause, his face serious, his face creased with concern. 'How dreadful.'

'Yes, I found it quite hard. She looked so beautiful, but then so did most of the women who had their heads shaved.'

'And what happened to him?'

'He was sent back to Germany in 1937 and according to the embassy, was killed in 1940.'

'And do you think Joseph knows the whole story?'

'What is the whole story?' she said. 'Can we really know this?'

'Come with me,' he said, standing. He waited for her to get up and in silence took her back to the main building and up stone stairs, surprisingly dark after sitting under the dome, to an upper floor and through a series of open doorways and rooms full of display cabinets, until he arrived at his destination. He stood for a moment and then pointed around him. 'This is history unknown,' he said. 'This is the world of Flotsam, give or take a hundred years or so. This is how much we know. And how little. From now on, you have to use your imagination.'

He led her lightly by the arm again, stopping at various cabinets, connecting the objects he showed her, their journey around the two rooms illogical in terms of geography, but perfect in reflecting the story of how Flotsam might have lived. He spoke gently about the objects behind the glass, isolated fragments, the corner of a pot, the handle of a sword, a reassembled tile, a model of an excavated boat, from which a history had to be made, to be guessed, to be imagined. She looked at him as he tried to put Flotsam in context, excited, exact and engaging, he built a picture from the scraps at his disposal and yet he made it real, as if it had been lived yesterday and he'd witnessed it happening. He saved the best until last. She followed him across to a long cabinet against a far wall.

'Perhaps Flotsam wore some of these.' She looked along the treasure trove in front of her, lines of silver rings, beautiful broaches of gilded bronze and garnets, clasps of gold and necklaces hung with pendants of coloured stones. She was astounded.

'They're so sophisticated. I had no idea.'

'The Anglo-Saxons were great craftsmen. Look at that ring, for example,' he said, nodding down at a gold ring mounted with a polished garnet which had lost none of its lustre. 'You could not find better today. But this, this is what I particularly wanted to show you.' He pointed to a necklace and she saw a slightly cloudy glass ball, held in place by long, thin silver fingers on a silver necklace. 'I think that would look beautiful on you.' She read the legend and saw that it was a rock crystal pendant, about a thousand years old which appeared to have survived those years with its beauty absolutely intact. Together with the ring, they might have been made today, so perfectly had they come down through time.

When she looked at him, she had her palm across the top of her chest. 'Do you think so?'

'I'm certain. It's rock crystal and back then, as now really, it was said to have special properties. It's magical, isn't it?'

Beatrice looked down on the necklace and tried to eliminate the years between then and now, to picture a young girl wearing the beautiful object around her neck but she could go no further, her imagination stopped, the days too distant and her knowledge too sparse.

'We have a rule of thumb that says the present began in 1950 and everything before that was BP, before present. So your search into the life of Joseph Troumeg's childhood falls into that category. More clues, more documents, moving images, photos, even some living testament, but it's still a form of archaeology, of sifting through the layers for a sort of truth.'

'A sort of truth,' she repeated.

'Yes. It's what I like about history. Although some dates might be finite, most interpretations are not. So we end up telling stories the way we see them, based on whatever evidence we have. The results can be fallible.'

She laughed. 'You'll never guess what I've just thought, and not for the first time?' she said.

He shook his head. 'Tell me.'

'How wonderful you would be on film. You put things so well. Most people don't.'

'That's another one of your compliments, is it?'

'I think it is,' she said.

'Well, it might be an opportune moment to ask you to lunch.'

'Are you sure? You know what happened last time.'

'Ah, yes, well shall we call that BP and try again?'

He took her to a small restaurant at the top of Drury Lane which looked on to a brutal new development on the other side of the road.

'I like coming here because I can remember the old buildings that used to be over there, many of them small studios of commercial artists doing work for Fleet Street. My father once took me with him and it was like stepping into a world which Dickens would have been more familiar with, men sitting on high wooden chairs with ink stained boards and jars full of brushes and nibbed pens. Now look at it. Ten years old and it already looks weary and ready to be pulled down.'

'What does your father do?'

'Did. He died a few years ago. He was in publishing. Children's books.' And, as if anticipating the next question, 'My mother and he split up when I was young. Bernard Makins, that's the name of the artist my dad used to visit. And your parents?'

'Dad, actuary, died when I was twelve. Mother still around, bit of a problem.'

'Why's that?'

'Why's that? I suppose she only thinks about herself and that can be very wearying. She doesn't understand what I do and is frankly not very interested.'

'And she doesn't approve of the men in your life and can't understand why you haven't settled down.'

'Something like that.'

'We've had some more reports in about Flotsam,' he said, changing subject. 'Dental pathology shows a distinct change in growth pattern and indicates that she might have lived in two different places. We see minor variations to do with periods of famine, or harsh winters, but this is quite different. And rather unusual. And...' He stopped. 'Sorry, we were talking about you but I knew you would be interested.'

'No, go on, I'm fascinated. Do we know where she might have lived other than London?'

'Hard to tell and it would be a huge guess, but the pathologist suggests that it was a healthier climate where the food might have been better, certainly more abundant.'

'So somewhere in the south, then?'

'Could be.'

'It must be so frustrating,' Beatrice said, 'not being sure. A life just out of your grasp.'

'But it gives us certain freedom, as well. Perhaps that's what I like. It's more difficult with Sebastian Traugott where the room to manoeuvre is less.'

'But still enough to make mistakes.'

'Sure. But why do you say that?'

'Because I have barely touched the surface of his life, or Odile's. I still have only scraps and we're talking only eighty years ago. It's like my parents. What I know about them I could write on the back of a postcard.'

'You'd want to write that much about your mother?'

Beatrice laughed. 'Far too much, you're right.'

Afterwards she wasn't sure exactly when things changed, when the balance of their relationship shifted, but it was about this point, when they exchanged proper laughter for the first time. What they went on to talk about was more serious, more personal, but it was perhaps this lighter moment of understanding which paved the way for this to take place.

'You said you felt upset when you realised that Odile might have been one of the women to have had her head shaved.'

'I think it was doing the shaving myself, if you like, creating the skull cap for the picture I showed you. I found that difficult.'

'What happened exactly?'

She saw that he was looking directly at her, wanting to hear more, almost willing her to explain. 'After I had done it, I felt very angry. I threw some things across the hotel room and left. I ran up the tow path of the canal, I can't remember how far, three or four kilometres maybe. I just felt terribly angry and sad at the same time. I still do, really.'

Harry nodded, encouraging her to continue.

'I suppose I'm not really sure why I reacted like that. Yes, as a woman I felt sympathy for the way Odile and the other women were made scapegoats and it was horrible to see them naked in public. I felt indignant for them.'

Just by the way he kept still she sensed him not wanting to disturb this moment and she felt strangely safe to continue, so for the first time she put into words the ill-defined feelings that had been shifting around her ever since the event.

'Maybe I understood her predicament on a more personal level, that she had reached this terrible point in her life because of a man. She had collaborated with a man and she had ended like that, head shaved and humiliated.' Now that she had said this, actually articulated the thought, she knew it was true and what Harry Wesley said next she would have said if he hadn't.

'Your collaboration with men has only ended in damage to you.'

'Precisely.'

There were so many facetious remarks that he could have made to this, but he remained silent and she was glad, for she felt she was on a tightrope high above the ground and a false word or gesture might have caused her to fall. 'But it was a collaboration and I have to accept my role in what has happened to me.' She thought, hoped, that at this point Harry Wesley realised why it was so difficult for her to contemplate another relationship and once again his response reassured her.

'Of course. The historian in me, though, agrees with you. We don't know about the relationship between Odile and Sebastian, how or why it ended. Some facts will help and I imagine, I know, that there will be facts to do with your, as you say, collaboration with men that will tell you more. We just have to study them. And how terrible,' he added, 'that I should have shown you the computer animation of Flotsam as a naked girl. How utterly foolish of me.'

The meal didn't end but drifted into the afternoon, nor was there any difficulty in their parting. He merely said he would call her and she knew that he would and was happy with that and she strolled eastwards, through Clerkenwell and Shoreditch to her apartment where she allowed the day to end in the same easy way.

CHAPTER FORTY-FOUR

The patterns of life give her strength, tell her she can cope, help take away doubt. Her mother had lost a husband and survived. She had found another and sailed with him across the seas to start a new life. After the summer has ended, she accepts her own husband is dead and the wheel begins to turn again. Her mother is buried on the hill and the reasons for being here diminish every day. By now, her daughter has stopped standing on the quay and begun to play again and she tells her they will return to the place where she herself had been born and the child accepts the decision, just as she had before.

They sail from the port which welcomed the Phoenicians a thousand years earlier and would welcome the liberating invasion at the end of a world war in another thousand years. She knows the voyage ahead, even though she had been only a child when she made it before. The boat is carrying spices, oil and wine and the smells are sweet and happy. Her precious stones, gold, silver and the tools that worked them are stored in the same chest that brought them out years before. The sea is more still than she had thought possible and she worries that this is too perfect. The child plays on the deck and she sees the round crystal bounce on her chest and reflect a glint of the sun. She looks up at the departing hill and brings the ring on her finger to her lips and carries her mother with her.

The seas which had almost claimed them before are calm and the journey, made at the end of the summer before the winds come, drift by so easily she sees it as another sign, both good and bad. The decision to leave is being blessed, but what is given can be taken and she fears that behind this benign gift harder days will follow. After less than a week, the westerly breeze which carries them past the rocks, which would one day claim a super tanker and destroy a coastline, pushes them easily towards the first sighting of the old country. A succession of blue days sees them to the wide mouth of the estuary and remains with them as they sail into the tightening jaw so that when she sees the town it is not grey as she remembered it, but colourful in the autumn sun. Even the bridge, the monument to her father's death, rests easily in the landscape, imposing but not threatening.

Only now, on the spot where St Magnus the Martyr would one day be built, at the point where the third London bridge will end, does the enormity of the decision strike her, for she has to restart a life she has almost forgotten. Moments before, the child had taken her hand and they had stepped ashore together. Everything seems bigger and busier. They climb the short hill to the old house and the sense of coming home is complete. Ownership belongs to her, not just in document, for this is her spiritual home and she knows it.

She sees herself in her daughter, the trusting acceptance of the new surroundings. She watches her begin to run and play, explore her boundaries. One day she walks with her towards the wall in the north to stand where she had once played with her friend, expecting at any minute to see the blonde haired child of her youth. Instead she sees a woman with the same face, only sadder, her hair straightened and dirty, who looks at her daughter in a way she cannot understand. Later she discovers the truth, hearing that the woman, her friend, had lost her child not long after his birth. The bewildered woman stares at the child in front of her, healthy and still brown from her time in the south and from the voyage and there is longing in her eyes.

Later she tells her daughter about her childhood friend, of how they had played on the foreshore, at the ruined house with no roof hidden in the trees up river and promises to take her there. She worries, though, that she might be tempting fate, that those days were over and could not be reclaimed. Her friend's face bore testament to this, made older by the pain of loss. What is given can also be taken.

She resumes where her mother had left off and works in the same position in the room so those who come to see them, who had known her mother before, stop and think that it is her. The ring that she wears and the other jewellery she makes bring comparison with her mother and she continues the tradition. The child finds the transition easy, accepting the change as part of a life that has been planned for her.

She thinks that once upon a time she had played with her blonde friend and watched the quays from the brow of the hill, but that for now seems a lifetime away, as out of reach as her mother lying still on a hill a thousand miles away.

CHAPTER FORTY-FIVE

If normal has a smell then it greeted Beatrice the following day in a quiet cul-de-sac somewhere north of Enfield where the cars were parked erratically half on the pavements and the sound of electric lawn mowers filled the air. The smell was unmistakeably lamb and it welcomed Beatrice even before she arrived at Amanda's front door.

'Ah, childcare is here,' Amanda said, leaning into her friend with a kiss and placing Harper in Beatrice's arms at the same time. 'Welcome to chaos.' A trail of toys led along the hallway and continued into a front room entirely taken over as an encampment for the child, a pen piled with more toys, a rug marked as a roadway and an old vacuum cleaner lying on its back. 'See what I mean. He's only been up since six. Drink? I'm desperate.' Beatrice had stopped wondering how her friend could live like this and saw that the joy of having the child came with penalties which included sleep, order, sensible conversation and, almost, sanity. Harper was just over a year old and Beatrice had no idea what to expect. 'He should go down soon and we might have a couple of hours to ourselves, but don't bank on it. He won't stay in the pen by himself, so you'll have to climb in.' When Amanda appeared with a glass of wine, her friend was waist deep in plastic balls under Harper's curious stare, about to be hit by a wooden duck on the end of a stick. 'Good to see you've got the hang of things. Welcome to the real world.' She thrust the glass in Beatrice's hand, just avoiding the well aimed lunge of her son.

An hour later, when he finally went to sleep and Beatrice had cleaned the wine from her blouse and readjusted her hair, she sat at the lunch table exhausted. 'Peace in our time,' Amanda said, presenting the dish in the middle of the table, 'and, like a phoenix from the ashes, I give you stuffed shoulder of lamb, á la Joseph Troumeg. A themed Sunday lunch. How's it going? Or are you too tired to talk?'

'It's a miracle you can cook and look after him,' Beatrice said. 'Hats off to you.'

'You get used to it. You forget you ever wanted a designer living room and spotless kitchen, let alone sex and candlelight.' She raised her glass and clinked it against her friends. 'Ah, that's better. So, I don't know what's more important, your hunting down of the aforementioned Mr Troumeg or your non-date with Mr Harold Wesley at the British Museum. Well I do really, but I'll let you decide.'

'Easy part first?'

'OK, then.'

Beatrice told her the story Odile and Sebastian, of Marguerite and Elliot, describing the unfolding chain of events leading her into the background of Joseph Troumeg, sketching in the characters, easier now that the account had been emptied of its emotion.

'Gosh,' Amanda said, cutting another slice from the shoulder, 'I'll never be able to look at this recipe in the same way again. It's a terrific story, isn't it. You must be really pleased.'

'To tell you the truth, Amanda, I can't quite see the wood for the trees at the moment. I've got a few more steps to take before I'm certain.'

'I'm picking up something here,' Amanda said. 'You've got plenty to go on. What's stopping you?'

'It's a good question. I'm not quite sure.'

'OK, we'll come back to that. Now, the main course. What about what's-his-name, our unpronounceable osteoarchaeologist?' She said the word slowly, syllable by syllable. 'He's got a nice voice, I know that much.'

'He took me to the British Museum, as you know.'

'It's a start.'

'And I must say he was fascinating. He showed me the world that Flotsam might have grown up in.'

'Flotsam?'

'Sorry. It's the name we have given the skull, or the person it once was. A young girl, we think.'

'So you have a child already. Nice going.'

'He showed me the most wonderful jewellery. I had no idea about the Anglo-Saxon world at all.'

'And what about this world, Beattie? What's he like?'

'Again, I don't really know. He's not like the others.'

'I told you that. And no bad thing, too.'

'He listens. He's full of information. And he tells me I've made quite an impact on him, although he didn't say so yesterday.' It was strange how, in the telling, aspects of the meeting seemed clearer. Harry, she now saw, had taken the measure of her and respected the boundaries which she had drawn, knowingly or not.

'Yes, I was led to believe that he was somehow smitten in our two phone calls. What do you know about him? He's not married is he?'

Beatrice brought her hand to her mouth. 'Heavens, I don't know. I know his father is dead and that his parents divorced a long time ago, but I've no idea about partners, married or not.'

'That's an unusual oversight, Beatrice.'

'Not really, since I hadn't been thinking of him in that way.'

'And now?'

245

Beatrice thought for a moment and felt sure in herself that Harry Wesley would have told her if he was married or involved, but Amanda had introduced an element of doubt.

'We'll see. Delicious lamb, by the way. I shall tell Mr Troumeg when I see him next.'

'And when might that be?'

'I can't be certain, but it won't be long. If I can find him again.'

She could see that Amanda thought that she was being deliberately opaque, but in truth Beatrice wasn't clear how and when the next stage would happen.

'And what about Harry Wesley? Is there another meeting in the diary? I do hope so.'

'We haven't fixed anything, but even if I didn't want to he would persist. That's what he's like.' She stopped. 'I told Joseph Troumeg something that I've never told anyone else, anyone else including me.'

Amanda, in the process of removing the lamb, looked at her friend and waited.

'I told him that I thought a succession of men had wasted my time.'

Amanda sat down again. 'You're being a bit hard on yourself. Mind you, it's probably true.'

'He'd asked me why I wasn't with anyone, how I'd got this far without, well, finding someone. It was a backhanded compliment, I suppose...' Amanda remained quiet and Beatrice added '...and a veiled criticism. At least, that's the way I took it.'

'That it was your fault.'

Beatrice looked at her friend to see whether this was an accusation or simply a confirmation of what Troumeg had implied. Whichever way, it was the same. 'Yes. I think so. And then, yesterday, I told Harry that I felt I had collaborated with men, that I was complicit and responsible for what happened.'

'You told him that?'

Beatrice nodded slowly. 'And do you know, he understood

and maybe realised why I'm not able to respond, why I am frightened of the loop repeating itself again.'

Upstairs the baby began to stir and moments later there was a gentle but insistent rocking. 'He's shaking the cot,' Amanda said. 'It won't be long before it falls to pieces. Along with me.' She brought him downstairs and handed him to Beatrice whilst she fetched two chocolate mousses from the kitchen. 'He might like a corner of this,' she said and stillness was restored as Beatrice fed the child.

'So what's next, Beattie?' Amanda said, watching the easy way her friend held Harper.

'I'm going to France again. There are too many loose ends for me to feel comfortable.'

'Does that mean you still might not make the film?'

Beatrice weighed the question before answering. 'To tell you the truth, I don't know.'

'Actually, Beattie, I wasn't really meaning the film. I mean, what's going to happen next with you and Harry, or you and anyone for that matter?'

'The answer's the same, I'm afraid. Actually, I'm not afraid. I feel better keeping my distance, more in charge of myself.' Harper smeared a finger of soft chocolate across her blouse, to join the faint island stain of wine.

'More than you are now. Here.' She beckoned for Beatrice to hand over the child, but she shook her head. 'No, I'm quite happy. I'm getting quite used to new experiences.' She shifted her position on the chair, crossed her legs so the baby tipped slightly back in her arms. 'But all I've done is talk about me. Shame James couldn't be with us.'

'Yeah, he's doing a studio shoot today, wouldn't you know. Got to take the work when it's offered. But can I return to you, please, miss? You talked about your dad. Take me through that again.'

'I told you he was fascinated about the future, about what might happen and about the consequences of things changing in years ahead. It was his job but somehow the here and now, me and what I was doing, he couldn't get his head around. At least, that's what I've come to think.'

'And what did this do to you, do you think?'

Harper raised a hand and hooked a finger in her mouth. 'I suppose it made me feel invisible sometimes, that I didn't exist.'

'Maybe he was unhappy?'

Beatrice licked the chocolate from Harper's fingers and he laughed at the sensation of her tongue. 'I tried to ask my mother about their relationship but it was like trying to herd cats. She's more like a parent from the forties than the sixties. Thinks there are things you shouldn't talk about with your children.'

'I think she's a bit miffed that you've been having the fun she never had,' said Amanda. 'And maybe just a tad jealous of your looks. I've seen it in her face. Competitive mothers, never easy.'

'She certainly disapproves of most of what I do.' Harper was now standing on her knees trying to pull her nose, which Beatrice was keeping just out of reach. She got up and carried him to the window and looked at the garden dotted with brightly coloured toys, a dirty yellow slide and deflated paddling pool.

'It's like a toy catalogue shoot gone wrong, isn't it?'

'My life, or your garden?'

'He's very happy with you. Had you thought of having children?'

Beatrice turned. 'Careful, I may throw something and it might just be your child.'

Amanda laughed. 'Well, we seem to be making some progress and I suggest further treatment with young Harper and probably another appointment with Dr Wesley.'

On the Tube home she was rather proud of the stains on her blouse, won in honourable conflict with Harper, a meeting he would never remember and which would never be recorded in history. Once upon a time, Flotsam would have been held in the same way, carried and loved and yet the events of her life were unknown, lost almost from the start and now completely eroded by the years.

CHAPTER FORTY-SIX

She feels at home.

There is still conflict from the north and there is no warmth, but the grey town settles on her like a familiar blanket. At first, just as her mother before her, she is a curiosity, a woman of rank, a widow alone, independent and noted for her craftsmanship. She is carrying on the tradition of making precious objects and it is this that brings her to the counsellor's attention. He makes the short walk from the old amphitheatre, on which the Guildhall would later be built and can still be found, to meet the woman whose reputation went before her, both for what she was and what she did. He wishes to commission a piece that he might give his wife, jewellery, he demands, that might be like no other. Even before he has finished speaking the images come to her, somehow stored without her knowing but rising to the surface at the right moment.

She has seen the birds in the south, pink and grey with long beaks and beautiful crests of white tipped with black. She had first been attracted by their strange, almost human calls and had sought them out. Later, with her daughter, they had watched them together, the exotic heads and raised crests. She knows their shape will be the centre of a large brooch of gold and enamel, fabulous creatures from lands far away.

First she draws them in charcoal on a wooden board, a pair of heads with beaks crossed and necks extended, the fingers of their crests extended above. Sometimes her daughter watches her, as she herself had watched her mother. She adjusts the position of the birds so that the tips of the crests define the upper boundary of the brooch, their half-spread wings the lower semi-circle. She then carves a smaller version in relief so that she can beat the gold over its outline, the birds emerging as they might on a misty morning, ill defined at first and then quite clear. As she often does, she wishes her mother could see the result, for she knows that she would have had no hesitation in praising the excellence of the work, of exalting the skill of her daughter. She will create a border to contain the two birds in which she will place four smooth garnets to give balance to the final piece. She knows her mother is the inspiration for the work for it was she who had given her the confidence to experiment, to go one stage further without fear of condemnation. And she remembers, quite suddenly, that it was one of these birds that had landed by her grave as she buried the ring. She shakes her head at the strangeness of memory.

She had worked for many hours, stooped over the bench, when her daughter tugs at her dress wanting to show her something new she has discovered. She runs ahead and she is reminded of herself, the same surefootedness. Today her daughter leads her to the fish traps that have been set up just beyond the bridge and they sit on the bank and watch as silvery fish are lifted out of the pens and put in baskets. Afterwards, it is her turn to lead and she takes her daughter further up river towards the clump of trees that she herself had played in as a child. They climb the bank and she feels a strange excitement at visiting a site which she had first seen when she was her daughter's age. The disused building is still there, the trees still growing through the strange floor, the roof partly fallen in, reminding her of the times she had sat with her blonde-haired friend and imagined who had lived here and why they had left. She tells her daughter of those days, of how they would play in these very ruins and how she came here after her father had died. She says she had seen him in the river, his arm raised in farewell, floating away, a warrior killed in battle and takes her to the spot where she had stood. Perhaps your father will come by, she says and wave at you. And the child nods, knowing that it is possible.

And just as she had felt a succession taking place even before the death of her own mother, so she looks at her child and knows that it is happening again, that into the hand she is holding the future is flowing.

She returns, hand in hand with her child, along the foreshore where for six hundred years fish will be unloaded for market until it becomes too difficult to bring them so far into the centre of the city and the ancient site will become offices where businessmen come and go and barely gave the river a backward glance.

CHAPTER FORTY-SEVEN

'I'm back,' her mother announced. Beatrice looked at her watch on the bedside table. It was slightly after nine in the morning and she imagined her mother waiting until now to make the call assuming that this is when Beatrice normally started her day. 'Are you free later?' Beatrice, in fact, had been up since just before seven and had already had coffee and croissant in her favourite café, a stylish glass cube recently opened within the heart of the old market. Whilst there, she had written an email to Graham Roth informing him of her progress with the Joseph Troumeg story, offering him no details but indicating that she was on to something very interesting and would need to return to France once more. It was both bait and smokescreen. She had thought about calling Harry, but had hesitated and now her mother, with immaculate timing, had come between them. Was she free later? She found it hard to answer, for in one sense she was and in another not at all.

'Not really.'

'You don't sound frightfully sure.'

'I'm not. Let me call you back.' And she rang off, not wanting to feel the guilt which her mother would have undoubtedly induced by whatever she would have said next. Instead, she made the call she wished she had made earlier.

'Harry, good morning. I wanted to thank you for yesterday. You got me thinking.'

'How nice to hear from you so early. About what, exactly?'

'I'm not really sure. A number of things, I think. I've got to go back to France and I just wanted to tell you.'

'I'm not surprised. It must be so tantalising to be on the edge of piecing all your information together. I'm excited for you. I know what it feels like.'

She hadn't expected this response, predicting that he might have been disappointed and so for the second time that morning wasn't quite sure how to continue the conversation. 'I'll call you from Paris. And let me know if you have any more news on Flotsam. I introduced her to my friend Amanda yesterday and she didn't know what I was talking about.'

'We never went back to the river. Maybe next time. Do give me a call. I'm really keen to know what more you find.'

It was with a vague sense of dissatisfaction that she rang off although she tried to ignore it and made a call to the Maison Clemenceau instead. Eventually she was put through to Elliot Honeywell, who, although perfectly charming, had no recollection of her visit.

'Beatrice who?' he said and she carefully took him through who she was and what she was trying to discover.

'I gather that your nephew is looking after some of Odile's possessions, letters and mementos, that sort of thing,' she said.

'You know Odile, do you? She was the love of my life.'

'I'm trying to find out more about her and I wonder if you would give me permission to look through some of her stuff.'

Beatrice wondered if he'd understood and waited, hearing his breathing on the line. 'What can it matter? She's dead now. She's beyond harm, no one can hurt her.'

'I don't want to hurt her, Mr Honeywell.'

'Do as you will,' he said.

Beatrice was uneasy about this less than satisfactory permission and was equally apprehensive about the call she had to make next. Simon Honeywell answered abruptly and his manner didn't change when she announced herself.

'Changed your tune have you?'

'I've been talking to Elliot,' she said, ignoring his hostility, 'and I asked permission to read Odile's letters. He said I could go ahead.'

'And what about my permission?'

'That's why I'm phoning. I wonder if you would allow me to see them?' Beatrice knew that he would procrastinate, use the moment to his advantage and she decided to pre-empt the counter proposal by offering a further inducement herself. 'And I'll tell you what I have discovered so far. You might be surprised.'

'And how do you intend to do this?' he asked.

'Well, we could have a drink. I'm coming to Paris tomorrow. We could meet at six, say?' It was, as she predicted, as easy as that and he agreed, giving her directions to a bar opposite the church of St Sulpice. She already knew that she wouldn't traduce the memory of Odile by revealing what she had discovered, not all of it at least. It was, like Simon Honeywell, a means to an end.

This left one more call.

'Hello mother. Sorry to have kept you waiting. How was your trip back from Toulon?'

'France would be fine without the French,' she said, 'but the cruise was lovely. I'll tell you about it later, shall I? The usual place? Good.'

Beatrice booked Eurostar for the following morning, wrote a note to Amanda to thank her for lunch, enclosing an old dry cleaning bill for Harper and then, having decided to walk, put on her trainers and set off for Oxford Circus taking in the three markets, Spitalfields, Smithfield and Covent Garden. She was feeling strangely light and could have broken into a run, an unusual experience given that she was heading for a lunch with her mother. She was preoccupied with other thoughts, though, and the two miles evaporated in what seemed the blink of an eye. Along the way, somewhere just north of Holborn, where the Fleet flowed unnoticed beneath her feet, she began to think of Flotsam and she wanted to hear Harry talk about her once again, building the picture of her life, his enthusiasm and knowledge giving her dimension and making her real. Somewhere around here, he had told her, she might have played, in the days when the river Fleet could be seen and flowed between banks that rose on either side of the Farringdon Road. It would have been quicker for her to go up to the right, along Holborn, but she veered slightly southwards, through Lincoln's Inn Fields and then across into Covent Garden where, Harry explained, the early Anglo-Saxons had lived and, who knows, even Flotsam herself. By the time she arrived at John Lewis she was ready to do battle with her mother and had the answer to what she knew would be her opening statement already prepared.

'You're late.'

'I walked here and it's hard to gauge time when you're on foot.'

'You look quite flushed. You're not ill are you?'

'It took almost two hours. I feel great.' Everything had to be a skirmish, no warm welcome and how-nice-to-see-you, but pistols drawn at once. Beatrice could barely conceal her smile. 'In some ways, mother, I've never felt better.'

'Goodness, what's brought this around? It doesn't mean you're going to question me again, does it? I sincerely hope not. Maybe it's another man.' She looked quickly at her daughter. 'It usually is.'

'Are you jealous of the men in my life, mother?'

'There, you see, you are going to question me. Of course not. Whatever gave you that idea? And I don't know why you've got that look on your face.'

Beatrice was still smiling. 'You were going to tell me about your cruise, I think.'

'Shall we order first.' Her mother bristled and tried to catch the eye of a waitress.

'Although I really shouldn't eat another thing after the meals on the ship.'

'I'm going to France again tomorrow,' Beatrice said. 'To continue my work.'

'With the man?'

Beatrice shook her head. 'I'm going to read some letters written by a German to a French Jew just before the last War.' Eileen Palmenter frowned at her daughter. 'I thought you might be interested to know more.'

'The things you get up to. And why would I be interested?'

'Because I am. He was with the German embassy in Paris and I'm intrigued that he had a relationship with a Jewish woman.'

'There are too many films about the Jews and the war. It's all they teach in school these days. It's like the Tudors and the Stuarts never existed.'

'Yes, what I knew about Anglo-Saxon England you could have put in a thimble before Saturday. I was taken to the British Museum by an expert and he showed me a world I'd never known.'

'Is this your man?' Her mother sniffed into her napkin.

'Not exactly. He's an archaeologist. He specialises in bones. Do you remember the skull I told you about?'

'Did you darling, I can't remember? What do you mean not exactly?'

'He's just someone I'm working with.'

'Well, he seems to have cheered you up. I wonder how long it will last.'

'Perhaps that's what you could do with, mum. A man to cheer you up. Unless you're keeping someone secret from me?'

'Really, Beatrice. I've told you I don't want to be questioned like that.'

257

Beatrice looked at her mother, a good looking woman not yet sixty, her hair fashionably straight and cleverly dyed blonde, not overweight, her age yet to show itself in her fingers and neck and assumed she must have had admirers after her father's death. This, however, was history that she didn't want her daughter to know about and so it would remain secret. 'But you're happy to ask about the men in my life.'

'That's different.'

'Anyway, as I was saying, I'm going to Paris again and then probably on to Marseille and perhaps even Germany.'

'Meanwhile I'm thinking of moving,' her mother said, as if she hadn't heard. 'Down to the coast, to be nearer to Jean. She's got a lovely place near Lymington. You might want to help me find somewhere.'

The point of the meal was now clear which brought the smile back to Beatrice's face. 'Of course, mother. What will you be looking for, a detached cottage with a rose covered porch?'

'Yes, something like that. I'm not very good with mortgages and contracts and I thought you could give me a hand.'

The pursuit of the truth behind the life of a woman who had her head shaved in front of a crowd on the boulevard St Michel because of a relationship with a German, the appearance of a doctor of archaeology with a special interest in the bones of our Anglo-Saxon forebears and the strange family history of the world famous Joseph Troumeg seemed to be of no interest to Eileen Palmenter whose world was soon to shrink even further into a corner of Hampshire where she would expect her daughter to visit but whose life she would continue to ignore.

'Of course I will.'

For the rest of the meal they talked about the proposed move, the sale of her current house, the state of the market, the coastline of the south of England, the need for more peace and quiet, the rise of crime in the suburbs and the atrocious rudeness of the French. Afterwards, when Beatrice walked home, her mood no less buoyant than earlier, she considered how her mother believed she had sovereign rights over her daughter, who was no more than a troublesome serf in her kingdom. It was not her duty to reveal anything of herself beyond the authorised version and this was why Beatrice could not fill the back of a postcard about the life and times of Eileen Palmenter.

She took a different route back, walking through Soho and picking up the river at Charing Cross and tracking the great curve to Blackfriars Bridge where the City began to rise up and present St Paul's at its peak. The tide was out and river was listless. Flotsam might have walked where she was now, although she knew the Embankment would not have existed and the river would have been wider, almost touching Whitehall and further on, held back by the steep rise to The Strand. She walked on to London Bridge and stopped to look down on the rotting timber stays which marked the limit of the old quays, split by a redundant cobbled slipway. She climbed the low slope into the heart of the City, through the passages to Lombard Street, her body curiously alive as she cut through the old rights of way, hemmed in on all sides by the looming presence of modern London which, despite its gleaming brashness, could not suppress and obliterate the signs of the past, the trapped graveyards, the old milestones, the corners of ancient walls and the unmistakable sense of the past just under the surface. When finally she turned off Moorgate and saw the solid whiteness of Christ Church standing at the end of her road, newly resurrected in all its glory, it was like an affirmation of the past and confirmed her own mood of satisfaction.

CHAPTER FORTY-EIGHT

She turns, thinking she hears someone move past her, but there is no one. She is standing near her home, at the point where Lombard Street would later meet the old footpath to Angel Court, not far from where the muscular bulk of the Bank of England will be built above the river Walbrook. She watches the stream curving away southwards in pursuit of the larger river and she walks along its bank, turning to wave at her mother framed in the doorway.

She is unlike her mother. Her hair lighter and thicker, her face fuller but they have the same eyes, deep brown, so that there is barely a shade between the iris and the black of the pupils. She also frowns when she stares, appearing to concentrate even if at that moment she is thinking of something else. Her mother says it makes her appear older and that she has wisdom beyond her years. Her fingers are long, as her father's had been and she has his certainty of balance. On her wrist she wears the bracelet of coloured stones.

She breaks into a run heading downhill to the quays where her mother tells her she used to play at the same age. She has learnt two languages in the south and has picked up scraps of many others and loves the look of surprise on the sailors' faces when they realise she can understand them. She marvels at her independence and knows that this has been handed down to her, a gift of freedom

Later she returns and finds her mother working at her bench. The golden brooch is almost finished and the entwined birds reminds her of other places, of wider horizons. In the border, between the deep red garnets, her mother has inlaid rounds of dark blue enamel and from time to time she takes the brooch outside to examine it in the daylight. When the counsellor comes to collect it he carefully lifts it from the table, glancing at her mother, its creator and as he does he lets it rest in the palm of his hand. The girl watches him examining it and listens to her mother telling him about the birds, creating a picture of their life under the southern sun, of their raised crests and strange calls. The sky there was truly this blue, she tells him and the birds were lovers. He carries it outside, just as she had done, so that the daylight catches the gold and emphasises the depth of the blue inlay. He takes it away with him, bowing as he leaves and she notices the sadness on her mother's face. She takes her hand and tells her she is remembering the brooch that her mother had made for her, at this same table and which now lies lost under the very blue sky that she has just been describing. She remembers her mother telling her the story of its loss and her delight at her own mother's response, her sympathy and her laughter and her simple joy in explaining that she could always make another brooch but never replace her daughter.

CHAPTER FORTY-NINE

It was raining on St Sulpice and its twin towers were lost in grey. Beatrice ran towards the bar, her umbrella twisted inside out by the wind, her hair attempting the same trick. Although she was on time, she knew he would be there and he greeted her coolly, taking in her dishevelled appearance and nodding at her to sit on the stool next to his. She was prepared for his attitude and found this sort of meeting, shorn of any possible romantic complication, very easy. She was in need of information and this, after all, was her job and one she did well. He pushed a drink towards her and waited for her to begin, knowing full well he had all the cards. Around them in the bar several other couples were also involved in similar games of give and take. Beatrice ran her fingers through her short, wet hair and unwrapped herself from her coat.

'So,' she said, 'thank you for coming out on such a terrible evening to see me. I appreciate it.' She watched him raise his eyebrows in disbelief. She noticed he was wearing cuff-links and that he had a gold ring on his little finger marked with the feathers of the Prince of Wales. 'Why is it that rain in Paris seems even wetter than in London?' She took a sip of her kir and looked at him over the rim of the glass before putting it down and arranging it in the centre of its black coaster.

'Look,' she said. 'I'm not going to trade myself for your permission to look at Sebastian's letters to Odile. It's not a swap I want to make. But I would be grateful for the opportunity to see them.'

'And what if I say no?'

'I had time to think about that on the train,' she said. 'Then, I suppose I would go to Germany, to find Sebastian Traugott's family. Maybe Odile's letters to him have survived. One way or the other, I'll find out what happened.'

She saw him weigh the odds, deciding which card to play next and she could see him decide to stretch the game out a little longer, hoping to trump her later.

'Sure,' he said. 'Why not.'

She could see that Odile meant very little to him, merely a distant adjunct to his uncle's life and since he appeared to have scant affection for his relative, why would Odile register on his radar at all?

'C'mon,' he said. 'Drink up.'

It wasn't far to the rue du Bac but it was into the wind and rain and he made no concessions as he strode ahead. Once inside, he pointed at the bathroom and when she came out the box was already on the table and she could hear him in the kitchen. 'Help yourself,' he shouted through. She would have preferred to be alone, to slowly immerse herself in an almost forgotten relationship which took place eight decades earlier in the most unlikely circumstances, but she had no option but to continue to be aware of the shadow of his presence. She saw that the two letters he had brought to the Brasserie Île St Louis were loose on the top of the tied bundle. When she saw that the others had been carefully arranged by date, this carelessness annoyed her, although by now it should have been what she expected. Her irritation was replaced by the tingle of apprehension as she slipped out the earliest letter, dated the winter of 1933. She noted it was written in French from an apartment on the rue du Louvre and, probably because French was his second language, Beatrice was able to read Sebastian's words quite easily. The letter spoke of joy and caution and Beatrice was able to deduce that Odile worked for one of the government ministries and that Sebastian had met her at a reception. He wrote, she gathered, because so often they couldn't meet, since he would have lost his job if it became known that he was seeing a Jew. He would meet her at night, in private and he spoke of the fear of being found out, yet as she read further letters, it was clear that he loved her and that he was prepared to risk a great deal for her. Beatrice broke the chronology of the letters by sliding out the last, dated November 1938. "You will know the worst by now. The assassination of vom Rath means that I am being sent home. I will see you tomorrow, *mon amour*, and we will decide what to do. Although these are difficult days, I remain always yours, Sebastian."

A pain had developed in her back, the tension of holding the thin blue paper on which he wrote and translating his words transferring itself to her body. She remembered that Joseph's birthday was sometime in November and she carefully removed several letters from the centre of the pile and quickly scanned them until she found what she wanted, one dated November 1935. The first sentence was all she needed to know. "A boy! My life is complete and yet the pain is doubled. I will see him tonight. What joy and how brave you are."

Beatrice hung her head and could barely continue. The tension she felt had frozen her fingers in position so that when she put down the letter she had to force them open and clench and unclench them to make them work. The back of her neck was also locked in position and when Simon came into the room she could not look up, even if she'd wanted to. Here it was, in dark blue ink, written with a thick-nibbed fountain pen, proof that Sebastian Traugott was Joseph's father. She was stunned at what she'd learnt and overwhelmed by the consequences and what she still had to uncover.

'Found what you want?'

She understood his flippancy. How could he be as engaged as she was with the pursuit of a story that was in the process of turning from a producer's quest for a good film into something far more personal? 'In fact, I have,' she said eventually, managing at last to look up at him, hands on hips, above her. Would he want to know more? She hoped not.

'I made you a coffee and I thought you might need this.' He placed a glass of brandy by the cup. 'You look as though you need it.'

'Odile was a remarkable woman,' she said, believing his kindness needed some sort of response. 'Her relationship with Sebastian at the German embassy did produce a son, Joseph. Can you imagine what anguish that must have created?'

'Tell me,' he said.

She averted her eyes from his as she spoke. 'It must have been difficult enough to be a Jew in those days and just as hard to be a single mother, with a child born out of wedlock. But for the child to be that of a German diplomat whose country was intent on eradicating the Jews.' She shook her head. 'Impossible.'

'It makes a good story for you, doesn't it? Sex, intrigue, Nazis. Forbidden love. You couldn't have written it better.'

For a moment she imagined this would be the reaction of Graham Roth in London and she suddenly saw him clearly, his face in close up, pressing himself on her, intent on getting his own way, and she was revolted not so much that he should make a sexual advance to her but that she should ever want to share the information she'd discovered with him.

'And imagine Joseph Troumeg's reaction.'

She could see that he was detached from the emotional repercussions of these facts and, again, she excused him for she saw how deeply involved she'd become.

'Can I ask you a favour?' she said. He waited for her to continue. 'Could you keep this information to yourself?'

'You don't want me to steal your thunder, is that it?'

She did not have it in her to explain how completely he'd missed the point, so she agreed. 'Something like that.' What she could see, though, was Joseph Troumeg in his kitchen in Marseille reading in the newspaper the story of his birth and she felt she wanted to protect him from this, even if some of it he knew already.

'May I photograph one or two of these letters, please?'

'Go ahead. I imagine there'll be a fee if they're used in the film?'

'Of course,' she said. 'But don't forget about the non-disclosure.'

'You should have made me sign an agreement.'

'I should have, you're right. But I trust you.' Whether she did or not, she couldn't say. She wanted to be away from him now, out of the room, back into the rain to feel it on her skin, to enjoy it on her face, to clean her hands and shake the tension out of her body.

Leaving was easier than she thought. He had clearly seen the intensity in her face and knew that any further overtures to her would be met with unconditional defeat. She said thank you with her back to him, slipped through the door with a promise to keep in touch about the progress of the film, took the stairs two at a time and pushed open the glass doors into the fresh air. It was still raining and after a while, her hair dripping down her neck, she stopped at a bar at the junction of the boulevard St Germain and ordered another cognac. Although she was aware of her surroundings, the football table in the corner, the zinc bar, the other tables, even her own reflection in the mirror on the back wall, what she saw was, if not out of focus, then distanced, unnecessary detail. She took out her phone.

'Hello, it's me.'

'Is everything alright? You don't sound yourself.'

A while later, when the rain had stopped and she was able to walk back over the Pont Royal and pause in the middle, she was not surprised she called Harry. She knew that his reaction to the events of that evening would be as correct as those of Simon

Honeywell were not, that he would instinctively understand the impact of the information she'd discovered and predict, as he did, the possible repercussions.

'Poor Joseph Troumeg.'

'That's exactly what I thought.

'Even if he knows some of it,' Harry had said, 'he'll find the rest difficult to take. From what you've told me, it will upset everything.'

It had been a comfort not to have to explain herself to Harry, to hear both support and sympathy in his voice and to have him second guess what she was thinking, sometimes arriving at conclusions before she did.

'You'll go and see him soon,' he'd said, 'but you've got some other decisions to make before then, haven't you? Like, will you go ahead and make the film anyway?'

Some of the tension had left her and she walked past the glass Pyramid of the Louvre, heading roughly in the right direction for the hotel, not wanting, for the moment at least, to take a taxi or the Metro. She came to rue du Louvre by chance and at first could not remember why the name was familiar. She took out her camera and looked at one of the letters Sebastian had written to check the address of his apartment and began walking northwards, looking for the numbers. The building was a grand affair, with two enormous doors on either side of which, five metres high, two muscular cariates supported a stone balcony above which several further stories rose into the sky towards a top terrace protected by elaborate wrought iron railings. She stood and imagined which one had been Sebastian Traugott's and tried to decide if Odile Leval had ever been able to visit him here or whether his neighbours, perhaps other diplomats, might have posed too great a risk. He would leave here, though, his coat buttoned up, his collar turned above his cheek, his hat pulled down, to take a cab up to her apartment by Buttes Chaumont where, for a while at least, they would be safe to discuss their predicament and later to play with the living proof of their impossible relationship.

CHAPTER FIFTY

The girl explores the river, drawn east as far as the great loop, where the marshes begin and to the west, as far as the monastery where, at low tide, there is a ford and she can watch the traders walk to the other bank with their loaded horses. But it is to the old bath house that she is drawn to most, playing there as her mother had done and where she feels a connection with her past and to the men and women who had built it and lived here before the trees took over, in a time that she tries hard to imagine but could not picture.

It is in the old bath house that she encounters the woman again, on a morning in winter so grey that snow could not be far behind. She is stepping on the stone stacks that had once held the floor, hopping from one to another until she reaches the part which has not yet collapsed and is covered with pretty little tiles that make up part of a broken pattern she cannot understand. Around the corner is an old window which looks along the river, through the tangle of the copse. Today, though, when she turns the corner, it is the woman's face she sees framed in the space and her heart jumps in her chest and not even her hand can calm it. It is her mother's friend, with the dirty face and hair and the eyes which penetrate her and seem to demand more. The girl stares at her and she can feel her beating heart beneath her hand. And then the woman is gone and in the space is left the outline of her head and the strange look in her eyes. The girl climbs up and stands on one of the remaining roof beams hoping to catch sight of her, but she is nowhere to be seen, and has disappeared directly behind the ruin, where the ground climbs steeply and is covered in bushes.

She returns along the river, watching for signs of her, wanting to make contact with her without knowing why. The snow comes, lightly at first, but then so thickly it is impossible to see. The shape of the ground changes, the mud of the foreshore flattened and strangely white against the dark river. Behind her she can see her own tracks and the coldness of her hands and legs are forgotten in the excitement of this new experience. The bridge looks completely different and lined in white against the grey of the sky and the water it appears to be floating. She wants her mother to see and turns around, thinking that she might be there, but there is no one. Further up the white shore, however, there is another set of tracks that leave the riverside and mark the steps that disappear into the quays.

She feels suddenly cold and becomes conscious of the silence all around her, the weight of the snow pressing down on the ground. But for the other footprints, she might be the only person in the world.

CHAPTER FIFTY-ONE

And so she made the walk that Sebastian Traugott might have taken many times in those distant and uncertain days, across north central Paris towards the railway stations, through the first and second *arrondissements*, then the tenth and finally the nineteenth, all the way turning over the new information that had begun to take hold of her in the past few weeks, not simply the pursuit of Joseph Troumeg, nor the fascination with the girl called Flotsam, but the arrival of Dr Harold Wesley, unexpected, at first a bit player on the periphery of her vision but who had gradually moved to the centre stage of her mind. By the time she had reached the hotel, almost two hours after leaving the bridge, she wanted to speak to him again but he beat her to it and the moment she walked into her bedroom, as if somehow he had been watching and waiting for just the right moment, her phone rang.

'And another thing I meant to tell you,' he said, carrying on from their previous conversation, 'will involve you having to come back to London. It's about Flotsam and I need you here for what I have to say.'

'Sounds serious.'

'It might be. Whatever, you owe me a trip to the river. I've been waiting too long.'

'I had thought about going on to Marseille.'

'You've made up your mind, then, what you're going to tell Troumeg?'

'Not really, no.'

'So come back here first and we can talk about it. I still think there are some pieces of the puzzle missing and until you have those you can't be sure what you'd say to him.'

'It's what I've been thinking, as well...'

'...like, for example, if Sebastian wasn't in Paris during the war, if he was indeed killed in 1940, why did Odile have her head shaved for collaborating?'

'Mmm, I'd been thinking about that as well. From what I can gather, immediately after the liberation lots of people were falsely accused of collaboration. Maybe she got swept up in that.'

'Terrible times. And lots to talk about. So, it's Tuesday tomorrow. Can you come to the museum, like before? Lunchtime?'

The next day, on the train again, the vast fields succeeding one another with frightening speed, she was glad of the pause between one thing and the next, although what she was coming from and where she was going were not necessarily clear. She needed to complete the picture, though, to explore the corners of the equation, to satisfy herself that she could go no further even if it meant leaving out a piece of the jigsaw puzzle because she had exhausted the possibilities of knowing more. The train galloped over the Medway and then down in to the Thames valley, to be swallowed under the river to emerge in the flat no-man's-land on the north side, where she saw birds turn and dive over the marshy fields bounded by fenced off industrial sites lined with imported cars, or full of rusting machinery. She couldn't quite see the river, but she knew it was there and thought of the Danish invaders moving upriver to leave behind them the arrowheads and armour, pieces of which Harry had shown her in the British Museum. The moment passed and she was down in a tunnel again, sucked under the accumulated suburbs of east London to arrive at St Pancras, three hundred miles behind her, time compressed and distance reduced in the blink of an eye.

He met her at the museum reception, enthusiastic and animated, his arms wheeling as he described what he'd been doing that morning, the assembly of a later skeleton which was laid out in his laboratory, almost complete as far as she could make out. 'Probably mid-eighteenth century, buried certainly and curiously close to the lowest tide level of the river. Not sure why yet. It's good to see you.' And he was off again, towards the far end of the room where she had first seen Flotsam's skull under the microscope and she followed, only for him to suddenly stop.

'Sorry,' he said, taking her hand. 'You must be tired and I haven't offered you a drink. I get carried away sometimes.'

It did cross her mind that he might want to put off telling her whatever it was he couldn't say on the mobile the night before and when, eventually, he did she thought she might have been right. She said she was fine and so he sat her down on his stool, tipped the computer screen to make it easier for her to see and brought up Flotsam's face with her fierce, brown eyes. It was a close-up without the naked body below.

'But we need to go backwards now,' he said, 'so prepare yourself.'

It was unnerving to see the life disappear from the face, the skin retreat to leave the remnant of the skull and the empty eye sockets.

'I particularly wanted to show you this,' he said and then hesitated before doing anything. 'Now that she's become so real for both of us, you may not like it.' With that, he zoomed into a small section at the back of the skull, almost at the base of the what remained of the dome.

At first Beatrice could not be sure what she was meant to be looking at until Harry pointed the curser at a small crack running from the edge of the remaining bone. 'It's hard to tell, but this may have been caused by a blow, perhaps the result of a fall, or something more sinister.'

Beatrice looked at the tiny crack, a minute line of evidence. 'In other words, she might have died unnaturally?'

'It certainly is a fracture and it happened before she died.'

'You can tell this?'

He nodded. 'I'm afraid so.'

'And we've hardly got to know her. Do you think she was buried?'

'There might have been a lower jaw if she had, the chances of it surviving from a proper burial in the right sort of soil being greater.'

'But more than likely not.'

'I'll show you another image and I don't know whether this will make things worse or not.' He moved the curser and then, in layers, the full version of Flotsam that she'd seen in Paris appeared, only this time wearing clothes, a cloak over what might have been a plain dress, held at the centre by a brooch. Around her neck was the silver necklace, similar to the one at the British Museum with at its centre the rock crystal ball. 'We've made her a young girl of rank, although we've no real proof that she was.'

He made no reference to the necklace, but she knew it was there for her and she felt herself grow even closer to the girl knowing that the necklace might just as well have been placed around her own neck. Her reaction to the image was the opposite of what he'd anticipated and she was glad to see the young girl given back her life and made real.

'That's what I'd hoped you'd say and why I kept this image until the end. It's low tide in about an hour and a half. Shall we grab some lunch and return to where we found her?'

As they walked over the road and into Smithfield market she told him about the journey from Paris, the sensation of time so speeded up and compressed that the past seemed to be pushed even further away, her understanding of Flotsam's world even more difficult to comprehend.

'We're beginning to learn more and more about the Anglo-Saxons, but it's still only fragments. Don't forget,' he reminded her, 'that Flotsam might have been quite unusual. There is that dental evidence that she might have travelled, so her world could have been considerably larger than was usual. Who knows? I'm not allowed to make things up,' he said, taking her hand to cut between a bus and a car, 'but a little licence is allowed. Funnily enough, when you came into St Pancras the train almost cuts through the graveyard of the parish church which would have been in existence in one form or another when she was alive. For all we know, she might even have walked there, out of London as it was and across country. You never know.'

He continued the theme over lunch, imagining the life of the girl called Flotsam and she watched him closely as he wove fact and fiction, building a world for the young girl out of the scraps of evidence at their disposal. He was a natural communicator and by the time they took the DLR to the tip of the Isle of Dogs, Flotsam's short life became once again full of possibilities and it would not have surprised her to see the young girl standing on this very foreshore where she may, once upon a time, have played.

By now she was familiar with the river at low tide, a sleeping beast in disguise, reduced and deceptively docile, shrunk back by the previous night's full moon to reveal more of the shore than they had seen before. The marker remained but she watched Harry work beyond this, exploring the extra few metres of river bed offered by the exceptional tide.

'It's a needle in a haystack, but we won't have a tide like this for ages, so we'd best make the most of it.' Harry was immediately engrossed and Beatrice found that the little she had been shown, the traces at the British Museum and the importance that he gave them, made the ground she was walking on almost sacred and everything beneath her feet became a possible clue. Looking down on the few metres of mud and stone the river conceded, she hardly knew where to begin. Next to her she watched Harry pick up and discard shapes that caught his eye, his gloved hands working quickly and she could sense his optimism that somehow a thousand years of tides might have sifted further clues to the life of Flotsam and left them just here for him to find. Her own hopes were set ridiculously high and she wanted to see a strand of silver at the end of which would be a clear, round of rock crystal. Time slipped by and the river inched towards them and they barely spoke, two figures stooped and focused on the ground beneath them.

'I've never been to Marseille,' he said, out of the blue.

She stood up, arched her back to release the pain of having been crouching for so long and saw that Harry was still bent over the river and had his back to her.

'What are you suggesting?'

'If you'd consider a research partner on your trip there. Bit like you being here with me today.'

'A professional relationship, you mean.'

'Sure,' he said. 'I thought you might like the company.' He stood up and took a pace towards her, leant forward and kissed her on the lips. It was momentary and he resumed his crouch almost immediately.

'Professional?'

'Indeed. A close working relationship.'

'OK, then.'

They continued searching, the tide slowly pushing them up the slope of the shore. They found nothing new and afterwards sat drinking tea on the river wall, waiting for the water to cover the ground in front of them whilst kicking their boots against the old bricks.

'Are you disappointed?' she said.

'Far from it. Did you know, the Golden Hind was kept in a special dock just over there, after it had finished going around the world?' He pointed along the river in the direction of an ugly block of council houses that had probably been built between the wars. 'It was allowed to fall to pieces. Incredible, isn't it? We might even have walked over bits of it today.'

Beatrice couldn't quite imagine what it would be like going to Marseille with Harry Wesley, but then again, once he'd suggested it, she couldn't now imagine going without him.

'I'll book, then,' she said.

CHAPTER FIFTY-TWO

The same moon hangs in the sky over the bridge, round and complete, lighting the river and the town but taking all the colour from the panorama in front of her. Down below, the fishermen are already at work and the birds, who think it is day, are crying to each other. She had woken during the night and called out, the face in the window as clear as the moon is now, the staring eyes more terrible, fixed and still following her even to this step above the water where she often sits. Her mother had come to her side during the night and she had clung to her warmth and listened to her words. There was nothing to be frightened of, she was reassured, you were surprised, that's all. Her mother says she should visit the woman so that she might understand her better. She lies in her mother's arms until they slept. When she woke it was still dark and her mother was not there, just the shape of her body on the bed. She knows the moon and the woman in the window are omens.

When the sun rises and the mists lift from the river, she walks up through the town towards the old wall to seek her mother's childhood friend, knowing that she is in need of help. A harsh winter cold deadens the air and groups cluster around a fire on the path, smoke drifting feebly in the damp air. She sees the woman in the fields beyond the wall, a haunted and diminished figure and when they meet she can see the suspicion on her face. She holds out her hand and at first the woman is surprised and looks at it unable to decide what to do. And then, tentatively, she places her hand on top, her cold dirty fingers uncertain whether to hold or merely touch. And then the hand begins to shake and she sees the woman is weeping, her tears clearing a line down her grimy cheeks to reveal the true colour of her face. She starts to talk, slowly and painfully at first, then more quickly, the words contained in her for too long and now bursting forth in a rush. She places her other hand on top of the woman's and listens to the story of the short life of her son, born one long, hot summer but who lived to see only another five. She describes him, his pale face and fine hair and makes him so real he might have been standing there beside them. She can feel the woman's pain as she tells of his brief life and then his sudden death, struck by a horse during the panic caused by another attack. She found him, she says simply, apparently untouched, perfect except for just a trickle of blood from his nose. He was a person, she pleads and he'd been taken and she weeps again in front of her and the noise of her sobs carry across the field and up towards the fading moon. Her shoulders are hunched and her head bowed. He is buried close to the river and she visits the grave every day and now she leads her to the place to stand above his grave, the river just visible through the trees. She looks at the old woman and feels that unfairness hangs between them, one child taken, another spared and understands insitinctively that her broken heart has produced a mix of sorrow and hate. The eyes that had woken her now look at her again and the coldness has returned. By the time they leave the grave the river has risen so high the water is seeping into the soil, bleeding into what lies beneath.

CHAPTER FIFTY-THREE

That Beatrice sat alone in the train pulling out of St Pancras, looking down at the old parish church as instructed, and that she was heading for Paris en route for Freiburg in Germany and not Marseille in France, was the result of a conversation that took place with Harry Wesley over supper after their trip to the river. He suggested they choose a place that neither had been to before and although he didn't explain why, he didn't have to and she agreed without question. So they found themselves sitting in a faux French interior under a covered shopping mall near London Bridge that, once upon a time in a more dignified era, had been a dock for tea clippers returning from their mammoth trips to south India. This, anyway, was the picture that Harry painted of their surroundings as they ate *entrecôte frites* and drank a carafe of red wine.

He was extremely courteous, as if the quickly stolen kiss on the foreshore was seen as a step too far and should not be misinterpreted. They were professional companions again and their mutual understanding of this made the evening all the more intimate. He worried away at the background for her proposed film, making her recount the various meetings and discoveries of recent weeks. He was properly involved and Beatrice watched him thinking about her replies, weighing the information he received.

'There are gaps,' he declared, clarifying her thoughts as the evening stretched out. 'Here is a five year old boy at the outbreak of war, almost certainly the result of a relationship with a German diplomat who is sent home a year before the invasion of France. It's doubtful that Troumeg can have had a proper memory of his father. But then the boy has to survive the war, a Jew when Jews were being rounded up and deported. When he's nine and Paris is liberated, it looks as though his mother is accused of collaboration. What happens to her then? Many were sent to jail. If so, what about the boy? What does he do?'

'Too many questions, Harry, although I may be able to answer one. I'm fairly certain that she may have been sent to Fresnes jail, just outside Paris.'

'Did she hide him during the war? Did she receive special protection, favoured status in some way?'

'More questions, Dr Wesley.'

'Yes, well, you've got to go to Marseille and talk to Joseph with only half the story. Do you think that's right? Don't you need a little more before you can begin to barter with him, swap what you know for his side of the story.'

'If he's prepared to do that.'

'And I've been thinking, I don't think it's right that I come with you. I think I'd get in the way.'

She knew this was correct the moment he said it and she put her hand on the top of his as her form of agreement, again no explanation necessary.

'I've been thinking that I might want to go to Germany first, to see if I can track down Traugott's family. I've seen his letters. I wonder if hers survived?'

They parted on the north side of London Bridge. They didn't kiss, she noted, pleased because the progress of their negotiations was still not clear and the heads of agreement had still to be finalised. It only struck her later, walking by the towering NatWest building, that she had forgotten to ask him a key question relating to those terms and conditions. Did he currently have a partner, married or otherwise? He didn't give the impression that he had, but then neither did the majority of men when trying to pick her up. She weighed the mobile in her hand, deciding whether to call him but somewhere by Liverpool Street station decided against it, slipping it back into her pocket as she crossed into Spitalfields.

****

The Traugotts were a well established Freiburg family, extensive and well connected, involved in local politics and business, deeply embedded in the community and keen to welcome Beatrice and her research. The patriach of the family, to whom she was routed after several phone calls, was Sebastian's brother's son, now in his sixties and retired. She arranged to meet him the following day, which was why she was now pulling out of St Pancras and watching the old church slip out of view. She could have flown, but she preferred the train and would change in Paris for the connection to Freiburg.

Harry Wesley seemed to move in the quarter of an hour ahead of her, she thought, dipping under the Thames yet again, if not guessing what she was thinking, but making connections just before she did. Instinctively he appreciated her caution in not wanting to repeat the mistakes of previous relationships and he'd pulled back, leaving her space and in this freedom there was a new comfort and what she'd experienced the night before in the restaurant, a closeness without the inevitability of sex.

By the time she'd changed in Paris a new series of thoughts had begun to compete for her attention, if not more important, then more immediate. The ripples of history might now be quite faint as far as Flotsam was concerned, but they were larger with Sebastian Traugott and it occurred to Beatrice that the existence of Joseph as his son might not be known to the family and that she would need to exercise enlightened caution when she arrived in Freiburg. On the phone she had explained that she was a film maker who wanted to know more about Sebastian and his time at the German embassy in Paris, but no more.

The neatness of Freiburg surprised her, even the geographical location, partly encased by the Black Forest, its boundaries precisely trimmed and not spilling ugly suburbs into the countryside. The home of Lothar Traugott was equally ordered, surrounded by an open garden, the lawns running into the pavement, the path winding towards an impressive house on different levels sitting comfortably in its grounds.

'Welcome, Frau Palmenter,' Lothar Traugott announced in perfect English, a beaming man wearing a pale yellow sweater over a white shirt, beige cords and brogues. He led the way into the house and Beatrice had already decided on an approach which would leave Joseph Troumeg's name unspoken until she judged it necessary, or safe, or both. What awaited her made this task easy, at least to begin with.

'There,' Lothar said, pointing to a large chart pinned on the wall of his extensive study. 'The family tree. I update it for every *familientag*, when as many of us as is possible gather here to celebrate.' He walked over and pointed to his own descent through the family tree, the drip of names through the ages. 'We go back until the mid-fifteenth century,' looking at her for approval. 'Not many can say that.'

Her eye had already been tracking along to discover Sebastian's name and she found it on an extension above Lothar's but before she could register it properly, he had moved across her line of vision and was offering her a glass of wine. 'Tell me about your uncle Sebastian,' she said and sat back with her Reisling and waited.

'What is it that you wish to know?'

Although smiling and raising his glass to her in a toast, she could hear the caution in his voice and detected a steeliness behind his soft-coloured exterior.

'I'm interested in his time in Paris, the four years up until he left. Difficult days on so many levels. He was clearly an important man at the embassy.'

'He was indeed. As you say, they were turbulent times that are constantly being scrutinised. What is the particular angle your film is taking?'

'I can understand your caution,' she said, having been through this hoop many times whilst preparing her films. Part of her wanted to come straight to the point, but her earlier apprehension prevailed and her reply, if not the complete truth, was close enough to be going on with. 'I have reason to believe that Sebastian may have had a relationship with a French woman during his days there. I thought this might have been unusual.'

'And what is unusual about a young man having a relationship with a woman?'

'It wasn't any old relationship.'

'Enough to build a film around?'

'If the relationship had any substance,' Beatrice replied, ignoring the scepticism of Lothar's response, 'it might be a useful focus for looking at what was happening in Paris in the thirties.'

'Such as?'

A pale wintry look had settled on Lothar Traugott's face and his drink remained untouched. There was more than one responsibility that now confronted Beatrice. She could not raise Joseph's name, for if his existence as Sebastian's son was unknown, then it would impact on both Lothar's family and on Joseph himself.

'Anti-Semitism,' for example. 'In both the French and the Germans.'

He put his glass down on a sideboard beneath the family

tree. 'Young lady,' he said with a backward nod of the head, 'this is my family and I feel naturally protective of it. In amongst all these people there are the good as well as the bad, as I imagine in all families, and I feel disinclined to open old wounds and to make life more difficult than it need be.'

Beatrice stood up and walked over to the family tree, where she put down her glass alongside Lothar's. She was now able to see that the branch of the tree that contained Sebastian's name had no issue leading from it and so she chose her next words carefully. 'I have some proof that Sebastian's relationship in Paris was with a young Jewish woman.' Again, there was no noticeable reaction from the man. 'And, given the nature of the times, this represented quite a risk for both of them, wouldn't you say?' She picked up her wine and returned to her seat.

Lothar had his back to her when he spoke, looking out on to the neat, well ordered garden of his home. 'What purpose would it serve, to reheat this well trammelled piece of history?'

'Considerable.' She waited until he turned around. 'What if the relationship between this member of your family and this Jewish woman was a loving one? This is not well trammelled territory, surely? Doesn't this offer a different perspective?'

'You have proof of this?'

'I have some proof of this. I have seen Sebastian's letters to this woman. Her name was Odile. Odile Levy, who became Odile Leval.'

'And what became of this Odile?'

'She survived the war, but not without penalty. She was accused of collaboration and, I think, spent some time in prison. She lived, though, until her nineties.' Beatrice was about to describe how the letters had been saved, but held back and waited for Lothar's response.

'You know what happened to Sebastian?'

'I understand he was killed in the Ardennes.' Beatrice was not sure if Lothar Traugott was now persuaded to be on her side, or remained entrenched in the defence of his family's name.

'He's in a cemetery up there, in Belgium. Recogne, it's called. Our war cemeteries aren't quite as dignified as yours. Perhaps that's our penalty, who knows. He's buried with two others. It might be that he knew them, maybe he didn't. Companions, let's say, one way or the other. It's not so long ago, is it?'

She shook her head.

'I was born two years after the war ended and my childhood is one of being told not to remember, only to look ahead. We did not want to address what had taken place but to put it behind us. This was forbidden history. My father, Sebastian's brother, was severe about this. He did not even visit his son's grave until the mid-sixties. Could not bring himself to do it. So sad, but then so understandable, don't you agree?'

It was not a question that he wanted an answer to and he returned to staring at the garden again. 'This is why our family trees are so important. It's an attempt to piece it all together again. This structure doesn't show the wars, just the family, the people.' He stopped and rubbed his forehead.

'This is the history I'm interested in,' Beatrice said. 'The personal history that takes place despite the wars and the great events.'

'Sebastian's things were returned to his father. He could not bear to keep them, this reminder of the way things used to be. He gave them to the Bundesarchiv, the military archive here in Freiburg. You may find what you want there. But I warn you,' he said, once again turning to face her, 'to tread carefully. You are not just dealing with the cold facts of history, but the people who made them and suffered because of them.'

Beatrice felt she was being addressed by a conservative historian in an old fashioned public school and chose to ignore his patronising warning. 'Surely you've seen what your uncle deposited in the archive?'

He gave her another wintry look, bowed and showed her to the door.

Both glasses of wine remained untouched.

CHAPTER FIFTY-FOUR

It is her birthday and she lies across her mother's lap and as she strokes her head is telling her about this very day in the south and the storm that had accompanied her birth. She listens, storing the facts for later telling, to pass on to her own children as the record of her arrival in this world. Her mother's fingers trace the outline of her head and she thinks of the child that had been taken from her mother's friend, the boy she might have been playing with now. Life was not fair, but she knows this by now and her mother has helped her understand the process of loss and recovery. Her mother has made a simple ring as a birthday present, twisted gold with a small garnet mounted also in gold and she wears it as they climb the low rise to the great church on the brow of the hill overlooking the river. It is newly built of stone and timber and the ringed hand holds her mother's as they enter the gloom of the interior. They are here, her mother tells her, to give thanks for her life, to remember the dangers of her birth and to ask for protection for the future. The great walls hold the outside at bay, the accumulated dangers and her mother pulls her towards her and she feels the warmth of her body.

CHAPTER FIFTY-FIVE

It was her birthday and one that Beatrice would never forget. Chance and persistence had given her the present that was now in front of her, another stage of the journey that she could never have predicted and whose destination was still uncertain.

From the fifth floor of the Bundesarchiv-Militärarchivs it was possible to see the dark green forest spreading over the hills like pubic hair, here and there perfectly trimmed to fit around a field or a farmhouse. The building was modern, made of concrete and glass and rose, ghostly white against a dark grey sky. Her surroundings were proof that you could create order out of chaos and give sense to events that at the time seemed random and pointless. In here a war was sanitised and made neat as if somehow its progress had been logical and not forged by chance. Beatrice was hesitating before reading what was on the screen in front of her, on old fashioned microfilm. To the archive, Odile Leval's letter to Sebastian Traugott was no more than social colour and whatever element of love it contained was useful merely to show how people addressed each other during those difficult days. Beatrice knew that she could not treat this document as anything but a letter laden with emotion and even before she began reading, held back by fear of what it might reveal, she pictured Odile alone in Paris as her child played at her feet. What was waiting for her on the impersonal screen was part of a leather wallet of possessions that had been found on Sebastian Traugott's body after his death in 1940. He was lucky, the archivist told her, that anyone should have retrieved the body for many lay undiscovered in the woods to decompose. He allowed her to hold his dog tag, a shiny oval with details of his rank and army number on one side and blood group on the other. She weighed it in her hand and even through her sadness wondered if his son had inherited the same blood.

The impending war had taken Sebastian Traugott away from Odile and the letter she was about to read was postmarked August 1939, just before the invasion of Poland. Did his one time diplomatic status enable him to receive and send letters in a way that might have been denied others? Whatever, the letter she was about to read had to be written with tact, bounded by obvious limitations, for it carried the threat of a hand-grenade liable to explode in both their lives. The letter was not addressed, merely dated and in the comfort of an air-conditioned office Beatrice began reading words that had been written on a summer's day in the strange months before the invasion of France over seventy years earlier.

Dear Sebastian,

Nothing changes, nothing at all. Our project, the one we worked so hard to achieve, continues to flourish without you and I wish you were here to help build what you started. There is talk of war and I cannot believe it has come to this, that we should be divided by our nations. But what are kilometres? Nothing. There is no distance between us.

My neighbour has a child who plays in the park opposite. His

father is away in the army and I think of how sad he must be and I
sympathise with him and his mother. But the child is often smiling
and he is much loved by his mother. He runs and runs and is full of
life and never complains. Everyday I think of you and try to imagine
what you are doing and when we will meet again. Here in the streets
of Paris there is not so much fear but apprehension about what will
happen. These are strange times and I cannot see the future, except
to know that it will always be with you.

I can hear the neighbour's child now. He is calling. I think he is
asking for his father. I'm sure he will return soon.

As you will.

My love, as always.
Odile.

A film would begin with this letter, Beatrice thought, twenty-
five lines in which were contained the events of the last part of
the twentieth century in miniature, the impending war which
would change the world seen through the prism of the forbidden
relationship between two people, a Jew and a German and their
inadmissible child. She continued staring at the letter, conscious
of the hum of the machine that displayed it and the ring of
distant telephones. Beatrice had seen both sides now and knew
that however intractable their situation, there was real love
between Odile and Sebastian, one which continued after their
separation. And in the middle, Joseph Leval, Levy, Traugott now
Troumeg a child forbidden on so many levels that his survival
must have always been in doubt, a pressure that Odile must
have lived with throughout the war. What had happened? How
did the boy and his mother get through those terrible years?
The film maker in Beatrice could see it clearly, a story of abuse
and innocence, ordered and contained in a documentary, the
emotions heightened by music, the confusion of those years
given focus and resonance, just as the state archive around her
had done with the countless documents that lay in the vaults

and drawers all around her. But it seemed to Beatrice that each answer produced a series of further questions, that the search for the exact truth was like catching mercury in your palm and that history was continually slipping through your fingers, elusive and always distant, a carrot on a stick. She thought of Lothar Traugott and the defence of his family, no different in a way from Joseph Troumeg's creation of his own history. Each left out some facts, reinforced others which were neatened and straightened for comprehension and comfort. She could reflect this inevitable conflict in her film, reject the sure judgement that television usually offered and suggest the facts were more ambiguous and open to interpretation.

She felt sure of one thing, though and called Lothar Traugott as soon as she left the building.

'What did you make of the letter?' she asked without preamble. She could picture him deciding how to respond, his well ordered life all around him.

'I saw it as a wartime affair, before the war started, if you see what I mean. Even before the war started, there were tensions and in this heightened state relationships begin which might not, in normal circumstances, have ever started. I'm sure you understand what I am saying?'

'Just a fling?'

'Precisely the word. Perhaps it meant more to her than him.'

And so history was made palatable for Lothar Traugott and the aberration of a relative smoothed over and reshaped to fit into his view of the past and the present. Beatrice realised that even if he was aware that the 'fling' produced a child, which she didn't, then it would have been written out of history.

'I see,' she said. 'Thank you for your help. You've made things much clearer.'

'It has been my pleasure, Frau Palmenter. And will you continue with your film?'

'I'm not certain,' Beatrice said, but this had nothing at all to do with Lothar Traugott.

'History would not choose to record such a small event,' he said with finality. 'Goodbye.'

It was too late to return to London, so Beatrice took the long train ride to Paris to stay at her now familiar hotel just off the canal. Somewhere in the low rolling plains to the east of Paris, where the vines that provide champagne for the world climb the long slopes and tall spires mark the isolated towns, a thought occurred to Beatrice which she felt compelled to share with Harry. It was based on conjecture and the sort of leap of faith that they had found themselves discussing on their very first meeting on the shores of the Thames. As well as facts, there have to be instincts she remembered him saying and as the train thundered past Épernay he had encouraged her thoughts.

'It would make sense,' he had said, and she knew in her mind it did and would explain so much. But would she be able to substantiate her hunch and realise the piece of the jigsaw that would give more logic to her pursuit of Joseph Troumeg? 'It will be a difficult interview,' he had concluded.

'And talking of difficult interviews,' she had said as darkness fell on the rushing train, 'I never did ask you if you had a partner, or were involved with anyone?'

'Do you think I am?'

'To tell you the truth, no, but then that's the impression a lot of men give, especially when they're married. But I asked you the question.'

'No, then.'

'Why the "then"?'

'Would it make a difference if I was?'

She thought about this for a moment, her body swaying with the train. 'Yes and no,' she said. 'I would be disappointed because my instincts would have been wrong and since we're talking about instincts, I'd like them to be right.'

'And you?'

'You keep asking me questions back. And you know the answer to this one. No, and no to the point of wondering if I'd ever have another relationship with a man.'

'And part of you still feels this.'

'It does. Part of me.'

'And what about the other part?'

'It isn't sure.'

'What will convince it?'

'What, indeed, Dr Wesley.'

'I was married, but my wife left me about five years ago. I've been meaning to tell you, but funnily enough your reluctance made me think that it would appear like overplaying my hand. So instead of telling you face to face I'm having to do so on a crackling line with the noise of the train in the background.'

'Why? Why did she leave you?'

'She was having an affair which I found out about.'

'I'm sorry,' Beatrice said, although part of her was relieved.

'Yes, I was. Looking back on it now, I can see that it was inevitable, but that's what hindsight brings.'

'You'll have to tell me more.'

'I was hoping I would. Does it change the way you think?'

'And what way is that?'

'I'm really not sure, but it's quite an important fact to take on board,' he said.

'I suppose it is, but I have yet to absorb it. I need some more details.' This was true, although Beatrice was conscious that the news didn't really change the way she thought about Harry, although she still had to define quite what that was.

'Are you still there?' he said.

'I am. I was thinking, does my past bother you?'

'I don't know much about it.'

It was black outside, no moon and the countryside without sign of habitation. The train continued its headlong dash westwards and she knew at that moment that she would probably tell him everything, that she would swap her background and trade it for his own, a barter that she saw as clear as her own reflection in the window.

'You've gone again.'

'No I'm here, very much here.'

'Good, because I miss you.'

'By the way, it's my birthday.'

'You didn't say. Happy birthday. I wish I could celebrate with you.'

'Me, too.'

'You're almost there. I hope it goes well.'

And with that he was gone but thoughts of Harry Wesley and a child called Joseph Traugott remained with her until the train snaked into Paris and she made the now familiar walk beyond the Gare de l'Est to the canal and finally to her hotel.

CHAPTER FIFTY-SIX

The woman who had lost her son sometimes appears at the ruined house, or she glimpses her among the crowd on the quayside and occasionally she finds her suddenly alongside her by the river, as though she had materialised from the very mud around them. She is a ghostly figure and sometimes the girl feels that if she stretches out to touch her and finds nothing, she would not be surprised. Although she knows that the woman is the same age as her mother, she sees her as much older, the lines on her face appearing to force down the corners of her mouth, her hair dirty and falling limply across her forehead. She remembers her mother's words, though, and speaks kindly to her, but in return the old woman is often silent and after a while she begins to dread seeing her, not knowing quite how to be with her and fearing her company. Occasionally she is followed and she can sense the old woman behind her, making no attempt to conceal herself, watching her with those eyes that continue to wake her at night, begging a question that she cannot answer.

It is late in the day, when the sun has softened the town and the wood of the bridge is warm to touch, and she crosses the river to the market on the south side. She likes to make this short journey, to be, her mother had told her, as she'd been as a child, a free spirit on the waterfront. She enjoys this special inheritance. The land is low and marshy and she watches the traders at a point where the brick columns supporting the railway will one day be built to carry trains that would rumble over and drown out the shouts of future stall holders working through the night to feed the city. Now, on the very spot where the next London Bridge would end and the glass-clad Shard would rise to dwarf the whole landscape, she wanders through the crowd. She sees the old woman in the distance and knows that she is not following her but going about her own business. She watches her pull her old cloak over her shoulders and across her mouth and begin to walk slowly away from the market, through the poorer dwellings which spread out from the bridge. Now she is the follower, unused to the role but compelled by reasons she does not question, curious to discover what the woman is doing. Just beyond, on a small track, she sees her stop. Ahead of the woman, on a triangle of land, open then as it is now, a body is being carried from a cart, loosely covered in dirty sack cloth. She sees the flimsy shroud slip to the floor to reveal the naked body of a young woman, her long hair hanging down from her lifeless head. A rough rectangle of ground has been prepared for her and she covers her mouth as the body is lowered out of sight. She has been told about this place, on the unloved side of the river, where the women were buried, without ceremony, because of what they had done. The woman who had lost her son is rocking to and fro, with her arms clasped around her and it appears that she is crying. Finally, when the earth has been shovelled back in to the ground and the body covered, the woman turns and walks away, passing close by but without seeing her, her head down, in the direction of the bridge. She walks closer to the plot, a rough patch of land, uncared for and isolated and sees that the earth has been broken in several places. She thinks of the women beneath and what had brought them to this lonely spot. Her fierce brown eyes scan the ground which for centuries afterwards will be the final resting place for women whose lives have been reduced to selling their bodies. Somehow she understands not only their pain but the unfairness of a life that ends here, under the thin soil, unloved. A thousand years later, by some strange chance, this forlorn place will become special and strangers will arrive to place flowers on the railings in celebration of the lives of these forgotten women and sing songs in their memory. She understands this too and sits by the river, not far from the improvised graveyard and watches the cold river flow by, as it still does to this day.

CHAPTER FIFTY-SEVEN

History is never perfect, never settled. It is constantly revisited as new facts are discovered and perceptions realigned. This room with its narrow view of the canal had seen the story of Joseph Troumeg develop like wet clay on a potter's wheel, misshapen at first, but gradually gaining form. It would never be complete, because history never is, always waiting to be further explored, a continuing mystery. She had spent barely eight hours in the hotel, but she was checking out again, leaving her bags at reception and calling Marguerite from the café where she almost expected Joseph to be sitting in his usual seat with a spill of croissant flakes over his trousers. Beatrice told her that there had been some exciting developments which she would like to share with her and they arranged to meet at her apartment at eleven. Inside her, Beatrice knew a decision had been made, although it had yet to be accounted for and given substance. She had the conclusion but the reasoning that had brought her there still demanded substantiation, an instinct in search of proof.

There was late warmth this autumn and Beatrice enjoyed the slow walk across to Buttes Chaumont. The more she walked, the surer she became, replaying her conversations with Marguerite Fourcas, mentally stopping and rewinding, going over her statements as she might in a cutting room. Eventually she had isolated several key statements, a second sifting of history, first as delivered by the old woman and now laid bare for re-examination. Marguerite was waiting, the coffee tray neatly prepared and biscuits on a china plate. What Beatrice was about to do would upset this neat order unless, of course, Marguerite refused to speak at all. The autumn sunlight, low in the sky over the park, was spilling into the room through the shuttered window and dancing on the far wall.

'So, what news do you bring me?' Marguerite's voice was bright and expectant and she held her coffee cup in front of her waiting for Beatrice's response before taking her first sip.

'I know who Joseph's father is.'

Without taking her eyes off Beatrice, the older woman raised the cup to her lips.

'I've just come back from Germany where I read perhaps the last letter that Odile wrote to him.'

Again, Marguerite's response was neutral, which was no more than Beatrice expected.

'She had a loving relationship with this man until the end, it appears. His end, that is. He was killed in action in the Ardennes. But I think you know most of this.'

The rectangles of light continued to play on the wall, in amongst the small pictures and curios. Marguerite put down her cup and walked over to the window and adjusted the blind.

'I think you knew Odile before the war,' Beatrice said quietly, pausing to drink her coffee and watch Marguerite return to her seat and settle herself. 'And you knew full well who Odile was seeing, didn't you? There was no American journalist, was there?'

Marguerite took another sip of coffee, wiping her mouth with one of the white linen napkins she had laid carefully on the tray. When she looked up at Beatrice it wasn't to speak but as a cue for Beatrice to continue.

'It is difficult to open old wounds and what I have to say next...' Beatrice hesitated, feeling her way forward '...will be painful. I am not certain when your son died, whether it was before or after Joseph was born. In a way, though, it makes no difference. I'm sorry about his death, but more sorry about its consequences.'

Marguerite held up her hand and Beatrice stopped and watched as she unclipped her handbag to take out a handkerchief which she rested against her nose. 'It was after. Go on.'

'You knew that Odile was seeing Sebastian Traugott, who worked at the German embassy and when Joseph was born I think you helped Odile. I think you admired her, am I right?'

The old woman, still holding the handkerchief to her face, nodded.

'But then came the loss of your child and the invasion. What happened next is so easy to understand, the atrocities committed by the Germans and yet, downstairs, the product of a liaison between a French Jew and a German. The unfairness was too great for you to take.'

Marguerite had dropped her head and now both hands held the handkerchief to her mouth. 'Whether you betrayed Odile directly, or accidentally, I don't know but the results were the same. She was one of the women you so clearly described to me, shorn and humiliated. You saw it happen, you made it happen. I have seen a picture of Odile, shaved and the object of derision.' Beatrice stood and walked over to the woman whose shoulders were shaking, even though she was making no sound. She knelt down and put her arm around the crying woman who now seemed to have diminished in front of her and become her age. 'I'm sorry Marguerite.' She watched the old woman's tears drip on to her skirt, the stain spreading across her thighs. 'What happened next, I don't know, but I'm going to guess. Odile went to jail, Fresnes perhaps, and you looked after Joseph, a strange period of joy for you. Joseph was nine, old enough to know what was taking place. Odile should never have been imprisoned but her affair with a German embassy official condemned her to an even longer stay.

By the time she came out, Joseph was older and, I don't know, when confronted with the situation found it too much.'

'He fled. Fled. So young.' She issued these statements between sobs, hardly able to speak. 'He despised us both. It is all my fault. Odile never forgave me and Joseph never forgave her. My fault. My fault.'

Beatrice found herself crying, in sympathy, in anger, it was impossible to separate the two emotions. Does history record emotion, the impossible dilemmas faced by women like Marguerite, she asked feeling the bony shoulders of the old woman? They remained silent for several minutes before Marguerite balled up the handkerchief and rose awkwardly to her feet. She walked slowly to the dresser and from a cardboard folder in one of the drawers extracted a photograph, which she handed to Beatrice. It showed a young boy in shorts standing between Odile and Marguerite. They were all smiling and in her arms Marguerite was holding a baby in a white shawl.

'The war had yet to begin. This was the last moment of happiness in my life. I have had a long time to regret what I did. I have wasted half a century. Make your film. I cannot suffer any more.'

Beatrice let herself out of the apartment, still feeling the tears in her eyes and the weight on her chest of contained emotion. In some ways she wanted to shout at Marguerite and condemn her for destroying the relationship between a mother and son, but what good would it do? She had lost her own son and her judgement had been impaired. Why had the two women carried on living so close together? Was it their terrible shared history that made them inseparable? Marguerite was to die soon and with her would have gone the truth of what had happened. Would it ever have been discovered? Beatrice now carried this vital piece of personal history and she knew that it was her job to hand it on, but not in the way she had first expected.

'It's me.'

'You sound exhausted. It was true, wasn't it?'

She was lying on her bed, back in the hotel, her body empty and bruised, having decided to stay another night after all and glad to be hearing Harry's voice for she knew that he would understand the impact of what she had just been through with Marguerite.

'Yes, it's so sad and in some ways it is hard to blame her. In some ways she can be excused for what she did.' She had told Harry the day before about her feeling that Marguerite might have known Odile longer than she admitted and that, following the loss of her son, may have become so jealous as to betray her friend.

'Do you think Joseph knows?'

'I'm sure he does. He's been watching me from the start, almost amused at my vague guessings at his past. I'm glad I can talk to you about this.'

'I'm glad I can help. It must have taken it out of you this morning.'

Beatrice quickly flipped back through her filing cabinet of relationships remembering the times she had finished a tough day on location or in the edit suite and had come home wearied to receive scant regard for her work. Why had she allowed this to happen? She screwed up her tired eyes and shook her head trying to loosen the reasons for punishing herself.

'Are you ok?'

'I don't know.'

'Can I come and see you? Now?'

Beatrice laughed. 'Yes, please. I'll tell you what, come to Marseille. I'm going to have to see Joseph now and I'll go there in the morning. Can you join me? I'll try and see Joseph around midday. Can you get down for the afternoon?'

'I could get down for the crack of dawn, if you liked.'

She laughed again. 'There's a bar called La Bouillabaisse just at the end of the old port. I'll see you there at four. And thank you.'

'For what?'

'Dropping everything for me.'

'No, no, because of you I've picked everything up. You'll see.'

She thought she did see, although this equation was yet to finally balance itself, just as the journey around Joseph Troumeg still had to be completed. For the first time in as long as she could remember, she felt unburdened, as though she had removed the tension from her body by shaking it down her arms, as a dog might. She opened her laptop and wrote about unpeeling the layers around Joseph Troumeg, finishing by photographing and storing the picture of him between Odile and Marguerite. Later, pleased with herself, armed with a book, she took herself to Jean-Paul's restaurant where, with unfailing timing, he appeared by her side as she was finishing her dessert, a delicious miniature *tarte aux pommes* with lavender infused ice-cream.

'A triumph,' she told him, remembering Joseph's words.

'You look different,' he told her. 'Still beautiful, but different.'

'Perhaps I am,' she said and wondered if some base male instinct in the chef had been alerted to the presence of a rival.

'You've met someone?' he said, proving the point.

'Is that what you think?' Jean-Paul's myopic logic would not allow that she could possibly resist him if she had been free and single.

'Perhaps,' she said.

'Well, let me know if it doesn't work out.' He rose from his knees without a backward glance and Beatrice couldn't help but think of the bouncing hind quarters of a defeated stag retreating into the woods. She took coffee and cognac but it wasn't just the alcohol that had finally loosened her shoulders so that they had now sunk into their normal position on her body, but her awareness that two decisions had been made even if they had yet to be conveyed. It still left one waiting for attention, but she knew that this would fall into place once she had completed the other two.

That night she dreamed of a little girl running free, her blonde hair bouncing in the sunlight and it wasn't until the following morning, when she was leaving the hotel to head for the station yet again, that she realised it was the figure that she had seen on the opposite side of the Thames in what seemed a lifetime ago.

CHAPTER FIFTY-EIGHT

The river flows in front of her and she knows that it links her past with the future and will never change. She is part of this river which had taken away her grandfather and guided her to and from distant lands. The tide is high and it tugs at the branches of the trees that dip into the clear water. It laps almost to the top of the quays and there is barely clearance for the small boats to shoot under the bridge. The traps are out of sight, beneath the water, waiting to catch the unwary fish. On the opposite bank, where she can see the church at the top of the hill, smoke from the surrounding homes rises in straight lines into the windless air. She sits on a tree stump where the prison would one day be built and the soft day reminds her of the south, except the smells here are of wood smoke and marsh and not the sweet mix from the hills. Would she go there ever again? On the other side of the bridge there are two vessels recently arrived from those shores and earlier she had recognised the language, to the surprise of the men on the quay. The world is open to her and she feels excited and for a brief moment thinks that she catches again the drift of those distant smells, the herbs and grasses that she would squeeze in her hands to release their special aromas. She feels complete and the old woman who wears the misery of her life on her face makes her happiness even more real. She thinks she sees her on the bridge, hunching her cloak around her, head still bent and not wishing to meet the eyes of others, but she is gone before she can be sure. From the tree to her side, she catches the blue flash of a bird diving into the water and sees it emerge with a fish.

She is lucky. She stands and begins to run back to the bridge, slowly at first but then more quickly so that she creates her own wind and her hair follows in strands. She weaves between the people on the bridge and then up the hill, past where the church of St Clement's would be built, upwards, enjoying the sensation of climbing without pause, feeling she could run forever, on and on into the future. She stops seeing what is around her and can hear only the sounds of her progress, the beat of her heart, the deep breaths she is taking, the rush of the air. She raises her arms to salute the moment and when she stops her arms are still outstretched, like the cross that she had seen outside the great church on the hill above the river.

CHAPTER FIFTY-NINE

Although it was the beginning of November, summer had yet to leave Marseille and Beatrice walked out of the station into strong sunshine and had to shield her eyes. Traffic was unusually heavy around the old port, with drivers hooting and shouting at each other. She began walking up the hill into the old town, passing one or two streets cordoned off with police tape, with cars jammed in the narrow streets. In the distance she saw several figures wearing white protective overalls and face masks and she assumed that a crime of some sort had taken place. She had decided to try Joseph's place before checking into her hotel and it was only as she was once again swallowed into the dark, narrow alleys and stairways of the old town that she considered the possibility that the restaurateur might not be there. She stood under the cherub and looked up to his puffed cheeks and couldn't help but smile at the process of events that had led her to this door once more.

'Ah, it's Flotsam,' he said the moment he opened the door, once again giving the impression that she was the first and only guest arriving for a lunch party he had specially organised.

'You've washed up here again,' he added, 'and I've no need to ask why I have the pleasure of your company on this beautiful autumn day. Please, come in.'

She was still smiling as she followed him into the familiar kitchen, where a camera on a tall tripod loomed over a plate of food on the counter.

'You've arrived just in time to help me. I wonder if you would mind pouring, gently mind you, the contents of that small jug just to the side of the fruit.' He pointed with his finger to the exact spot on the dark green plate he wanted it to take place. 'No, don't stand that side, you'll block the light. Yes, that's it. Now wait.' He climbed on to a silver camera case and looked through the lens. 'OK, my dear.' She poured and she heard the shutter click several times in rapid succession before he shouted 'Perfect. It's for my next book, "Winter in Provence". Good title, don't you think? I'm glad you're amused.'

'And I'm glad I was so useful,' she said. 'Is this the strawberry and pink peppercorn dish you made for me last time I was here?'

'It is and it was vital that I caught the cream before it dissolved into the syrup. And, thanks to you, I did. Look.' He turned the screen on the camera so that she could see the luscious close-up of two strawberries, several pink peppercorns and a neat boundary line where the white of the cream and red of the strawberry juice and reduced lime juice had met but not yet fused.

'Now, coffee, or a glass of wine? You're looking great, I must say. Let's go for the wine.' He flicked back through the images in the camera's memory and showed her a glass of white wine through which he had shot the corner of a fish and the edge of some ratatouille, so that it looked almost like an abstract painting. He opened the fridge door and handed her the glass. 'Here's one I made earlier,' he laughed. He took the bottle and poured another glass and then switched it with the one he'd given her. 'Might be tainted and we can't have that for Flotsam.

Although more people than ever come down here in winter,' he continued happily, 'it's still pretty empty and a real delight. Hence "Winter in Provence". Tourist Board loves it, let me tell you. I've had lots of help from them.'

Beatrice continued to smile, amused that he had immediately swept her back into his life without a hint of being put out.

'Come, tell me why you look so radiant. Is it because you want to direct the television series to go with the book? Wouldn't that be fun?'

He was irrepressible and Beatrice realised that she had a choice, just as she had in Germany. She could leave matters like this, with Joseph Troumeg living life in the present, the past just a forgotten toy left at the back of dusty cupboard, or she could upset this careful construction.

'But you've got things to tell me, I detect. Of course you have, that's why you're here.'

'I'm not going to make the film,' she said.

'My goodness, was my past *that* boring?'

She laughed. 'Tedious.'

'Well, you surprise me Flotsam. I thought you had your teeth into me good and proper. Did you discover something hideous that you don't want to tell me?'

So, here is the fork, Beatrice thought. She could take one route and lie and say that she didn't think there was enough to make an interesting film, or she could tell him the truth. Once again, he was there before her and pointed her in the right direction.

'You'll have to try me, Flotsam. Tell me what you discovered and I'll let you know if you're right.'

'What if there's stuff you don't like?'

'I'm a big boy, Flotsam,' he said, again laughing and refilling her glass and waited. 'What intense brown eyes you have,' he said, 'especially when you concentrate. C'mon.'

'We should be recording this,' she said and raised her glass to his. She felt as though she was about to direct a live studio with the clock counting down the seconds to the moment they would be live. She launched straight in.

'Your mother, Odile Levy, Leval, had a relationship with Sebastian Traugott, a high ranking member of the German embassy in Paris. It started in the winter of thirty-four, thirty-five.' She looked at him, but his face didn't move. 'You were born sometime after, in November thirty-five. Difficult days, but not as hard as the ones that would come. Sebastian was sent back to Germany two years later and your mother was left alone with you. She had a friend, Marguerite Fourcas, who lived in the same block, who helped her through those days and during the occupation.' Still no response and she hesitated before offering the next piece of information. 'Your father was killed in the Ardennes in 1940.' Joseph nodded, just one tiny dip of his head and she continued. 'He's buried in a German military cemetery near a place called Recogne, in Belgium. His nephew told me this. I went to see him in Germany.' She raised her eyes to his. 'Neither he, nor his family, knows about you.' Again, the single nod. Did he know this already, she wondered?

'Were you aware that Marguerite had lost a son, a baby, sometime in the thirties?' Again, no response. 'It's important to remember this in relation to what happened next. I think she became very close to you, a replacement son, if you like, and her judgement became distorted. You were the product of a relationship with a German and I don't think Marguerite could forgive Odile for this, particularly as the war went on and the atrocities increased. I think she saw a way of keeping you for herself and in the immediate aftermath of the war, she betrayed her friend, directly or indirectly, I'm not sure.' She paused. 'Do you want me to go on?' A further nod gave her permission, but Beatrice hesitated, not wanting to wound the man whose exuberant high spirits she always found so rewarding. She realised, though, that there was no correct order or gentle way of presenting this information.

'Your mother was revealed as a collaborator. She had her

head shaved, in public and I believe was sent to prison as a result. I have a picture of her at that time, but perhaps you don't want to see it.' The nod came quickly this time and again Beatrice felt that this information was not new to him.

She pulled her laptop out of her bag and turned it on. She found the photograph of the shaven but defiant Odile, looking out beyond the crowd that had gathered to taunt her, and moved the screen towards him. She watched his face as he looked at his mother as no son should ever have to, but again he showed no emotion.

'I was there,' he said. 'She was looking for me, hoping, praying, I think, that I wasn't there. But I was. I was indeed.' He carried on looking at the photograph, matching his memory with the image in front of him. She was certain now that most of what she'd said so far and shown him had come as no real surprise. As such, it might give logic to the fact that Joseph did not see his mother for more than half a century, but she wondered if what she would show him next might explode this reasoning.

'I want to show you a letter, two letters, in fact,' and as she said this she could not help but feel an intruder into the intimacies of his family. 'As I said, I've just come back from Germany, where I read this one in the state archive.' She slid the screen around again and this time Troumeg put on his glasses and slid them down his nose to read. If he was surprised, he didn't show it and looked up at Beatrice as a signal for her to continue.

'Odile Levy, Leval, was writing to your father Sebastian about you. It is a letter full of love, as were the ones he wrote her.' She leaned across the computer and brought up one of Sebastian's letters and left him to read. She watched his eyes move along the lines but again his face betrayed little emotion. 'This was a proper relationship and not a wartime fling, or pre-wartime fling, as Lothar Traugott, the nephew would have it. They loved each other. Clearly.' She saw him tighten his mouth, the first physical reaction to the information she was giving. He pushed the screen back to her and stood up and moved to the end of the room, looking out through the conservatory to the garden. She saw him lean against the work surface, spread his fingers on the wooden surface and lower his head.

'So, she loved my father. You're sure?'

Beatrice waited. 'I'm sure.' There was another long silence.

'By the time she came out of Fresnes prison, I never wanted to see her again. Did you know that, Flotsam?'

'I imagined it, Joseph, yes.'

'And was I wrong?'

This was the sort of question that Beatrice thought she would never hear from Joseph Troumeg, always so sure of himself and not given to this sort of introspection. She remained silent and eventually he turned to face her.

'I was, wasn't I?'

'I think she was protecting you, not wanting to humiliate you any more. She was in an impossible position.'

'I was almost sixteen when she came out of jail. I found out from the papers. I fled, did Marguerite tell you that? I came down here and this is where I have escaped to ever since. Poor *maman*.'

'The more famous you became, the more difficult it was for her to contact you. In a strange way, she colluded with your fantasy about her. It was a way of disguising the past.' He came over and sat by the computer and looked again at the two letters, reading them slowly, scrolling up and down, confirming the information that had changed his perception of the past. His eyes began to glisten. This is a man, thought Beatrice, who had learned very early in life to contain himself, to create his own world when the one he was living was falling apart around him.

'My dear, you've almost made me cry. I haven't done that for years, except when I listen to opera.'

'That's why I don't want to make the film,' she said. 'I don't think I have the right.'

'The right to upset me?'

'Yes, and the right to upset the past you have created for yourself and which has served you well. To change that would be simply selfish of me.'

He absorbed what she said before replying, not in his usual jocular tone, but in a slow and measure way. 'Flotsam, I knew there was something special about you from the moment we met. It must be those eyes. Where do they come from, I wonder?'

He made her a late lunch, his favourite he said, French beans sautéed in garlic with a slice of foie gras and a glass of sweet wine.

'Did you see all the fuss outside when you arrived?' he asked. 'They found some bodies on the hill, when they were digging the foundations for a new building. Plague victims they told me in the café this morning, hence all the protective gear. They say that some jewellery was found as well, although they don't know why. The past, a mystery as you know only too well.'

CHAPTER SIXTY

She tells her mother about the old woman and the graveyard, describing the burial and how it had made her sad and then, afterwards, happy in contrast, how she had run back home, her feet not touching the ground. She sees her mother smile, knowing that she doesn't have to explain the way her old friend earns her money. She looks at her mother who stretches out her hand to touch her cheek and agree that life can be very cruel and that her old friend deserved better. Her mother takes her hand and leads her to the table where on a piece of wood she draws the outline of a girl with wings on her feet, who seems to float over the ground. Her mother tells her that she will make a silver broach with this figure on it and she should give it to her old friend as a present to lift her spirits.

She works with her mother, familiar now with many of the techniques she has been told about, excited at the process of creating an object of beauty from misshapen lumps, absorbed by the processes, knowing without question that one day she, too, will stand in the place of her mother. When it comes to the figure, the girl's face is turned away, hidden by her trailing hair, her light clothing billowing to emphasise her progress, her feet sprouting wings whose delicate feathers are unfurled as they transport the apparently weightless girl. She is on a path that snakes into the future towards which she is running without fear, a timeless figure. Or perhaps it wasn't a path, but the river, flowing in and out forever.

She continues to see the old woman, often on the bridge crossing to the other side, sometimes turning to find her watching from a corner or trailing after her in the distance and she puzzles over how or where she will present her with the brooch now approaching completion. Somehow she knows that it will be difficult for the woman, that it will confuse her and that she will search for the true meaning of the present and think, for a moment at least, that she is being mocked.

The sad faced woman was still living up by the wall, against its southern flank so that this sunny morning she sees her resting in the warmth, her eyes shut and her face tilted upwards. It is possible to see the face of the girl she had been once upon a time, the distant trace of beauty. She waits until she opens her eyes, the eyes that had so frightened her and when they see her the hunger appears in them again. She walks forward, feeling the sun on her back and bows before handing over the package wrapped in golden cloth. As she had guessed, the woman's face is a mix of query and suspicion and she hesitates before opening the gold bundle. The brooch lies in the palm of her hand and the woman continues to be wary, not touching the elaborate round of silver but continues to examine it, looking for clues as to why it should have been given to her this bright autumn day. She could find no reason and looks up, her eyes still questioning, still wanting more than she could deliver. This act of affection was in the process of being misunderstood, as she had feared it would be, a gesture beyond comprehension. The sad woman runs her fingers over the figure and turns her head to stare into the distance, perhaps remembering her childhood along the foreshore or, perhaps, closer and more painful, the brief youth of her lost child. Her fingers close over the silver broach and her head drops to her chest. She kneels before her and puts her hand over the woman's and feels the coldness that not even the sun can penetrate.

When she walks away, she knows the eyes of the woman are still on her and that they posed the same question for which there was no answer.

CHAPTER SIXTY-ONE

He was late.

She waited at La Bouillabaisse and watched Marseille go about its business, the old port perfect in the mid-afternoon sun. She had confirmed that the train was on time and even in their brief relationship she thought his lateness rather out of character. When, half an hour later, she saw him walking quickly down the hill towards her, he was busy on his mobile and distracted enough to almost collide with a couple of pedestrians. She thought he was going to walk past the café until at the last minute he looked up, registered its name and, finally, saw her sitting there.

'You must have laid this on for me,' he said, leaning forward to kiss her on the cheek. In many ways she had, but sensed this was not what he was talking about.

'The bloggers and Tweeters have been going mad about it. What a wonderful coincidence.'

She was still none the wiser. He leaned over and kissed her again, this time on the lips.

'What they've found on the hill, up there,' he said, pointing towards the old town. 'The plague pit. Amazing stuff.' He fiddled around with his phone and handed it to her. 'Just look at that.'

She had to shade the screen from the sun and eventually found a shadow which allowed her to see the image which was so exciting him. He had come round behind her and was pointing at the photograph of a ring held by dirty finger tips. It was hard to make out the details, but it appeared to be a dark stone set in a square mount on what might have been gold.

'Beautiful.' He looked at the ring and then across at her.

'It is,' she said and she saw him shake his head and smile.

'The curious thing is,' he said, once again bending his body towards her, 'that the ring is similar to one in the British Museum, which we saw on our visit. That was unearthed in London. It would be astonishing if it was made by the same person and yet discovered so far away. Can you imagine?' He put his hand on hers and his enthusiasm coursed through his fingers and into hers and she felt it rise through her body. 'Its about a thousand years old and already helps us date the body on top of which it was found.'

He was animated and she listened as he explained about the small circle of people who always came together when this sort of discovery took place, now linked electronically so that within moments they were able to share their knowledge, a group beyond boundaries, he said, linked by pre-history.

'Outbreaks of plague happened down here, although the big one didn't arrive until about a hundred years later. They had to live with death like we don't. The average life span then was about thirty-five years and I would be surprised if any of the skeletons that are up there now are older than that.'

The discovery of the plague pit was a blessing, she realised later, taking any awkwardness away from this odd but inevitable meeting and allowing them to be involved in something outside themselves.

'Who knows,' said Beatrice, 'they might even be connected to Flotsam? And that reminds me, Joseph has taken to calling me that all the time. Said that he was not surprised to see me wash up here again. In fact, every time I see him he gives me the impression that he's been expecting me.'

'I'm sorry, Beattie, I should have asked you straight away how it went. I was just so excited with the folks on the hill.'

She thought of several things to say, to do with dead bodies being more interesting than live ones, but stopped herself. 'I think Joseph knew a lot of the stuff I was telling him, although I'm sure he didn't know about Marguerite's betrayal. In one way, I'm glad I was able to show him the letters his parents wrote to each other, but I think it hit him when he realised that his separation from his mother need not have happened. He was quite philosophical about this, but then he long ago learnt to be self sufficient and set the boundaries of his own world.'

'How clever of you to piece all this together,' Dr Harry Wesley said and she accepted the statement because of the way it was said. She considered his hand on hers, the comfort of this single gesture. 'Why does what you've just said mean so much to me, do you think?'

'Do you want the long answer, or the short one?'

'I imagine I might get both.'

'The longer version might take a few years.'

How had this man crept up on her, she wondered, to become so close, intimate almost, even though they had never slept together and she could number their meetings on the fingers of one hand? And then she worried that sex would spoil it, render useless this long and comfortable preamble. His mobile chirruped again and when he clicked on the message, he stood up and walked further into the shade of the terrace before returning to thrust the phone triumphantly back into her hands.

'Look, look. This is the ring at the British Museum. They've just sent it to me from their records. It's almost identical. It must have been made by the same person. Can we walk up there?'

He had half risen before she replied. Romantic weekends

on the south coast of France don't often begin with a visit to a plague pit, Beatrice thought as he took her hand and pulled her up the slope towards the old town, the site pinpointed by GPS on his phone. 'Joseph lives up here,' she said, nodding towards the dark steps leading off to one side.

'Will you take me to meet him?'

'Of course,' she said, 'I'm sure he's expecting you already.'

The brow of the hill was disguised by a rash of buildings of various heights and the sea, somewhere down to their left, was entirely obscured. The site, bounded by black and yellow tape, looked no different from any other building site, but for the figures in white overalls and masks on hands and knees at the base of a neat rectangle that had been cut out of the dry earth. One of the group, looking up, saw Harry and raised her arms in greeting. Clearly Dr Harold Wesley had been expected. Before the figure had time to clamber out of the pit, Beatrice whispered in his ear. 'And I thought you were here to see me.' Seconds later the woman in white was embracing Harry, removing her mask as she did.

'Beatrice, let me introduce Dr Miriam Larose, who's in charge of the dig here.'

She shook hands with a pretty dark haired woman, probably a few years younger than her, who immediately turned back to Harry to look at the photograph on his mobile sent from the British Museum.

Down below Beatrice saw the skeleton emerging from the earth, the bones of the fingers placed across the swell of the rib cage. The skull looked upwards to the blue sky, revealed for the first time in a thousand years, seemingly at peace. Beatrice stared at the figure and then at Harry and saw, in that very instant, a whole world open up to her, the curtain on a stage rising to reveal an unexpected and beautiful set. She was registering Harry Wesley for the first time. It had nothing to do with jealousy, quite the opposite, but the thrill of recognising that somehow she had been handed the key to a puzzle that she had been seeking to answer for years but had given up hope of ever finding. Until this moment, Harry Wesley had been someone she had looked at but not seen, part of her peripheral vision. He had ghosted through her preconceptions of how these things worked until he was suddenly there, by her side. She acknowledged the wave of pleasure and surprise that lapped through her and she put her hand on his arm, a gesture which caused him to turn and face her. She saw, when she looked into his eyes, that he instantly knew that something had changed, that they had stepped towards each other and moved on to a different level. She could not unpick the collision of events that had brought her to this point but she knew she had crossed a divide and high on a hill in Marseille, above the remains of an ancient body, she felt alive in a way she knew she hadn't before.

The day before she had been going to book a hotel in Marseille but had stopped herself, unable to decide whether to reserve one room or two, but when Harry took her arm and guided her away from the site the question had already been answered.

'There's a hotel on the Corniche which I've read about,' she said and he watched as she called and booked a double room. They didn't speak as the cab took them around to the other side of the city, climbing above the old port beneath the outstretched arms of the Virgin Mary. There was an easiness between them, a complete lack of tension and ahead they watched the blue of the sea intensify. The same blinding colour filled the window of their room and they stood on the balcony anticipating the logical conclusion of their extended and unusual courtship. When it happened it was much more than she had expected, their sex the result of what had gone before rather than a physical act waiting afterwards for justification. When she stood before him naked and felt him outline the shape of her body with his fingers, she had the sensation of being observed for the very first time. What followed next, though, seemed like the conclusion of a much longer process and one that put her in touch with a part of her that was ancient and undiscovered and which had remained hidden for a very long time.

Afterwards she lay like the woman in the excavation, her hands crossed over her chest, naked on the bed. 'Did that just happen?' she asked the ceiling.

'I doubt if history will record that it did,' he said.

'That depends, of course.'

'On what?'

'Well, you didn't ask if I was on the pill.'

He rolled over to face her but she continued to look straight above. 'Do you mind?'

'No.'

'And *are* you?'

'No. Do *you* mind?'

'No.'

They bathed together and then he lay on the bed as she wandered around between the bedroom and the bathroom preparing to go out.

'I have brought a dress in honour of the occasion,' she said, holding up a crumpled ball which she opened out and slipped over her head before pulling on her jeans. She went into the bathroom and regarded herself in the mirror. The brown eyes that stared back were undoubtedly hers but what they saw was quite new, quite different. She called through to him that they would be eating at Joseph's old restaurant and that they would stop by and see if he was at home first. He came up behind and joined her face in the mirror. They didn't have to say anything.

It was as Beatrice had predicted. Joseph opened the door and she saw him take in the presence of Harry.

'Ah, perfect,' he said. 'You're the reason she's been looking so ravishing. Come in, come in, I've just made a *pissaladier*. I must have known you were coming.'

'This is Harry Wesley,' she said and he ushered them in.

'Well, he's a very lucky man,' he said without looking

around. 'You've kept him very quiet, Flotsam.'

'Even from me,' she said and she heard him laugh.

'Took you by surprise, did he? What do you make of her, Harry?' He was now opening a bottle of wine.

'She's the best thing that's ever happened to me,' he said.

'So, Flotsam's finally come to rest are we saying?' handing him a glass of pink wine. 'How's she's gone this long, I really don't know.'

'I feel the same way.'

'Will you come to dinner with us, Joseph, at your old place?' Beatrice said.

'And come between you two? Is that wise?'

'It is,' said Harry.

Later, in the restaurant, Beatrice watched as Joseph unfurled for Harry the now familiar stories of his life and she saw them laugh, the restaurateur in his pomp.

'This young woman,' he said, 'has rewritten a lot of the history you've just heard. Do you think she'll do the same to you?'

'She already has,' Harry said.

'So, if you're not going to make a film about me, what are you going to do instead?' Joseph said, turning to Beatrice.

'I have an idea,' she said, 'but it's still forming. But can I ask you something first? Were you serious about wanting me to direct "Winter in Provence"?'

'My dear, nothing would give me greater pleasure. But I wouldn't have to talk about my childhood, would I?'

'Only your version.' She sensed Harry looking at her.

'But what makes you think,' Joseph said, 'that you can persuade your controller chappie, Graham Roth, to commission it?'

'Oh, he will. It's part of a trade, you see.'

'My dear, how mysterious you are. Are you going to tell us what this trade is?'

Beatrice turned to Harry. 'Not yet. I need to talk about it

with my partner first, although I think he may already know.'

'Never mind, I'll send you my proposal for "Winter in Provence" anyway. I'm sure you'll be able to improve it.'

They parted at the edge of the old port on stones worn smooth by the passage of history, the old man winding his way towards his home to leave them to walk along the quayside in search of a cab.

'Did you know that it would turn out like this?' she asked him.

'Do you know, I think I did. It was just a question of getting your attention.'

'Well, you have.'

CHAPTER SIXTY-TWO

The girl walks back into the sun, taking the right fork at the end of the path that will one day become Bishopsgate, where the roads still split in exactly the same way today, downwards towards the river. Along the way, near the point where, three hundred years later, Leadenhall Market would begin, she overhears that another attack from the Danes is close, so she changes direction to what, in time, will become Lombard Street. Beneath the fields to the north, where sheep now grazed, later called Moorgate, scores of passengers would one day be killed in a Tube accident. At the very spot where she stands on this golden day, a bomb will fall during the Second World War and kill an ambulance driver and two nurses. Just behind her, a century earlier, a footpad would murder a young woman for a halfpenny.

The girl passes by the ditches being dug to repel the invader and sees the recently unearthed golden dagger, lost in a fight by the previous invader. Further along, closer to her home, the flames from the great fire would, half a millennium later, be at their fiercest. She begins to run, her legs carrying her faster and faster, her arms outstretched so that soon she cannot feel the path underneath her. She is free, alive, the link between the past and the present and there is in her, on this bright autumn day, the feeling of eternity, that what she is, at this very moment, would last forever. She was complete and along this path, with her home just in front, she feels she can go on forever.

Wrapped in her own happiness, she does not see the woman waiting in the shadows of the old wall, her eyes narrow and cold and hidden. When she runs alongside the Walbrook, down the slope of the hill, her feet light on the banks, she does not see the woman shuffling after her, the one figure weighed down by life and poisoned by its disappointments, the other unburdened and seemingly weightless.

She reaches the edge of the water, where the tributary flows into the larger river and sees the mud it brought curl into a tick in the darker waters, instantly to be washed away. She does not feel the blow, aware but briefly of the huge darkness which follows. Like her grandfather before, she never knows this moment and her body is lifeless before it drops into the water, pulled into its cold embrace where it will be washed in and out with the tides, each motion reducing it further until only the bones remain.

The river is still alive, still breathes in and out and still, when it chooses, reveals its secrets, offering clues to the past, of lives come and gone.

CHAPTER SIXTY-THREE

The train pulled out of Gare St-Charles and for the third time in two weeks she was speeding through the portal of bleached rocks that protect the northern reaches of the city. Only now it was different, of course and Beatrice considered the figure of Dr Harold Wesley sitting opposite, tapping away at his computer in response to the latest information about the excavation in Marseille.

'You're going to ask me something, I can tell,' he said without looking up from his screen.

He was right and it was tiny details like this, his instinctive awareness of her, that she realised had been there from the start, although she had been painfully slow in recognising it. Last night, after they had left Joseph, when they lay in bed and his hand rested on her stomach, he had said something which remained with her now, so obvious but, as is the case with many truths, unseen until they are spoken.

'I've noticed,' he said, after she'd admitted to a series of unsuccessful relationships, 'that you expect the worst, as if you've decided beforehand that things will go wrong. Perhaps you chose men who merely confirmed your expectations. If what you tell me about your mother is true, you're used to being criticised, or ignored and so, despite your success, this is what you feel about yourself.'

She had lain awake thinking about this and could see that it was true and that she had found herself with men who did just that, confirmed the criticism she expected, apparently content that they showed no interest in her beyond the sexual. 'Is that why I ignored you to begin with?'

'Probably. Either that, or you didn't fancy me.'

'I couldn't see you. I wasn't looking.'

'That's what I'd hoped.'

The train sped on through the morning and he continued to tap away at his keys.

'I was wondering what might have happened to Flotsam,' she said.

'We can't really tell. She may have fallen, or been bashed from behind by a blunt object. Who knows? She might have been hit by a horse, or a Viking, or killed by the broken mast of a ship.'

'So we can make up what finally took place, you mean?'

'Up to a point. History is a bit treacherous. It's like the currents in a river, hidden, shifting, dangerous and often contradictory. Sometimes it's hard to put your finger on the truth.'

'In answer to your original question, I was thinking about last night,' she said, 'and tomorrow morning.'

'And what's happening then?'

'I want you to meet my boss.'

'Is this part of your mysterious trade?'

She nodded. 'I've fixed a meeting for eleven. Could you get away?'

'And you're not going to tell me until then?'

'I will if you want.'

'No, like before, I'm prepared to wait.'

That night he stayed with her in Spitalfields and they made

love within seconds of arriving at the apartment. Later she noticed that on the empty shelf opposite the bed he had placed a print of the ring that had been found in Marseille, the first of an accumulation of objects she knew would fill that space and, she thought with some certainty, would remain.

The next day they walked across to the offices of The Digital Corporation, which occupied two floors of an anonymous block just off Kingsway. Along the way they swapped more information about themselves, gradually unpacking their backgrounds, piecing together their histories, the beginnings of an exchange that would never be quite complete. She was greeted by several of her colleagues, who regarded Harry Wesley with undisguised interest.

'Trust me,' she said, just before they were ushered through to Graham Roth's over-large office. He was sitting on the edge of his desk, in front of a wall covered with commendations, award certificates and photographs of him with the great and good, finishing a telephone call. He waved them in and rang off.

'You sort of disappeared,' he said to her.

'I sort of did, didn't I. Let me introduced you to Harry Wesley.' The two men shook hands and Beatrice smiled as she saw Roth's eyes assessing Harry, trying to work out exactly where he fitted into the scheme of things, a predatory male on guard in case he was in the presence of superior opposition. 'Harry is an osteoarchaeologist, about which more later.'

Graham Roth raised his eyebrows in mock admiration. 'So, what do you have for me?'

She slid across a two page proposal that she had reworked that morning from the information that Joseph had emailed.

'"Winter in Provence"?' But this is not too different from what I wanted in the first place.'

'True. Joseph doesn't want me to make a documentary about his life and I respect that, although I do know that what I have subsequently learnt about him will be reflected, one way or the other, in these programmes.'

'Such as?'

'Such as fleeing to Provence as a young man and starting his first restaurant in Marseille. He talks wonderfully about those days. And you'll be pleased to know that he's got the tourist board on his side.'

She watched him scan the proposal again, but she knew that its acceptance was a formality, that the deal with the publishers he had mentioned weeks ago, allied to support from the French, would see it through.

'Fine, then. When do you want the production period to start?'

'But there's something else, another film. I want to make a deal with you.' Graham Roth looked at her quizzically as if to say I'm the one the makes the deals and not you. 'I'll trade "Winter in Provence" for your backing for a very different sort of documentary. Let me paint a picture for you.'

Both men were watching her and Beatrice stood up and walked over to the window, where she could see the traffic negotiating the semi-circle of Aldwych.

'Its about the unexpected death of a child. A real child. And a real mystery. Perhaps even a murder.' Without looking round she knew that she had Graham Roth's attention. 'And it's about three generations of the same family, the child who died, her mother and her grandmother.'

She came towards them, her head turned to one side, her eyes focusing elsewhere. 'The story begins with the discovery of a child's skull on the foreshore of the Thames, a dirty fragment of a human being, eyeless and without a lower jaw.' She walked behind them as she spoke. 'The film cuts between the past and the present for the skull, it turns out, thanks to the work of osteoarchaeologist Dr Harry Wesley, is a thousand years old. It holds some of the clues to what happened to her. Was she murdered, or did she die accidentally?

'The skull is real, the child was real, but her history is lost, like the histories of so many people. So, on one level, this is a film about the elusiveness of history. It will be presented by Harry, who is one of the world's leading archaeologist and he will take us through the clues that the skull offers and the techniques involved in dating and examining bones and teeth and the evidence they give about geography and diet.'

She saw Harry smile at her, a smile she reflected before a new seriousness took over her face.

'But I want the film to be about much more. You see,' she took a step closer to them, 'I want to give these three Anglo-Saxon women a story, which may or may not be completely true on one level, the factual, but will be on another, the emotional. I imagine a woman, an important woman, who makes jewellery and her daughter and granddaughter and what happens to them. The grandmother begins her life not far from here, down there on the river,' she pointed to the window, 'where she lives before moving down river, to where the City is now. Her husband is killed by the Danes when London Bridge is attacked. His body is lost and for all we know his bones are not five hundred metres from where we are now sitting. Later the woman meets a sailor, who commissions a necklace from her and persuades her to leave with him and her daughter for a new life far away and they sail to the port that will become Marseille. There is evidence, from examination of remaining teeth in the skull, that for a while she lived somewhere else, probably in the south where the weather and the food were better. There she continues to make jewellery and her daughter learns as well, the skills handed down from one to the other.'

Beatrice looks across to Harry before continuing and she could see the smile was still on his face.

'She dies here of the plague and is buried in a communal grave on the hill above the old town.' She saw Harry watching her, willing her on, hearing the story of fact and fiction being woven together. 'The daughter in turn marries and has her own child and when her husband dies at sea she returns to London, the place where she was born. Before she leaves she makes two identical rings. One she leaves above the body of her mother at the plague pit, the other she always wears. Somewhere, somehow it is lost but a thousand years later it is discovered and now everyone can see it in the British Museum. And to make the story complete, the companion ring has just been found in Marseille, along with the bones of a woman.'

Harry flicked through to the photograph and pushed the phone across to Graham Roth.

Beatrice came away from the window and walked back to the table. 'As I have said, her daughter is killed, deliberately or accidentally, we don't know. But she was real, as were her mother and grandmother. They existed and I, with the help of Harry, will give them life. It's about three generations of strong women and the support they give each other.' Beatrice stopped and closed her eyes, raising her head towards the chrome lamp which hung from the ceiling.

'I have the beginning of the film in my head, the image of a young girl running downhill, her legs carrying her faster and faster, her face intense and worried. We see two shots of her, from her own point of view, which shows London as it used to be a thousand years ago, the old streets, the thatched houses, the old wooden quays on the river and then, in a series of wider shots, the same progress, in exactly the same places, as the scene is now, her progress between tall buildings and across busy roads, to the new bridge but the very same river. We will bring this girl alive, for the emotions she goes through are no different then from what they are now.'

Beatrice stopped and looked at both men. 'But she's forgotten. And it's too easy to be forgotten. We'll bring her to life.'

'Brilliant,' Harry said.

Roth looked disapprovingly at him. 'Sounds more like a drama than a documentary,' he said.

'It did happen,' she said. 'In one form or another, it did happen. And we have to put flesh on those bones, on that skull. The assumptions we make will be based on the best facts that we have. We can save this girl from obscurity.' She stared at Harry as she said this.

'Do you have a title?' Graham Roth asked and again Beatrice knew that she had his approval for the film, if not his understanding of its real purpose.

'I do,' she said. 'It's "A Girl Called Flotsam".'

Beatrice could sense Harry looking at her and shaking his head. 'How long have you been thinking about this?' The question, which had it come from Graham Roth might have been laden with criticism, was instead said with an element of awe. She looked at him and in that moment Graham Roth didn't exist, his views, one way or the other, entirely irrelevant.

'After I'd held the skull,' she began, opening the palm of her hand and offering it to his imagination, 'I felt it charge me in a way I couldn't understand, or give dimension to. Not long after I sat down by the river wall and dozed off to sleep. What you've just heard, the opening of the film, came to me then, not as a film at that stage, but a vivid picture of this girl, running, free somehow linking the past and the present, as her skull did in my hand.'

Harry was nodding, wanting her to continue. 'And the rest?'

'I don't know, I don't know. I can't explain how it worked. In a way, I don't want to know. Flotsam became something I wasn't, but I could glimpse her and the more I thought about her the clearer she became.' She paused. 'And then you came into the picture and gave another dimension to it all, not that I saw this at first. I would find myself thinking about Flotsam as a real person, which of course she was. But, and I've only just realised this, the more I could see the...' she searched for the words '...well, what did Troumeg say, washed up state I was in, the more I created a world for Flotsam that perhaps I didn't have. Three generation of self supporting women who were able to do something that I realised I couldn't... trust their instincts.'

She stopped and felt a great weight come off her chest. 'And so the two stories began to appear in parallel, often in opposition, the events of my life and that of Flotsam and I would find myself dreaming of her and waking and wondering where I was, neither here nor there.'

Not far behind where she was now standing, a grassy slope had once run down to the river where she was sure the three woman had walked and played. How she knew this she couldn't say, but peering out of the window she quite expected to see them, hand in hand, emerging from the underpass, strong, sure of themselves and pausing now to look upwards to raise their arms in her direction to wave a salute.

So now Beatrice, facing away from the two men, saluted back, a gesture that spanned a thousand years.

ACKNOWLEDGEMENTS

I am indebted to Thames21 for setting me off on this journey. Cleaning the foreshore of the Thames, the valuable task this charity undertakes, is an odd but fascinating way to spend a few hours and clearly inspirational. I was given valuable help by the City of London Archaeological Society and by the Museum of London. If you get the chance, visit Billingsgate House and Baths on Lower Thames Street, not far from the Tower of London and get a sense of what London was like a thousand years ago. The Anglo-Saxon jewellery in the British Museum was a delight. Thanks, as ever, to my wife Sally, who along with Richard Barber, Rita Dallas and Chiara Messineo helped guide and inform the manuscript. Finally, my thanks to the late Doreen Fiol, writer, poet and teacher, who always believed in *Flotsam*

Also by John Tagholm

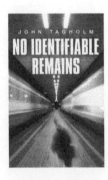

No Identifiable
Remains

Bad Marriage

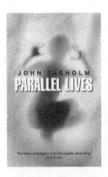

Parallel Lives

Non fiction

elsewhere

www.johntagholm.com